PRAISE FOR
The Labyrinth of Lost and Found

★ "First-time author Lees writes with confidence and fantastic imagination, crafting a complex world that layers both original and classic mythologies. Benjamiah and Elizabella's antagonistic dynamic evolves in a compelling way, leading to heartbreaking yet necessary revelations. Readers attracted to the dark storytelling of Neil Gaiman and Philip Pullman will adore this captivating first installment in the haunting Whisperwicks series."

—*Booklist*, starred review

"Completely fantastic."

—A.F. Steadman, *New York Times* bestselling author of the Skandar series

ALSO BY JORDAN LEES

The Whisperwicks Series
The Labyrinth of Lost and Found

The Whisperwicks

VOLUME 2

The Impossible Trials of Benjamiah Creek

JORDAN LEES
Illustrated by VIVIENNE TO

SIMON & SCHUSTER BOOKS FOR YOUNG READERS
New York   Amsterdam/Antwerp   London   Toronto   Sydney   New Delhi

SIMON & SCHUSTER BOOKS FOR YOUNG READERS
An imprint of Simon & Schuster Children's Publishing Division
1230 Avenue of the Americas, New York, New York 10020
This book is a work of fiction. Any references to historical events, real people, or real places are used fictitiously. Other names, characters, places, and events are products of the author's imagination, and any resemblance to actual events or places or persons, living or dead, is entirely coincidental.
Text © 2025 by Jordan Lees
Originally published in Great Britain in 2025 by
Penguin Random House UK as *The Impossible Trials*
Jacket illustration © 2025 by Isobelle Ouzman
Jacket design by Lizzy Bromley
Interior illustration © 2025 by Vivienne To
All rights reserved, including the right of reproduction in whole or in part in any form.
SIMON & SCHUSTER BOOKS FOR YOUNG READERS
and related marks are trademarks of Simon & Schuster, LLC.
For information about special discounts for bulk purchases, please contact Simon & Schuster Special Sales at 1-866-506-1949 or business@simonandschuster.com.
The Simon & Schuster Speakers Bureau can bring authors to your live event. For more information or to book an event, contact the Simon & Schuster Speakers Bureau at 1-866-248-3049 or visit our website at www.simonspeakers.com.
Also available in a Simon & Schuster Books for Young Readers paperback edition
Interior design by Lizzy Bromley
The text for this book was set in Adobe Garamond.
The illustrations for this book were rendered digitally.
Manufactured in the United States of America
0425 BVG
First Simon & Schuster Books for Young Readers hardcover edition June 2025
2 4 6 8 10 9 7 5 3 1
CIP data for this book is available from the Library of Congress.
ISBN 9781665950169
ISBN 9781665950176 (ebook)

For my family

ONE
WITH THE STRANGE PARADE

The Festival of Midsommer will forever be the merriest and most magical time of year in Wreathenwold, a time for celebrating the rich and mysterious folklore of our world. Magic forged at Midsommer is the strongest and truest of all magic—both fair and foul.

—*The Book of Barely Believable Stories*,
Mildred Fogge

THE PARADE CAME the first night of Midsommer, beneath the blossoming bonewoods and a smoky moon.

Claris Songwood sat on the front steps, knees drawn beneath her chin and her face trapped in a scowl. Her older brother was being mean again and she refused to go inside until he was properly punished—ideally shipped off to a boarding school for horrible boys. Even as darkness set in and the day's warmth slipped away, Claris could not be coaxed home.

"I'll just leave this here, then," said Mum.

She set a mug of hot treacle tea on the stone step beside Claris, where its sweet smoke climbed upward and made Claris's mouth water. Still, Claris only took her first sip when her mother had gone. The taste flooded her, warm and deliciously sugary.

Claris stared at the sky, studying the moon in its shawl of thin cloud and the scatter of surrounding stars. Wind sighed through the bonewoods, which always erupted into blossom at Midsommer. They swelled with petals of a purple so pale they were almost white. The street was quiet otherwise, nothing moving but the shivering trees.

Feeling lonely, Claris cast her poppet—called Tya—as a tortoiseshell cat. Tya curled in Claris's lap, purring as Claris scratched the back of her head.

"Horrible boy, isn't he?" she said.

Tya meowed in agreement.

"We should run away," said Claris.

Tya was less convinced by this. Getting lost in the great labyrinth of Wreathenwold often meant never finding home again. Claris took another sip of treacle tea—Mum really knew how to hit the spot. She could wander the entire labyrinth and never find anything that tasted so good. Then she heard the drum.

At first, it was a deep, steady beat, like a great heart

pulsing from the depths of the earth itself. Then, as it grew louder and clearer, Claris perceived the patter of smaller drums surrounding it. A tingle traveled down her neck. Could it really be . . . ? Claris was nine years old and had never seen the Strange Parade—had never allowed herself to believe it was anything more than legend.

Her eyes fixed on the end of the road, a tight turn of mossy stone beneath an archway. The drumming grew. Claris rose, her heart chattering, while Tya meowed nervously in her arms.

The parade came. First was the drum major. He had long, sinewy limbs and wore a regimental coat and cape, twirling a bonewood baton as he danced at the head of the column. Embers spouted from the baton with every flourish, forming cartwheels of fiery specks. On his head was a tall top hat. A silvery masquerade mask covered the upper half of his face, shimmering like liquid starlight.

Music filled the street as the parade followed, a column of drummers and pipers in regimental coats, their knees rising and falling in perfect rhythm as the horns cried and the drums beat. Surrounding them were dancers, leaping and twisting, ribbons streaming and twirling from their elbows and knees. Some carried batons, splashing fiery embers upon the dark air. All were masked.

It was a spectacle marching straight from a dream. By now, others had joined Claris on the street, whooping

children in nightcaps, and grown-ups, baffled and astonished. Poppets cast as stags, their antlers festooned with ribbons, hauled wagons from which masked men released flurries of sugar-flies—plump, fluttering sweets that had to be caught to be enjoyed. This set the children, Claris included, to frenzied, jubilant chasing, using their poppets to catch the delicious treats.

Meanwhile, the music swelled, embers showered, and the ribboned dancers leaped and spiraled like flames. While enjoying a sugar-fly, Claris saw that the drum major had taken the hand of old Mrs. Hundercliffe and was dancing with her at the head of the column. She was eighty-two years old, wearing a nightgown and slippers and having the time of her life.

Masked dancers gifted ne'er-do-wells—slender, smoky-white flowers. Small batons were handed to children, which spurted glowing sparks when twirled. Sugar-flies swarmed. Tya, cast as a sparrow, chased another through the maelstrom of delirious children.

"Ooh, look!" exclaimed an excited voice.

On the next wagon, masked women held large birdcages. Inside were birds made entirely of bonewood blossom. They hopped around, chattering, before the women opened the cages. Out the blossomy birds soared, the crowd cheering as they took to the sky, streaks of light purple petals cutting through the darkness.

Claris watched as one landed on the bough of a bonewood tree. It twittered, bouncing happily as an expectant hush fell. Then it erupted with a bang like a pistol shot, throwing an enormous flurry of blossom against the night sky. The petals leaped and whirled, joyously alive; Claris felt her heart sigh.

From roofs and windowsills, from streetlamps and bonewood branches, blossom birds exploded in billows of splendid petals. The crowd gasped and applauded. Claris spied her mum, her eyes filled with light and color. Claris set off in her direction, but was quickly distracted.

"It's the Pyrate Queene!" squealed a boy among the crowd.

From the next wagon, a beefy woman in breeches, a silk coat, and a bandana waved to the children. Hanging from her belt were five fake poppets, a tribute to the story of the Pyrate Queene—betrayed by the four other pirate lords, she claimed their poppets as punishment and became the most fearsome buccaneer in Wreathenwold history. From treasure chests, the Pyrate Queene threw coco coins.

The Strange Parade brought more figures from Wreathenwold folklore. After the Pyrate Queene came a woman dressed as the Two-Headed Magpie, then Lyly Well-I-Never, then the Half-Bears of Wychbrooke. Each had their own story—captured best in Claris's favorite book, Mildred Fogge's *The Book of Barely Believable Stories*.

The procession continued—drummers and pipers, figures from fairy tales and folklore. Claris had never seen her street so joyful. Neighbors danced and clapped and children were giddy, gorging on sugar-flies and writing their names with the ember-throwing batons, while blossom eddied and drifted.

"*Claris!*"

It was a sharp whisper, knifelike, startling her. Turning, she found a child in the gap between two houses. The boy was a little shorter than her, dressed in rags and with something on his face that swiftly chilled Claris to her core.

It was a skull mask of pale stone. The boy's real eyes were fixed within its eye sockets as though it had fused with his face. The mouth was even more frightening—a lipless, skeletal mouth with rows of skinny, stony teeth.

The masked child took a step backward, absorbed by the shadows, beckoning Claris toward him. Following the creepy boy into the darkness felt like a bad idea to Claris, but curiosity got the better of her. She drew a little closer, but lingered in the mouth of the passageway, staying where she could be seen.

"Who are you?" she said.

"I don't know my name," whispered the boy.

The skull mask, chalky white, glowed in the shadows.

"What do you mean?" said Claris softly. "And what's that mask? Why is it . . ."

"Part of my face?" said the boy. "The same reason I don't know my name. I am one of the lost children of Midsommer. They call us snatchlings."

Claris gasped. It was a story she knew well. Agatha Drake, the Witch of Midsommer, and the snatchlings . . . Surely it couldn't be *true*?

"That's just a fairy tale," she said.

"Does it look that way?" said the boy.

Claris shivered, fighting the urge to run back into the crowd. Sympathy rooted her in place.

"How do you know my name?" she asked.

"We've been watching you," replied the masked boy.

"Why?" said Claris, horrified at the thought.

"We're only free to walk Wreathenwold during the month of Midsommer," said the boy. "We use that time to look for somebody who can save us. A child who is brave, and clever, and good. We believe that's you, Claris."

"But *why*?"

"You are special," said the boy.

"I'm not," said Claris, shaking her head. "I'm sorry, I can't help. . . ."

Fear swarmed in her chest. She backed away, toward the street and the music and safety.

"Please . . . ," whispered the boy, a tear snaking from his eye down the surface of the stone mask. "Please? There are so many of us. We can't remember our names. Our families. We're trapped like this forever until somebody saves us. Only free at Midsommer. For the rest of the year . . ."

He trailed off with a shiver. Claris didn't have the courage to ask for more detail on where the snatchlings spent the remainder of their time.

"There's nothing I can do, I'm sorry," she said.

The masked boy was devastated.

"You can save us," he whispered. "Just . . . Will you please think about it? We believe you're the one who can finally free us. I'll be outside your house at midnight. If you still don't want to come, we'll leave you alone."

Claris's mind whirled. Disoriented and frightened, she backed away until the boy was out of sight and rejoined the crowd. Her heart hammered like the drums of the parade.

It wasn't long before the drum major reached the far end of the street, leading the parade toward the next branch of the labyrinth. The crowd surged alongside, cheering and clapping, bunching round the archway to wave them on their way. Few followed round the corner—not even the parade was worth the risk of never finding home again.

Claris joined the throng, still shaken up by her encounter with the snatchling. Children fought over the last of the sugar-flies and an almighty roar went up as the final blossom birds rose high into the sky and shattered into great weeping willows of petals. The music grew steadily quieter, until the last of the marching band had threaded away. Gradually, the sound of drums and pipes grew muted until Claris could hear it no more. Some of the younger children started to cry.

An arm flowed round Claris's shoulders.

"Come, chicken," said her mum. "To bed with you."

She chatted away while she put Claris to bed, checking that her daughter had seen every marvelous sight the parade had to offer. Claris did her best to reply enthusiastically, but the bony-masked boy plagued her thoughts.

"You're exhausted," said Mum, mistaking Claris's solemnity for tiredness. "Sleep. That's an order."

Her mother kissed her forehead and rose to leave. But before she could Claris had a question.

"Is the story of Agatha Drake and the snatchlings true?"

Her mum gave a wide, patient smile, tucking Claris's hair behind her ear.

"I wouldn't think so, chicken," she said. "Just an old fairy tale. There's nothing to be afraid of. Promise."

"But what if it *is* true?" said Claris. "Those poor children, tricked by the witch."

"What's brought this on?"

Claris buttoned up. Mum would never believe her about the snatchling. She wasn't even sure if she believed it herself.

"It's just a story," said her mother. "Like all the other stories Mildred Fogge wrote. They're not real, but they still mean something. Who knows? Maybe there once was a real person called Agatha Drake. But that would have been long ago, chicken. And I rather doubt she was a witch."

She leaned down for another kiss, rising with another gentle stroke of Claris's forehead. Then she blew out the oil lamp, which died with a tremble and a trail of smoke.

In the darkness, Claris did her best to take her mum's word for it. But, no matter how hard she tried, all thoughts spiraled back to the snatchling boy—his mask of chalky stone, the haunted undercurrent to his pleas, his conviction that Claris was special and that she could free the snatchlings from their curse.

When midnight came, Claris crawled nervously from her bed and peered out of the bedroom window.

Standing on the street, mask turned up to her window, was the little snatchling boy. He was tiny, really—all fragile and mouselike in his tatty clothes. He gave a hopeful, tentative wave upon seeing Claris. Could she leave him—him and all the others—to their fate? What if she really could save them all?

Quietly, Claris threw on some clothes, fastened Tya to her hip, and crept out of the house.

After the jubilant scenes earlier, the street felt eerie in the pale moonlight. Blossom fluttered along the cobbles, but all else was still. The snatchling had vanished. Claris looked in every direction, finally spotting the skull mask. The boy peered out from an alleyway beside the color-broker's, beckoning frantically.

Though her stomach lurched, and despite the almost overwhelming desire to dash back to bed and take refuge beneath her blankets, Claris followed.

At the mouth of the alleyway, she paused. Ahead was deep shadow and no sign of the snatchling.

"Are you there?" she asked.

"Yes!" called the boy. "Thank you for coming. This way...."

Claris took a few steps forward, hand drifting instinctively toward her poppet. Something felt suddenly amiss, something she couldn't name or shape.

"Where are we going?"

"I'll show you," whispered the boy.

A few more steps and Claris's resolve failed. Or perhaps common sense finally triumphed. She stopped.

"I don't like this," she said. "I'm going home."

"Please, no!" said the boy.

Up ahead, she saw him, his skull mask shining in the shadows. The boy held out his hands pleadingly.

"We need you," said the snatchling.

Then Claris heard a sound from somewhere close.

Tick.

It sounded like a clock. Or something clockwork. Claris felt her blood run cold. Keeping an eye on the snatchling boy, she backed away.

"What's going on?" she called.

"We need you," repeated the snatchling, only now he sounded neither sad nor desperate—just matter-of-fact.

Tick. Tick. Tick.

Whatever it was, it was right behind her now.

Claris whirled, her mind a frenzy of panic and fear. Briefly, she glimpsed two other skull masks, human eyes glowing in their sockets and skeletal mouths drawn in leers. Then a handful of drowsipowder was thrown, the world disintegrated, and Claris saw nothing more.

TWO

WITH THE BOY IN THE LIBRARY

> A bookwyrm is the bane of any library. Almost impossible to catch, the beastly wyrm will eat its way through the pages of books—boring its holes precisely where plot twists are introduced, vital information is given, or the solution to a mystery is revealed.
>
> —*The Book of Barely Believable Stories*,
> Mildred Fogge

WYVERN-ON-THE-WATER had only one library. It was once the cottage of an eighteenth-century explorer called Smythe, widely regarded as one of the most inept navigators the country had ever seen. Later in life, a drunken Smythe was said to stagger around the Wyvern-on-the-Water streets, raving about a chain of phantom islands off the coast from where—Smythe claimed—giants came to eat children. Upon his death, his home was converted into a library, though Smythe's study—with its collection of erroneous maps, raving letters, and pamphlets about places that simply did not exist—was preserved.

Given the study was about the only historical curiosity Wyvern-on-the-Water had to offer, it was no surprise that Benjamiah Creek had visited many times throughout his childhood. Every few months, Mum, Dad, Grandma, and Benjamiah would come to Smythe's study to read the diaries in which Smythe described his fantastical voyages, and the letters he wrote to politicians and newspaper editors warning them of the child-eating giants.

Afterward, they'd have fish and chips by the water, or ice cream on warm days, watching children crab from the pier and boats swan up and down the river. Standing in Smythe's study now, one cold January afternoon, Benjamiah found those memories acutely painful. The days of family outings were over.

The study was hexagonal-shaped. On the walls were various framed editions of Smythe's nonsense maps: the chain of islands with the child-snatching giants; a network of secret canals revealed only by moonlight; a map that allegedly revealed a secret entrance to one of the hills overlooking Wyvern-on-the-Water, where legend said a dragon slept.

Benjamiah had come to Smythe's study straight after school, as he often did. Most days it was not uncommon to see the short and slight Benjamiah there, with his messy, mousy hair; his brown eyes; and the nose that speared strangely to the left. He wore his school uniform, including a school tie and blazer of a particularly offensive pickle green.

The Wyvern-on-the-Water library had been Benjamiah's sanctuary in recent months, a haven amid the turmoil of home life. Smythe's study now fascinated him. Throughout his childhood, he had thought Smythe utterly ridiculous. The explorer's study wasn't the least bit interesting to Benjamiah, who would much rather have been in the main library, digging into some fascinating book about landscape architecture or oceanography. But that was before Benjamiah's adventures in the summer when he'd found his own impossible, magical world.

While Benjamiah studied one of Smythe's pamphlets—this one explained how to secure your home against invasive giants—there came a cough from behind him.

Benjamiah turned and saw Hassaan, a boy from school. Hassaan had an oval face and shiny black eyes, brown skin and floppy hair. He was dressed in the same miserable green uniform as Benjamiah, except Hassaan's tie was shorter and scruffier and his shirt was untucked.

"All right?" said Hassaan.

"Hi," mumbled Benjamiah.

Hassaan gave an awkward smile, then hastily shuffled off to examine one of Smythe's sketches. With only the two of them in the study, the atmosphere thickened.

Over recent months, Benjamiah had begun to suspect that Hassaan wanted to be friends. A few times, Hassaan had trotted up and walked to school with Benjamiah, which for Hassaan—as shy and bookish as Benjamiah—was quite a gesture. Needless to say, conversation never exactly flowed. More than once, they'd run into each other at the library—Hassaan sitting nearby with his own book. A couple of times, he'd even offered Benjamiah some potato chips or sweets when the librarian wasn't watching.

Not that Benjamiah was an expert on making friends. In any case, it was uncertain and unwelcome ground for him. He had a best friend, Elizabella Cotton, whom he missed dearly every day. Nobody could replace her and nobody could fill the void she left in his life. Benjamiah had no interest in a new friend, thank you very much.

Hassaan coughed again, now much closer to Benjamiah. Was Hassaan ill or trying to get Benjamiah's attention? This was a minefield. Unsure how to handle the situation, Benjamiah plotted his escape.

"Um . . . ," said Hassaan.

Benjamiah turned. Hassaan was right behind him, chewing his bottom lip with his hands crammed in his pockets.

"Hi," croaked Benjamiah, before remembering he'd said that already and feeling intensely stupid.

"I was wondering if you wanted to come round

mine...," muttered Hassaan, talking to his own shoes.

"Oh," said Benjamiah. "Um. I have to meet my mum..."

"Not now, but..."

"Maybe another time..."

"Yeah, cool," said Hassaan. "Cool, cool."

"Cool," echoed Benjamiah, wishing he were dead.

Quiet fell—the most painful quiet Benjamiah could remember. Mercifully, Hassaan broke it.

"Oh, I almost forgot."

He dipped a hand into his knapsack and pulled out a shabby-looking pack of playing cards.

"You said... When we walked to school one time, you collect them? Or something?"

Benjamiah blushed. It was an act of kindness that knocked him off-kilter. Hassaan hadn't found it weird that Benjamiah collected playing cards; he'd remembered, and actually bought some for him.

"Thanks, that's really...," murmured Benjamiah.

"Saw them in the charity shop," said Hassaan, bobbing his head.

Benjamiah took them, grateful but still absolutely adamant he didn't want a new friend. He'd been collecting packs of playing cards for the last few months, hoping he'd need them again. Already there were five packs stashed in his knapsack.

"Thanks," said Benjamiah again, feeling stupid for not having anything else to say.

"Right, well, I'd better head off," said Hassaan. "See you at school?"

Benjamiah nodded. When Hassaan was gone, he opened his knapsack and stowed the playing cards—next to a doll of red, leatherlike fabric, with a tuft of black string for hair and white buttons for eyes. Every time Benjamiah saw the poppet, the grief at his center renewed itself.

Before heading off, he took another long look around. Surrounding him was evidence of how fiercely Smythe had mourned the wonderful places he'd apparently been—Benjamiah knew just how he felt.

Benjamiah set off for the riverside. The Wyvern-on-the-Water main street was a sloping and slaloming lane of cobbles, cottages, and shops. Benjamiah passed the bric-a-brac stores and the drugstore, the pottery studio and the church, the chip shop and Once Upon A Time bookshop. Through the window, Benjamiah spied Grandma doing her crossword at the counter. She didn't look up and Benjamiah didn't go in.

Mum and Dad had separated last summer. Dad and Grandma remained in the flat above Once Upon A Time, while Mum was renting a small flat overlooking the quay.

Everybody was at pains to impress upon Benjamiah that this arrangement wasn't final. Mum and Dad owned the bookshop together, so time was needed to work out the best way forward. As far as Benjamiah could tell, life lurched from one uncertainty to the next.

He was free to stay where he liked. Rather than impose some kind of schedule, his parents encouraged him to make his own decisions about where to be. He was welcome whenever and wherever. They wanted him to feel he had two homes, but Benjamiah knew he had none. Mum's place smelled wrong and the bookshop, with her gone, no longer sounded like home.

Mum waved from a bench by the quay. It was low tide, leaving the moored boats around the quay wedged in slopes of sticky mud. Masts rattled and creaked in the quick winter breeze. The sun hung low and cold.

Wearing her big yellow coat, Mum rose to clasp Benjamiah in a hug that was slightly longer and tighter than those of old. Benjamiah looked up to return her smile, seeing the features—the bent nose, mousy-brown hair, and coffee-colored eyes—he'd inherited from her.

"How was school?"

They walked the trail, weaving between the glittering shallows of the river and the woodland thronged with birdsong. On the other side of the water, where heathery slopes traveled up toward the pale blue sky, two horses ambled and ducked their heads to graze. They spoke about school, and Mum's latest research—on Titan, one of Saturn's moons—and whether they should get fish and chips for dinner.

Benjamiah contributed very little. Not long ago, school, astronomy, and battered cod would have represented a great day. Now none of it excited him. Nothing did.

"Is everything okay, Ben?" said Mum.

Benjamiah shrugged. Absolutely *nothing* was okay. His world felt strange and broken; another world, the one he missed with every fiber of his being, was lost to him, out of reach.

"I wonder what Hansel's doing right now," said Benjamiah.

The effect upon Mum was instantaneous. She stiffened, lips pressing into a tight line as she made a noncommittal noise in reply.

At first, when Benjamiah brought up Wreathenwold, Mum had been an enthusiastic counterpoint. They'd spoken in hushed, happy tones about treacle tea and plumpkin broth, about ne'er-do-wells and poppets and majestic bonewood trees. Though Benjamiah hadn't told Mum everything about his journey with Elizabella, he'd regaled her with the highlights—the less dangerous ones—to which she listened with wide eyes, rapt and animated.

But, over time, she became more restrained whenever the subject came up. She held back, withdrew, as though trying to diminish Benjamiah's enthusiasm for Wreathenwold, doing whatever she could to divert conversation back toward *this* world: to school, to books, even the weather. It was yet another thing that Benjamiah couldn't understand.

"Do you wish you could see him again?" he prodded.

"Hm?"

"Hansel. Do you wish you could see him again?"

"I don't know."

"I do," said Benjamiah. "Before I left, he was bragging about his toadstool stew. Said it was the best in Wreathenwold, but I never got to try it. Have you ever tried any?"

"Ben . . ."

"Did you ever visit a Root Folk street? They're like little forests and—"

"Enough, Ben!"

It was loud enough that Benjamiah actually started. Mum, so softly spoken, almost never raised her voice. She had a way of commanding attention and respect without needing to shout. Benjamiah looked up, finding a panicky expression upon her face. She took a deep, slow breath, staring out across the water. Even the horses on the other side of the river eyed them with alarm.

"Why?" said Benjamiah. "Why is it enough?"

"You live *here*, Ben."

Mum set her hands on Benjamiah's cheeks and drew her face closer to his. Fear had changed her eyes.

"I know that," he said. "But it doesn't mean Wreathenwold isn't real. Why can't we talk about it? It's not like I can talk about it with anybody else."

"Maybe it's best to stop discussing it at all," said Mum.

"Why?"

"Because you belong *here*," she said, as kindly as she could. "All of you, including your mind and your heart and your imagination. Time spent thinking about Wreathenwold is time wasted, Ben."

"So you *never* think about it?"

"No. Not when I realized there's no way back. I'm happy you saw it, Ben. I really am. But it's time to let it go."

"I don't want to," said Benjamiah.

"You have to!" Mum's voice rose again. "You can't go back, Benjamiah. Neither of us can. I don't know why a door opened for you, but there is absolutely no reason to expect it again. And I know, Ben. Don't you think I longed to go home? That I searched, for years and years, for a way back? Don't you think I *grieved*, Ben? I don't want that for you."

A volley of birds took off from a nearby tree. Crickets chirped in the long grass. Benjamiah felt suddenly, totally exhausted.

"You could have fooled me," he said.

"What do you mean?"

"That I belong here." He shrugged free of Mum's hands. "Doesn't feel like it. I don't belong anywhere anymore."

He turned to leave.

"Ben, please?" said Mum.

Benjamiah stopped, tears gathering in the corner of each eye and his heart charged with sadness. Mum stepped forward and enveloped him in a long, firm hug. They stayed that way for a while, until she said it was time for fish and chips.

Benjamiah woke suddenly in the night.

Some vague and formless excitement surged in his chest. Sitting up, the dreamy shroud of sleep falling away, he looked around. It took a moment to process where he was—not in his old bedroom above the bookshop, but his other bedroom at Mum's quayside apartment. It didn't have much character yet, only a few star charts and a periodic table stuck to the wall. On the bedside table was a book: *Jamima Cleaves and the Book-Eater*. Elizabella had given it to Benjamiah, since when he had read it four times. It was the kind of book he'd never have picked up before Wreathenwold; now he couldn't get enough of stories about magic and epic adventures.

Nuisance sat propped up on the bedside cabinet, lifeless. Just where Benjamiah left her, as he did every night. The sharp thrill that had woken him gave way to a familiar sorrow. He'd been dreaming about Wreathenwold—about Nuisance fluttering around as a nightjar, living and singing and wonderful. But it was only a dream.

"Nuisance?" said Benjamiah, sitting up.

Nothing. Where once Benjamiah had felt the living, breathing presence of the poppet in his mind, now there was a yawning emptiness.

"Please..."

Benjamiah reached out and held the doll, fingers pressed into the fabric, biting his bottom lip so hard it began to sting. His mind strained, tensed, against nothing at all. Nuisance would not spring to life.

"I really miss you," said Benjamiah.

Still nothing happened. Maybe Mum was right. Maybe he was never going back. *Don't you think I grieved, Ben?* And now it was Benjamiah's turn to grieve. Sitting there in his chess-themed pajamas, clasping the lifeless poppet, Benjamiah thought—not for the first time—how horribly unfair it all was.

He was sliding back beneath his covers when he heard a creak from the next room. Popping on his slippers, Benjamiah crept through the shadowy stillness of Mum's flat. From the living-room doorway, he saw that the balcony door was open. Mum was sitting out there, swaddled in her fluffy white dressing gown, holding something in her hands.

What was she doing outside? It was the middle of the night and icy cold. Benjamiah watched Mum's breath smoke. He crept forward, unsure whether to disturb her. What *was* that in her hands? It was flat and pale, with jagged edges and a hole in the center. It looked like a fragment of pottery.

Unaware of Benjamiah's presence, Mum lifted the strange object toward her face, holding it close to her eye without letting it touch her skin. Then she peered through it, up toward the black sky dusted with stars.

"What is that?" said Benjamiah.

Mum started, swirling in a panic and quickly stowing the peculiar object in her dressing-gown pocket.

"Ben! You made me jump."

Benjamiah shuffled forward to join her on the balcony. The air was witheringly cold. Boats creaked in the dark quay below. Mum looked flustered, which frightened Benjamiah—she was ordinarily so composed.

"I thought you were fast asleep," she said.

"What was that thing?"

"Oh, nothing," said Mum. "Come on, let's get you back to bed."

She stood, attempting to usher Benjamiah back inside.

"Let me see it," he said.

"It's nothing, sweetie."

"Why are you lying?"

"Benjamiah. Enough."

Like earlier, it was said with a force Benjamiah did not expect. Though Mum looked regretful, there was a steely resolve in her eyes that refused to soften. Whatever the object was, she was not prepared to discuss it.

Which, Benjamiah thought, could mean only one thing. He left Mum without another word, hurrying into his bedroom and closing the door. Then he kicked off his slippers and perched on the edge of his bed, his mind a hurricane.

Mum had never refused to answer a question from Benjamiah. In fact, she had actively encouraged his curiosity at every stage of his life. She'd explain and illuminate any mystery that Benjamiah asked her about—no matter how strange—clearly and patiently and happily. There was only one reason Mum would refuse to tell him about the object through which she'd been looking.

It came from Wreathenwold.

THREE
WITH THE IMPOSSIBLE MOTHS

"You have seen all the world," said the Queen to the Traveler. "What more do you seek?"

"I seek a door," said the Traveler. "A door that is only mine—a door through which nobody else has ever passed, which waits only for me."

"Does such a door exist?" asked the Queen.

"For us all," said the Traveler.

—*The Book of Barely Believable Stories,*
Mildred Fogge

BEFORE MUM WOKE, Benjamiah snuck out of the flat.

It was Saturday, so there was no school. Benjamiah had hardly slept for obsessing over what he'd seen. What was the strange fragment? Why had Mum been looking through it? And why had she lied? It was clearly *something*. Benjamiah couldn't recall a single time in his life where Mum had pushed him away like that. That was the most disturbing thing of all.

It also made him angry. Which, in turn, made Benjamiah resolve to find out the truth about the object, whatever Mum said.

He scampered through the dewy Wyvern-on-the-Water morning, yawning and rubbing his eyes, until he reached Once Upon A Time. Grandma, in her many cardigans and large tortoiseshell glasses, cocked a surprised eye when Benjamiah entered the bookshop.

"You're up early on a Saturday," she said.

She set her crossword down and studied him from behind the counter. Benjamiah was sure Grandma could sense when something was wrong—it was one of her many talents.

"Everything okay?"

"I wish people would stop asking me that," snapped Benjamiah.

"Do you now?" said Grandma. "If the day ever comes when nobody cares how you are, you'll feel very differently. Believe me."

Benjamiah snorted, grasping the straps of his knapsack.

"Enough of that," she said. "Do you want to tell me what's happened?"

"Not really."

"You'd rather just sulk about it instead?"

"That's right."

Before she could respond, Dad emerged from the cellar, an unruly stack of paperbacks climbing higher than his head. His widow's peak was still damp from the shower.

"Oh, hello," said Dad, a lopsided smile peering round the books. "Are you home today?"

"Home?" said Benjamiah. "Where's that?"

Dad and Grandma both made some kind of reproachful noise, but Benjamiah was already striking a course for his bedroom. Blood throbbed in his ears as he hurried upstairs. With his bedroom door shut, he slumped on the bed and immediately felt regretful. Dad and Grandma had done nothing wrong and he knew that. Nobody was to blame for the way Benjamiah's life had changed, but that didn't stop it hurting.

And a single question, like a black hole at his center toward which everything else fell: *What was Mum hiding?*

Feeling guilty, Benjamiah helped around the bookshop throughout the day—serving customers, shelving and unshelving books, sweeping up. Grandma went off to play tennis, while Dad drifted here and there, butchering Led Zeppelin songs while he worked and making bad jokes that made Benjamiah smile, reluctantly, once or twice.

In quieter moments, Benjamiah's mind drifted back to last night. A plan took shape in his mind. That evening, Mum was attending an astrophysics conference on the university campus. Keen to stress that Benjamiah was welcome anytime, Mum had given him his own key to her flat. So, when she was out that evening, he'd go and find the peculiar object she was so determined to hide.

Dad was in the kitchen when Benjamiah came for lunch, dolloping an absurd quantity of peanut butter onto a slice of bread. An enormous wedge of a book about dragons and warriors was propped open against the sugar jar.

"Sandwich?" he said, spotting Benjamiah.

"I can make my own," said Benjamiah grumpily.

"But it doesn't taste like mine," said Dad, smiling broadly.

"It's a peanut-butter sandwich. There's only one way to make it."

"You'd think so, wouldn't you?"

So Benjamiah sat while Dad made Benjamiah's sandwich and poured him some pineapple juice. He delivered the meal with an overly enthusiastic *"Voila!"*

Benjamiah ate—and he had to admit it *did* taste good. How did Dad do that? There were only two ingredients. Dad sat opposite, hands interlocked round a mug of honey-smelling tea, the steam fogging his glasses.

"Are you okay?" he said.

"I really, *really* wish people—"

"—would stop asking you?" said Dad.

"Yes."

"Well, is there anything you'd like to talk about, then? Anything on your mind?"

A thousand things, Benjamiah thought ruefully. *Why is Mum hiding something from me? Why did Wreathenwold make more sense than here? Where do I belong?* None he could bring himself to say aloud.

Dad sipped his tea. "Well, I'm always here if you change your mind."

"Thanks," replied Benjamiah, willing the conversation to end.

There was an intensity to Dad's stare, a desperation to make a breakthrough. Benjamiah felt his stomach lurch, unable to bear it any longer. He finished the sandwich as quickly as possible, then rushed downstairs to the bookshop.

The day passed with painful slowness. Thankfully, Dad made no further attempts to draw Benjamiah into any kind of heart-to-heart, for which Benjamiah was grateful. As darkness fell and the customers thinned out, Benjamiah's anxiety increased at the prospect of his plan. Mum had given him a key because she trusted him, because Benjamiah was honest and good and reliable. This was no way to repay her. But he had to *know*.

Finally, it was closing time. Benjamiah had just finished

sweeping up when Grandma returned. Dad was upstairs cooking.

"I'm going out," said Benjamiah, slinging his knapsack over his shoulders.

"Oh, where?" said Grandma.

"Just, you know . . . See you later."

Seeing Grandma's suspicious glare, Benjamiah fled—quickly enough to avoid further questions, but not so quickly that it resembled an outright sprint.

Every step of the way, he felt like a wretched criminal. Mum trusted him and this was an abject violation of that trust. Benjamiah Creek was a follower of rules. Unlike most children his age, he thought them sensible and necessary for the smooth functioning of society. There had even been times when Benjamiah had suggested new rules to teachers, which for some reason his classmates didn't seem to appreciate.

Maybe all criminals begin this way, thought Benjamiah. *Some small act of wrongdoing.* Before long, he'd be wearing a balaclava and robbing elderly couples on the river trails.

With a squirm of the stomach, he reached the horseshoe of flats overlooking the quay. Mum's windows were dark. She'd gone to her conference, oblivious to her son's nefarious plans. Benjamiah paused, his conscience pulling him like a strong wind back toward Once Upon A Time. But curiosity got the better of it.

He felt like a burglar as he entered Mum's flat and closed the door. All was dark and quiet. Benjamiah crept on, skulking into his mother's bedroom.

It smelled of her—her deodorant and hand cream and the chocolate mints she liked to nibble while watching movies in bed. Mum's fluffy dressing gown hung from a hook on the back of her bedroom door. It was into its pocket that Benjamiah had watched the strange object disappear—so it was that pocket he tried first.

And there it was.

Benjamiah's emotions flurried as he withdrew it—excitement, guilt, fear. Something else happened too. The moment his fingers made contact with the object, the hairs on his neck prickled and shivered—as though suddenly in the presence of some impossible, unearthly energy. It was a feeling he remembered from the summer.

The object wasn't ceramic but stone, chalky-colored and threaded with veins of a very faint violet. It was roughly circular, as large as Benjamiah's palm. Half its edge was a smooth, crafted curve, the rest jagged as though broken from a larger object. The hole in its center, Benjamiah now saw, was oval-shaped—as though purposely designed for an eye.

Whatever it was, Benjamiah had not been wrong—this stone fragment was from Wreathenwold. He could feel the shadow of magic traveling along his skin, making his heart pulse and his palm tingle. But what exactly *was* it?

Just as Mum had, Benjamiah lifted the stone and looked through the hole. Nothing happened. So he pulled it closer, pressing it over his left eye—finding it fitted snugly over the contours of his eye socket and nose. It had no immediate effect. Mum's bedroom looked exactly the same, her untidy bed and her dresser loaded with toiletries and her bedside table stacked with half-read books.

Then, suddenly, something flared in the darkness—something incandescent, violet-colored, and *alive*.

Benjamiah flinched so fiercely that his grip slackened. But the fragment stayed where it was, clinging to his eye. Assuming simple friction, Benjamiah went to remove it. Then panic took root—the fragment refused to come off. When he pulled, it tugged at the surrounding skin as though glued in place.

Heart throbbing, chest tightening, Benjamiah lurched to Mum's mirror. No matter what he tried, he couldn't pry the stone fragment from his eye socket. The panic was sheer and dizzying. Drawing closer to the mirror, he found the edges of the pale stone fragment had merged with the surrounding skin. It was a part of him now and wouldn't come loose, the purple strands glowing brighter. Why would Mum have something like this?

Mum . . .

She must have known what it was. Benjamiah had

to find her. Perhaps this explained why she hadn't let it touch her skin last night, and why she'd hidden it from Benjamiah. Why hadn't he listened? On the cusp of a panic attack, he turned to leave.

Then he saw her. In the mirror, Benjamiah caught sight of a figure filling the doorway behind him. He whirled round and found the doorway empty. But, returning to the mirror, there she was—a tall, severe, featureless shadow. Horror swept through him.

"It was not made for you," she said.

Benjamiah flinched, reeling, his heartbeat filling his skull. Though the figure could only be seen in the mirror, her voice filled the room, husky and ashen and ancient. Staring into the mirror, Benjamiah perceived the gleam of two eyes amid the shadows, one oddly brighter than the other.

"Who are you?" he breathed.

"It was not made for you, but it fits all the same," said the figure. "So tell me, boy. Would you like to play a game?"

Benjamiah was baffled, his mind careering, ears full of white noise and the thump of his heart.

"Who *are* you?" he said again. "What is this thing? And what game?"

"Decide quickly," said the figure. "The door is closing. Do you want to play?"

How was Benjamiah supposed to answer when he understood so little? Mum would know. Mum would be able to explain. But then he remembered last night, recalled recent months, with Mum shutting down all talk of Wreathenwold. Would she explain if he asked her?

"Hurry, boy," said the shadowy woman.

"Will it mean going back to Wreathenwold?"

A moment's hesitation followed, before the figure said: "Follow the moths."

It was then that the incandescent shape returned, joined now by others. Around Benjamiah, a handful of big moths rose up from the shadows. Their wings were dark but patterned with luminescent violet—the same shade as threaded the stone fragment—leaving behind trails of purplish dust as they flapped like ponderous comets in the darkness. The woman had vanished from the mirror.

The moths fluttered, weaving brilliant circles above him. For a moment, Benjamiah's confusion subsided, his heart swelling—here was magic again, impossible and wonderful and mysterious. A shiver traveled down his spine, both thrilling and frightening.

He held up a hand and one of the moths settled on his finger. Benjamiah felt a vague, magical heat. Elation spread throughout him, as warm and bright as a sunrise. This was real. This was happening. When Benjamiah covered his left eye, the moths dissolved: only looking through the stone fragment revealed them.

The moth on Benjamiah's finger took off and suddenly

they all fluttered in the same direction—out of Mum's bedroom and into the hallway, trailing lines of violet dust. He hesitated, torn between seeking out Mum and following the moths, between terror and hope, between the safety of Wyvern-on-the-Water and the intoxicating mystery of the woman in the mirror, her game, and Wreathenwold.

What if this was his only chance to go back?

Benjamiah rushed in pursuit of the magical moths, barely keeping up. They crawled beneath Mum's front door, down the staircase, out into the cold Wyvern-on-the-Water evening. Benjamiah hurtled after them, the stone upon his eye and his chest tight with the effort of running.

As the moths swooped onward, past cottages and streetlamps and picket fences, questions lanced and tangled in his mind. What was the fragment now fixed upon his eye? Why did Mum have it? Who was the woman in the mirror and what did she mean? And where exactly was Benjamiah being led?

He soon got his answer. The flurry of moths descended upon the Wyvern-on-the-Water library. Before Benjamiah reached them, one of them crawled right into the keyhole. Benjamiah watched it fill with dazzling purple light before it clicked. The moths fluttered through as Benjamiah reached the door.

Struggling to catch his breath, Benjamiah entered the library. Now he could add trespassing to his burgeoning list of crimes. There was something unsettling and forbidding about the place after dark, titles and colors erased from the rows of shadowy books. All was eerily quiet.

The moths flurried, incandescent in the darkness, swarming across the library, along a corridor paneled in dark wood and lined with oily portraits. Ahead was Smythe's study. The moths soared inside, Benjamiah surging in pursuit.

By the time he entered, the moths had gathered round a door between Smythe's bureau and the bookshelf. A door that hadn't been there yesterday when Benjamiah had had the painful conversation with Hassaan. A door that had not been there the many times Benjamiah had visited with his family.

A door that had never been there before.

Four of the moths perched on the frame, the other on the doorknob. All else was dark and unmoving. Benjamiah trembled, ransacked by excitement and tension. He took a step forward, the moths flexing their luminous wings.

Something tugged at him from behind and he spun round, but nobody was there. It was then that Benjamiah, breathing furiously, checked his knapsack.

It was unzipped. And Nuisance was gone.

Benjamiah cast around wildly. Not for a single moment in the last few months had he been without Nuisance. Panic crested in his chest. Had he lost her? Had somebody taken Nuisance?

Or . . . had she let herself out?

"Nuisance?" he whispered.

Benjamiah peered high and low, breath sticking in his throat. "Are you here? It's me. Benjamiah."

A tweet.

Benjamiah's head cranked upward. There was Nuisance, in the form of a nightjar—her feathers black and red, her eyes white buttons—perched on the antlers of a stag head.

Benjamiah's heart soared as the little bird speared joyfully toward him. Before landing, she transformed into a capuchin and it was in this form that Benjamiah—after the longest and loneliest time—was able to embrace his poppet. They hugged, while Benjamiah laughed wildly and Nuisance hooted. Benjamiah sank to his knees and drew Nuisance's head toward his own, their foreheads pressed together, staring into her white button eyes.

"I missed you so much," said Benjamiah.

Nuisance howled mournfully in agreement. The living, breathing feel of her beneath Benjamiah's fingers felt so precious—only now did he truly appreciate the void she had left.

"I thought you were never coming back," he said, fighting to send a sob back down his throat. "Why did you leave me?"

The monkey stamped her feet, turned up her hands, and hooted argumentatively—and loudly.

"Okay, okay!" said Benjamiah.

The capuchin folded her arms, looking sulky. Benjamiah smiled, holding out a finger. Nuisance closed her hand round it. Happiness flooded Benjamiah.

"Look," he said, pointing toward the door.

Nuisance hooted and danced, wildly happy. Benjamiah laughed—he knew just how the poppet felt.

She transformed back into a nightjar, fluttering up to perch on Benjamiah's shoulder. She trilled happily in his ear. A nervous smile sprawled across Benjamiah's lips. This was really happening. He was really going back. Wreathenwold might not be Benjamiah's world, but his own world had never felt blander and less welcoming. He'd been so desperate to get home safely the last time, only to be left wondering if he really belonged here at all. Maybe Wreathenwold was where he was supposed to be.

As Benjamiah approached the door, the hairs on his arms and neck prickled and shivered. The shadowy margins at the door's edges seemed almost to stir, as if the air lived—churning like dust in sunlight. As Benjamiah's hand made contact with the doorknob, he perceived keenly some secret and quiet immensity behind it, a vastness that climbed up from his fingertips and set his body quivering.

Taking a deep breath, he opened the door. With his poppet on his shoulder, Benjamiah stepped through. They were going back.

FOUR
WITH THE FALLEN MAPMAKER

The bard sang of a library, an upside-down tower spearing downward into the earth. This library was kept by the insidious Chained Monks. It is said that all stories, past and future, are contained in the library—even the story of one's own life. Many have lost their minds chasing a glimpse of their own future, a madness on which the Chained Monks feed.
—*The Book of Barely Believable Stories*,
Mildred Fogge

BENJAMIAH FOUND HIMSELF in a dark, cold room of gray stone lit by a few shivering torches in brackets. Above was shadow so deep that he had no sense of how far it traveled. A cold, dreary draft plunged from the dark heights. On the walls were books—huge, ancient tomes of frail parchment, bound to the shelves by heavy chains so that they could be taken no farther than the wooden ledges beneath. The air smelled of crackling torches and brittle paper.

"Where do you think we are?" whispered Benjamiah.

Nuisance twittered from his shoulder. The room was circular, with only a door of weathered white bonewood. Benjamiah was not surprised to find the door through which he'd arrived had already vanished. Still, he felt an anxious squirm in his stomach. So keen to return to Wreathenwold, Benjamiah had overlooked the fact that Wreathenwold decided when he came and when he left. There was no immediate way back. And where exactly was he? This place already gave him the shivers.

"Only one way to go," said Benjamiah, as much for himself as Nuisance.

His steps echoed as he crossed to the bonewood door. It opened with a series of shudders and shrill creaks.

Benjamiah gasped. He'd emerged on a stone staircase spiraling round a vast chasm that plunged endlessly downward. Tomes covered the walls, thousands of them, every one chained to its shelf. There was no end in sight, either upward or downward. Peering over the edge, Benjamiah found only an abyss.

"It's a tower," he whispered.

He could see neither the top nor the bottom, nor another soul. Torches were the only light, arranged in fiery spirals traveling infinitely up and down. Nuisance crooned, drawing Benjamiah's attention to something.

It was a window—really just a square carved out of the stone. As he peered out, Benjamiah's stomach lurched. At first, he thought it was pitch-black outside. But, as his eyes adjusted, he perceived distantly the sleek, craggy shape of rock sparkling with minerals. The tower seemed to be enclosed within a vast cavern.

Then Benjamiah heard the clanking of a chain.

Spinning, Benjamiah found a small, crooked figure coming down the stairs. He was encased entirely in folds of mustard-colored robes, including a hood that sagged over his face. A bulky chain trailed out of the man's sleeve and rose high above, fixed to a thick loop in the stone wall.

"Admiring the view?"

The man's voice was hoarse and slow. He took another step toward Benjamiah, dragging the chain with him.

"Who are you?" said Benjamiah, backing away.

Nuisance trilled mistrustfully. The man paused.

"I am Brother Cayne," he said, "of the Order of the Chained Monks, the keepers of the library. Who might you be, young man?"

"I'm Benjamiah Creek. What is this place?"

"Surely you know? This is the Library Without End."

"Oh," said Benjamiah. And then, to keep the sinister monk talking while he considered how on earth he was going to escape, he said: "What's that?"

A dusty laugh gusted from Brother Cayne's hood.

"You are a very lucky boy," he replied, spreading his arms. "Look around you! All you could ever hope to know is contained within this tower."

"So it *is* a tower?" said Benjamiah. "Only out of the window . . ."

"Not all towers travel upward," said Brother Cayne.

It took Benjamiah a beat to process his meaning.

"An underground tower? But that's impossible!"

Even as he said it, he chided himself. It was impossible in *his* world. Wreathenwold was an entirely different matter.

"And yet it is so," said Brother Cayne, taking another step toward him.

"How deep does it go?" said Benjamiah, glancing over the edge of the steps. Vertigo made his legs momentarily flimsy.

Brother Cayne drew closer, his chain clanking. Benjamiah shifted backward, now pressed up against the books. Brother Cayne smelled of cloth and teeth.

"Who can say? There is more in this library than can ever be known or understood. Every story ever told can be found here. And every story not yet told, too. All eternity is written here—backward and forward. Every story that has ever been or ever will be. Including your own, my child. Somewhere here, among these books, is the story of Benjamiah Creek—from beginning to end. Would you like to read it?"

A shiver scaled the length of Benjamiah's spine. Could it be true? He examined the nearest books. Each was a vast ream of ancient parchment, the titles illegible.

"That would mean my story is already written," said Benjamiah.

"Quite so."

Brother Cayne gestured again to the cavernous library around them, twisting endlessly up and down.

"It waits for you somewhere here. And think of all the other things you will learn along the way. All the wisdom, all the secrets. You shall know everything. You shall be a *god* by the end."

Benjamiah scrambled backward as the Chained Monk laughed, a nasty, shuddering laugh that sent Nuisance squawking and flapping in terror. With every backward step, Brother Cayne drew closer again. How was Benjamiah going to escape?

From below, suddenly, a howl carried upward.

"Please . . . ," screamed a miserable voice. "Help me. Help me find my book. . . ."

Terror flared in Benjamiah. Clearly, he had to run upward to escape the tower, but how was he to elude Brother Cayne without the risk of tumbling over the edge and careering into the void?

Nuisance cried and then Benjamiah felt it: that presence in his mind, that network of magical nerves, which connected not to the muscles of his own body, but to the poppet on his shoulder. Nuisance grew still as Benjamiah assumed agency of his poppet. Suddenly he had two minds—his own and that of his poppet.

"You are most welcome here, Benjamiah Creek," croaked Brother Cayne. "Welcome to all this knowledge. Welcome for this day, and every other day to come!"

The Chained Monk cackled.

At Benjamiah's command, Nuisance speared at the hooded face of Brother Cayne, drawing a baffled howl from the monk and giving Benjamiah the chance he needed. Beneath Brother Cayne's grasping arms, Benjamiah wriggled. Then he charged up the stone steps, heart thumping, as the Chained Monk swatted at Nuisance. Benjamiah had the nightjar flash into his hooded face again, pecking his dusty old skull, while Benjamiah fled.

Then, at Benjamiah's command, Nuisance flapped upward and rejoined him.

Panic pursued Benjamiah every step of the way. The stone stairs coiled and coiled with no end in sight. Finally, just as he began to fear the tower really was infinite, he saw light above. Struggling to breathe, his legs about to give way, Benjamiah chased up the staircase and emerged into merciful fresh air.

It was early morning, still dark. Stars blinked above, arranged in patterns Benjamiah didn't recognize. The entrance to the Library Without End was carved into the trunk of a mossy bonewood tree. A sign hung from one of its boughs, reading: FINEST LIBRARY IN WREATHENWOLD! ALL WELCOME. STAY AS LONG AS YOU LIKE.

"Trust us to arrive *there*," said Benjamiah, scratching Nuisance's feathers.

He looked around. There were more bonewoods, though they were different from when Benjamiah had last been in Wreathenwold—the branches brimmed with incredibly pale purple blossoms. There were toadstools nearby, and smokeberry trees, and flowers of snowy white. All was quiet, save the mournful creaking of trees. Above Benjamiah, the purple moths flurried, grouping and separating frantically.

He walked on, wondering where he was and what he was supposed to do next. Last time he arrived in Wreathenwold, one event had led to another until, by chance, he'd met Hansel Cotton. But this was not a place Benjamiah had been before. Even if it were, Wreathenwold was an endless and impossible labyrinth—Benjamiah had no way of navigating it and finding Follynook, Elizabella and Hansel's bookshop. Fear tightened in his midriff.

The forest gave way to gentle slopes on either side, before taking an abrupt right turn. The wild became a Wreathenwold street.

A cold morning, and the cobbled street was coming to life: a ruddy-faced boy delivering newspapers, shops opening up, a tall woman dressed like a court jester playing mellifluous music from a three-pronged pipe. People hurried one way or another, dressed in top hats and frocks and waistcoats, in dress shoes and button-up boots. Poppets of infinite colors and designs hung at every hip.

Benjamiah also noticed people wearing masks. Two children came racing past in wolf masks—their poppets, cast as wolverines, scampering alongside. There were masked adults, too. A pair of women passed Benjamiah, arms interlocked, red-and-white masquerade masks covering the upper half of their faces. Wherever Benjamiah looked, he spotted more. Relief coursed through him; the many peculiar masks at least made the stone upon his eye less conspicuous.

"A hot brew for you, my lad?" said a voice.

Benjamiah turned. A man with coily black hair and a bushy mustache was serving cups of treacle tea from a stand. He wore an intricate mask—one half a bear's face and the other a man's.

"Only one piece," he said.

Benjamiah beamed. The sweet, sticky smell was blissful, the scent of wonderful memories. The man eyed Benjamiah's clothes (thankfully, he was wearing nothing colorful, which might otherwise have attracted the dangerous attention of color-poachers)—not to mention the stone encircling his eye—with some bemusement. Benjamiah dipped into his knapsack and drew out a two of clubs from one of the six packs of playing cards. In Wreathenwold, playing cards were money and Benjamiah had brought plenty with him.

The man gave him an ace of clubs in change, before pouring him a tall, steaming cup of treacle tea. The taste was paradise, like nothing back home. The hot, syrupy drink swept through him.

"A Merry Midsommer to you," said the man, doffing an imaginary cap.

"Merry Midsommer," returned Benjamiah, though he had no idea what it meant.

Midsommer might have explained the masks. There were other signs of festivity too. Dangling from tree branches and streetlamps were plumpkin-shaped paper lanterns of black and white, candles flickering within. Benjamiah walked on, sipping his tea beneath the bonewoods, their boughs swelling with blossom. He smelled poppysyrup and plumpkin broth, freshly baked sweetdough and pipes giving off trails of lemony smoke. Benjamiah bought a small bag of wyrm's eggs—delicious sweets that hatched on the tongue in a flood of sugary flavor—for when he was reunited with Elizabella.

But that thought gave him pause. Really, what hope was there of finding Follynook? Wreathenwold was an endless labyrinth and there were no maps or signs pointing the way. It was only by chance he'd met Hansel at all. It was a frightening realization. For all the weeks and months he'd longed to return, Wreathenwold was not without its dangers—particularly for Benjamiah, who still knew so little of this world.

As if to reinforce the point, he passed a street bulletin board plastered with missing posters for three different children. It was all too easy for children to stray too far in Wreathenwold and never find home again.

Nuisance cawed from his shoulder. Benjamiah slipped away from a woman wearing a mask of black and white feathers, jostling a sack of painted bird skulls, which—she claimed—would reveal his fortune.

"What do we do?" he asked the nightjar.

A happy trill was Nuisance's only response. At least his poppet wasn't afraid. Benjamiah regarded the little bird on his shoulder. If Nuisance had brought him to a specific place the last time Benjamiah had come to Wreathenwold, perhaps she'd done the same this time.

So Benjamiah walked, finishing his treacle tea among the carnivalesque Midsommer atmosphere. There were stands selling masks. A tall woman juggled fiery batons. Wagons and hansoms pulled by clockwork horses sent Benjamiah darting out of the way. He dodged a pair of Hanged Men, sackcloth covering their faces, their poppets—cast as formidable leathery-gray tigers—patrolling menacingly beside them. The Hanged Men policed Wreathenwold and were best avoided.

The street grew busier and Benjamiah's apprehension increased. Nothing presented itself to him, no reason for being here. The violet moths continued to flutter above, trying to lead Benjamiah on—perhaps toward the mysterious game he'd agreed to play. He wouldn't follow them without understanding more. For that, he needed Elizabella and Hansel.

He planted himself on a stubby rock wall, beneath the branches of a crooked bonewood tree. Above was one of the grotesques he remembered well from his last adventure in Wreathenwold—a stone gargoyle with the head of a bull, eyes bulging and mouth slanted in a silent scream.

"What are we supposed to do now?" said Benjamiah.

A bard in motley was telling a fanciful fairy tale from an upturned crate to a crowd of rapt children. It starred a mischievous young girl named Lyly Well-I-Never, who apparently found it impossible to do as she was told.

"Spare some change?" said an exhausted voice.

Benjamiah turned. On the other side of the rock wall was a boy, a little older than Benjamiah, in torn breeches and a frayed jacket.

"Sure, just let me . . ."

While retrieving some playing cards, Benjamiah noticed a spyglass at the boy's waist. Then, beside the boy's poppet, a cutlass.

When the boy looked up, Benjamiah gasped.

"*Silas?*"

Silas Weaver was a lieutenant of the Company of Mapmakers, whom Benjamiah and Elizabella had met when visiting the House of Mapmakers last year. Back then, despite his grumpy and despairing demeanor, Silas had nevertheless presented a serious, regal appearance. Now he looked utterly bereft.

"Do I know you?" he mumbled.

All pomp and grandeur had been stripped from Silas. His black hair was uncut and lank and his dark brown skin was grubby, crisscrossed with scratches and streaks of dirt. He seemed to have lost weight, too, his face drawn in around pointy cheekbones and colorless eyes. His poppet was icy blue with white stones for eyes.

"We met once," said Benjamiah, "at the House of Mapmakers."

Silas shrugged. "I don't remember," he said. "Be happy you got to see the House, though. Before she threw us all out."

"What do you mean?"

"The Viper," spat Silas. "She disbanded the Company. Said making maps is *illegal.* Which it always has been, but even the magi never broke up the Company. We're the seventh oldest in Wreathenwold!"

Benjamiah, with a shiver, recalled the Viper. She was Captain of the Company of Colornomics, which made her among the wealthiest and most powerful of all the ninety-eight Captains. She was also an awful person.

"But what does it have to do with the Viper? She's from another Company."

Silas studied Benjamiah as though he might be mad. It was a familiar experience for Benjamiah when it came to Wreathenwold.

"Have you had a bang to the head or something? The Viper rules now, with the Minotaur . . ."

"The Minotaur is dead?" blurted out Benjamiah, devastated.

"Not yet," said Silas. "But soon, by the sounds of it. Whatever the case, he's not well enough to rule."

"And he chose the *Viper* to rule in his stead?"

Benjamiah, who had met the Minotaur and found him a harmless old man, struggled to believe he'd choose such a cruel successor.

"So they say." Silas shrugged, as though it didn't matter. "Soon the ninety-eight Captains will vote. Not that there's any doubt. The Viper will win. She'll buy up most of them and terrify the rest. Then the Mapmakers really will be doomed. She'll burn the House down and hang the lot of us, I expect."

Silas slumped, a shipwreck of his former self, and Benjamiah reeled. It made no sense that the Minotaur would choose the Viper. He also felt great sympathy for

Silas and the Mapmakers, whom he'd always thought of favorably—probably because theirs was such a hopeless task. It was impossible to map Wreathenwold.

"Oh no . . . ," mumbled Benjamiah.

"What?" snapped Silas.

"Elizabella and Hansel . . . ," said Benjamiah.

"Who?"

If the Viper ruled now, the Cottons would be in as much peril as the Mapmakers. Through little fault of their own, Benjamiah and Elizabella had upset the Viper during their last adventure and Benjamiah knew she wouldn't rest until she'd exacted an unjust and excessive revenge.

"Where are we?" he asked, crouching in front of Silas.

Silas frowned. "Well, let's see. . . ."

It was then that Silas withdrew a disheveled notebook—really just an unruly stack of pages held together by a crumbling spine—and began leafing through it. Every page was a chaos of sketched streets, and woods, and illegible notes. Silas looked up and down the street, back to his notebook, increasingly despondent as he tried to orient himself. Benjamiah knew it was futile. Every page in Silas's notebook would be nonsense.

The Mapmaker sighed, shoulders slumping.

"How will you find your way back?" said Benjamiah.

"Who cares?" wailed Silas. "It's all over. The Mapmakers were Wreathenwold's only chance. Only a map can free this doomed city. The Viper will destroy our last hope. And, even if she hadn't, we never did find..."

He trailed off, burying his face in his hands. Benjamiah knew where the unfinished sentence would have led. The Mapmakers once had a magical thread that could help people navigate the labyrinth. That was until the thread was stolen from the House of Mapmakers by Elizabella's brother, Edwid, setting in motion a sequence of events that ended with Edwid's death.

"I know," said Benjamiah, patting Silas on the shoulder. "Ariadne."

Silas's head shot up, eyes bloodshot and tight with sudden suspicion. But Benjamiah was distracted. The moment he'd said "Ariadne," something had moved on the rock wall above Silas's head.

It looked like a tiny reddish snake, about sixteen inches long. Except she had no head or eyes or tail. She was only string—the most wonderful and welcome string in the world.

Ariadne rose like a cobra, head bobbing. Benjamiah's eyes widened, stunned.

"What did you say?" snapped Silas, who hadn't spotted Ariadne above his head. "How do you know about Ariadne? Who exactly are you? Come to think of it, what are you *wearing*? And what is that thing round your eye?"

Benjamiah ignored him, staring at Ariadne with

intense relief. About halfway up was a knot—this marked the spot where she'd been cut in half, apparently killed, until Benjamiah had retied her.

He reached out a hand and Ariadne latched on, swinging between Benjamiah's fingers like a monkey between branches. Benjamiah laughed. From his shoulder, an overjoyed Nuisance the nightjar plunged toward Ariadne. The poppet and the thread embraced, rolling around in euphoric reunion.

Finally, Silas spotted Ariadne. He fell back, struggling for purchase on the rock wall as he staggered up, his eyes orblike and his mouth opening and closing in mute shock.

"It's . . . It's . . . ," he muttered.

The Mapmaker rubbed his eyes. Ariadne wriggled up Benjamiah's sleeve and sat nervously on his shoulder.

"Ariadne, it's me," said Silas. "Don't you remember me?"

Coyly, Ariadne nodded. But when Silas reached out a hand, his eyes watery, Ariadne recoiled.

"Why?" said Silas, running despairing fingers through his hair.

"Because she came for me," said Benjamiah. "Isn't that right, Ariadne?"

Ariadne nodded.

"But how?" said Benjamiah.

Gently, he lifted Ariadne from his shoulder, letting her coil in the palm of his hand. As Benjamiah understood it,

Ariadne was unable to find people in the labyrinth—only places. So how had she tracked him down? And, perhaps more worryingly, why?

"Are Elizabella and Hansel okay?" he whispered.

Ariadne—as best as a length of thread could do so—gave a meek, noncommittal wiggle.

"Are they in danger? Is it the Viper?"

Another shrug. Benjamiah felt his chest tighten, felt the world around him tilt and teeter. What had the Viper done? Though Ariadne was a marvel, her inability to speak was immensely frustrating in that moment. Try as he might, Benjamiah could only glean that they were not at Follynook, were alive, not harmed, but in some kind of nameless trouble.

"Can you take us to them?"

Ariadne shivered upright, giving a formal bow before swinging from Benjamiah's hand and back onto the rock wall, ready to lead the way through the labyrinth.

"*Us?*" said Silas, still shellshocked.

Benjamiah nodded. "Come with me," he said, "and Ariadne is yours. We should have given her back, anyway."

The scruffy Mapmaker, unable to draw his eyes from Ariadne, gave a quick nod.

FIVE
WITH THE MANOR IN THE WOODS

> In the depths of the Weird Wood lives a great stag named Ogbo. Legend says that the truth of the world's origin is carved into his antlers. For generations, hunters have pursued Ogbo in order to learn the secrets he carries. Ogbo lives to this day, while the hunters do not.
> —*The Book of Barely Believable Stories,*
> Mildred Fogge

BENJAMIAH AND SILAS traveled all day. So anxious was he to reach Elizabella and Hansel, Benjamiah scarcely had time to absorb the remarkable fact that he was actually back in Wreathenwold. Since the moment he'd left last summer, he had craved to look upon the magical world once more: the people in their Victorian-style clothing, a poppet doll hanging at every hip; each street the branch of a seemingly endless and unmappable labyrinth with the rows of crooked buildings its walls; the bonewood trees; the clockwork horses; the miasma of exotic smells and smokes.

The thrill of being back was tempered, though, by his need to find Elizabella and Hansel. A frantic Benjamiah hailed a hansom cab.

"I can't . . . I have no money," said a despondent Silas, head drooping.

"I do," said Benjamiah.

Perched on the hansom's pitted leather bench, Benjamiah and Silas swayed in unison as it rattled along the cobbled street. Nuisance was in doll form, flopped in Benjamiah's lap, Ariadne poking out of his breast pocket. Through the window, Wreathenwold was in good spirits amid the soft, warm sunlight. There were masks and music and lanterns, a carnivalesque feel to the city.

Benjamiah thought of Elizabella and Hansel, his mind a carousel of dreadful speculations about what the Viper might have done. He remembered Odith Murdstone all too well. Spiteful and greedy, there was no telling what retribution she might have concocted. But for a timely intervention, she'd have sucked the color from Benjamiah's eyes with a ghastly instrument called a spectractor. He shivered at the memory.

"This is as far as I go, lads!" called the driver.

Benjamiah groaned rather rudely. The hansom drivers tended not to travel more than a street or two in

Wreathenwold; the labyrinth had a way of fogging people's memories, so that even straying two or three streets from home could mean never finding your way back.

After Benjamiah paid the driver with a three of spades, Ariadne led them round a narrow stone corner, passing beneath a mossy archway upon which perched another stone grotesque. When they emerged on the next street, rain hurtled from a smoke-colored sky. In Wreathenwold, the weather changed with every street. It was another reminder of how terribly Benjamiah had missed the marvelous, nonsensical charm of this world.

They traveled for hours, in hansoms and on foot. They journeyed through sun and fog, snow and rain. They turned corners, crossed bridges, took winding stone staircases up and down—the marvelous Ariadne leading the way like some gymnastic serpent, a puffing and panting Silas doing all he could to keep up with Benjamiah's demanding pace.

It might have been a symptom of Benjamiah's anxiety, but he couldn't help noticing a lot of posters for missing children. Almost every street had one or two. On one rainy street, a sobbing grandfather was accosting passersby, asking if they'd seen a small redheaded boy named Pip.

"Why are there so many lost children?" asked Benjamiah.

"Why do you think?" said Silas miserably. "Children will forever be getting lost until the curse of this labyrinth is lifted. That's why the work of the Mapmakers is so vital. Only we can free this accursed land!"

It seemed more than usual to Benjamiah, but he'd learned there was little point in arguing with Silas at his most melodramatic. Everything about him was thinned out and bedraggled. The spyglass hanging from Silas's belt was cracked, and even his poppet dangled forlornly. Silas had told Benjamiah he was called Griffyn.

Unwilling to accept the hopelessness of the Mapmakers' task, Silas consulted his slew of useless maps as they traveled, sketching and making notes, mumbling miserably to himself. No matter how he tried to orient himself, Wreathenwold had him bewildered and defeated at every turn. Regardless, he did his best to pretend otherwise.

"I *knew* it would be this street . . . ," he'd declare, adding another fruitless note and sticking out his chest importantly.

At other times, Silas would blather on about his favorite historic Mapmaker, Ernold Lacer, who had voyaged around Wreathenwold for forty years, attempting to plot the unplottable. Benjamiah neglected to remind Silas that Ernold had failed and ended up dead at the bottom of a well—lured there by a malignant well-lurker.

Another thing Silas liked to do was complain, particularly about how poor and unfortunate he was. Losing patience with this, Benjamiah shoved an entire pack of playing cards into his hands.

Silas stared at it as though it were some unfathomable object, his expression drawn into blankness.

"What . . . ," he finally said. "This is . . . Where did you . . . I can't . . ."

Clearly, Silas had never seen so much money. His hands began to tremble and he shook his head from side to side, throwing a frantic, bloodshot look in Benjamiah's direction.

In Benjamiah's world, the playing cards were almost worthless. In Wreathenwold, a full deck was a lot of money—the equivalent of over a thousand pounds back home.

"Where did you get this?" said Silas fearfully. "Are you some kind of pocket-picker? Or color-poacher? Or *worse?*"

"You're welcome," said Benjamiah, trying not to be offended. "It was my money and now it's yours. Keep it. I have more. Buy whatever you want, whatever makes you happy. As long as we can *hurry up.*"

For a moment, Benjamiah thought Silas was going to cry. Then, finally, the Mapmaker pocketed the cards. The latest hansom rattled onward, Silas stony with shock beside Benjamiah.

In the afternoon, Benjamiah bought lunch on a busy market street—sweetdough sandwiches, sticky opples, and milk punch to drink. With his new wealth, Silas had nervously bought himself an enormous plumpkin pastry and was now loudly devouring it.

Benjamiah sat nearby, beneath a gnarly bonewood tree, relishing his own food. The market was a hive of noise and movement, merchants hawking all manner of oddities: magical powders and serums, glass jars of impossible sounds and scents, toadstools, and bouquets of strange flowers.

Nuisance, now a capuchin, was playing with Ariadne. Above all else, having Nuisance back brought Benjamiah such happiness. She did turn his thoughts toward Mum, though. His first few hours back in Wreathenwold had been so frenzied that he'd barely paused to consider home. Already the alarm would have been raised that Benjamiah was missing. His stomach twisted at the thought of what he was putting his family through again. Only Mum would suspect the truth, particularly when she found the strange stone missing from her dressing-gown pocket.

Benjamiah had asked Silas about the mysterious fragment, explaining he'd found it and now it wouldn't come off. Unfortunately, Silas offered nothing useful. He only boasted of the wonderful archives at the House of

Mapmakers, where the answer to any question could be found. This set him off muttering furiously about the Viper again, forgetting Benjamiah's question entirely.

From his reflection in a tavern window, Benjamiah regarded the stone clasped upon his face. Chalky-colored, spiderwebbed with faint violet threads. The oval in its center looping perfectly round his left eye. What exactly was this thing? And who on earth was the woman in the mirror?

Elizabella and Hansel would know.

Elizabella and Hansel . . .

Apprehension gathered again, a storm in his belly. They had to get moving.

The next street was a forest bisected by a stream babbling upon a bed of glassy, orblike stones. The trees were vast, webbed tightly together on either side and coated in pinkish lichen. Birds muttered strangely from the undergrowth. Trudging along the bank, Benjamiah asked Silas a question he'd wondered about all day.

"What exactly is Midsommer?"

Silas shot him a look that was all too familiar for Benjamiah in Wreathenwold—as though Silas were trying to work out if Benjamiah was teasing him or otherwise heavily concussed.

"I'm not from around here," said Benjamiah, which didn't help.

"Meaning what, exactly?" said Silas.

"It's . . . difficult to explain."

"I'm a Mapmaker, don't forget," said Silas, tugging at the lapels of a new—somewhat extravagant, Benjamiah thought—tweed jacket he'd bought with some of the playing cards. "We've heard of many strange places. A lot of them made up, no doubt. But better we hear about them than not."

As briefly as possible, Benjamiah explained he was from another world entirely—one that was not a vast labyrinth, where people were not dollcasters, where there was no magic at all. Afterward, there was only the sound of the stream rattling along its bed. Silas's expression gave nothing away.

"Midsommer is a monthlong celebration of folklore and fairy tales," he said. "It's a little murky where it all began. It's long been said that the month of Midsommer is the most magical time of year. *Magic forged at Midsommer is the strongest and truest of all magic—both fair and foul.* That's from Mildred Fogge's *The Book of Barely Believable Stories*, which is a collection of folktales. Actually, the Captain of the Mapmakers, Josabella, is a distant descendant of Mildred's."

Silas had given nothing away as to whether he had believed Benjamiah's story or not—Benjamiah wasn't sure what to make of that.

"Midsommer is a time to celebrate," continued Silas. "People give each other gifts and wear masks. There are parties in the streets, bonfires. The midpoint of Midsommer is called High Dusk, which is when the Grand Masquerade happens, a fancy ball for only the wealthiest people in Wreathenwold. The stories say Midsommer is when figures and creatures from folklore live again, too. But that's likely all humbug. The most important thing is that it's a happy time for Wreathenwold. . . ."

Silas trailed off, hurt and bitterness rallying upon his face once more. This Midsommer was not a happy time for him and the Mapmakers. The Viper had seen to that. And, if Benjamiah had understood Ariadne correctly, it was not a happy time for Elizabella and Hansel, either.

The day brought no sign of Follynook. After spending the night at an inn, they continued the next morning with yet greater urgency. Silas grumbled, though a little less than before. Nuisance fluttered or scampered about, as either a nightjar, capuchin, or dormouse. Ariadne swooped and swung, leading them on.

Every step nearer cranked up Benjamiah's fear. What if they were too late? Were they moving too slowly? What had the Viper done to Elizabella and Hansel?

That afternoon, Benjamiah had the answers.

After many more streets, left turns and right turns, bridges and tunnels and staircases, after streets swimming in luminescent Midsommer sun and streets swept with fog or lanced by hail and ice, Ariadne delivered them to a gate of black iron, rising into ominous corkscrew spikes and set within a stone archway. A bullheaded grotesque was crouched upon it, a long forked tongue falling from its mouth. Beyond the gate a gravel driveway twisted away through rows of naked, spindly bonewoods. The forest was blanketed with snow.

A plaque on the gate read:

OGBO'S REST

ALL VISITORS

UNWELCOME

Benjamiah looked up at Ariadne, coiled round an iron spike.

"Here?" said Benjamiah.

Ariadne nodded and he swallowed. What was this place?

"Is it safe?" he asked Ariadne.

Ariadne gave a noncommittal shrug.

"Thanks," muttered Benjamiah. "Really comforting."

"How do we get in?" said Silas, trying—and failing—to sound brave.

At that, Ariadne snaked downward and descended upon the gate's lock. She threaded inside, nosing around within the mechanism until it unlocked with a *thunk*.

Benjamiah was impressed. "Did you know she could do that?" he asked Silas.

"Of course," said Silas, beaming like a proud parent. "She's full of tricks."

Silas held out a finger as Ariadne emerged. Ariadne regarded it mistrustfully and instead slithered onto Nuisance's back—then cast as a nightjar. Silas looked hurt.

"Give her time," said Benjamiah.

The iron gate opened with a loud, treacherous squeal. Nobody came rushing to apprehend them, so they followed the driveway, boots crunching in the snow, as it weaved between the trees. Snowflakes tumbled from a sky of endless glaring white. The leafless bonewood branches formed a matted snarl above them, snow tufted on every bough.

Ariadne still rode Nuisance, now perched nervously on Benjamiah's shoulder. Silas had unhitched Griffyn from his belt and held the doll tightly, though Benjamiah noticed the Mapmaker's hand was shaking. Large bone-colored moths fluttered among the trees.

Finally, the manor came into view.

It was a spooky, rambling, L-shaped house clad in grim timber and sprawled with blackish ivy, the slate roof smothered in snow. Every window was unlit. Columns of smoke unfurled from two of its chimneys. It was like every haunted house Benjamiah had seen from Grandma's scary films. Outside was a half-collapsed stable and a large well and a shed of chopped bonewood logs.

"I think we should go back . . . ," whispered Silas.

Before Benjamiah could respond, a grim rumbling sound carried from the trees.

Coming down the snowy slope was a hound, as large and fearsome as a panther. Its fur was slate-colored, its eyes red coat buttons. It growled and snarled, teeth bared, strings of saliva swaying from its gums.

Benjamiah's body locked up. He couldn't breathe, couldn't think, as the monstrous creature drew slowly toward them, head low and its snarl gathering in volume and intensity. Nuisance twittered uselessly. Beside Benjamiah, Silas had fallen backward—Griffyn remained uncast in his hand.

A furious bark erupted from the dog's mouth, as stark and terrifying as a gunshot ringing through the woods.

"No trespassers!" despaired a wispy voice.

A thin, hunchbacked man limped out through the snow, joining the growling poppet hound. He looked around sixty years old, with waxy skin, a white beard, and badly chopped white hair. There was a milkiness to his pale green eyes, and Benjamiah noticed an involuntary tremble in his left hand. Furs wrapped his shoulders and he leaned on a bowed walking stick.

"There should be no trespassers here!" moaned the man.

The poppet barked again, spraying saliva.

"W-we're so sorry, sir," stammered Silas, down on his haunches. "We'll leave right away, right now...."

Before Silas could scramble up, the hound unleashed a volley of booming barks that reduced him to whimpering.

"The gate is locked," said the man, limping forward. "Why did you come here? There should be nobody here, nobody!"

"We're looking for someone," said Benjamiah, finally finding the strength to speak. "We thought..."

But the man was working himself into a passion, the poppet snarling and barking and lurching forward. Benjamiah stood paralyzed, fear blotting out all thought.

"Who is it, Clover?" came another voice.

It was one Benjamiah recognized. Mercifully, trudging along the driveway, came Hansel Cotton.

He was just as Benjamiah remembered him, short and wizened with a mad bush of white hair—he had always reminded Benjamiah of Albert Einstein—and soft, colorless eyes.

Those eyes widened as they settled upon Benjamiah.

"Can it be...?" he muttered, overcome with shock. "Can it really be you, Benjamiah Creek?"

Forgetting Clover and his horrid poppet, Benjamiah bolted forward and buried himself in Hansel's midriff. Hansel laughed, his shabby waistcoat smelling of lemony smoke and books and safety.

"You're not hurt," said Benjamiah into Hansel's torso.

"No, dear boy. Whyever would I be?"

"Elizabella?"

"Safe and well," said Hansel. "And here. But how can *you* possibly be here, Benjamiah?"

Benjamiah drew back and looked up. It was then that Hansel regarded the stone encircling Benjamiah's eye—and instantly Benjamiah knew he was in trouble. Horror played upon Hansel's face, his lips parting in baffled shock.

"This thing, it's stuck—" began Benjamiah.

"Later," said Hansel, flicking his eyes toward Clover.

It was so good to see Hansel again, even if his reaction had chilled Benjamiah to the core. And Hansel was safe, and Elizabella, too.

"Why are you here? What about Follynook? The Viper . . ."

Hansel's eyes dimmed, looking strained.

"A misunderstanding," he said half-heartedly. "An issue with taxes. Fines, interest . . . All a little boring. Everything will be put right—don't you worry about that."

"Odith Murdstone has repossessed Follynook and turfed them out," said Clover over Benjamiah's shoulder. "There will be no going back, as much as we'd all like it. It's up for auction."

Hansel studied the old man with a look far colder than Benjamiah would have thought him capable.

"You've met my brother, Clover," said Hansel.

Hansel's brother? *That* was a surprise. Benjamiah supposed, now he looked for it, that there was a resemblance in the nose and chin. But Clover was taller, gaunter, and more crooked than Hansel—not to mention completely devoid of all Hansel's easy goodness.

"Clover, recall that hideous beast," said Hansel, pointing at the dog.

Murmuring under his breath, Clover limped forward and ran his fingers through its fur. As quick as a click of the fingers, the hound shrank, reshaped, and became a doll in Clover's hand—slate-gray, with red coat buttons for eyes.

Hansel eyed Clover with considerable distaste as he introduced Benjamiah Creek—as a friend of Elizabella's—and allowed Silas to introduce himself. Silas and Hansel shook hands heartily. Clover looked, above all else, deeply unhappy.

"Master Weaver, come inside and get yourself some treacle tea," said Hansel. "I will hear everything—absolutely everything—about the famed Company of Mapmakers."

A prideful smile spread across Silas's mouth, his chest puffing up importantly.

"You'll have a cup too, Benjamiah Creek," said Hansel. "But first . . . She's through there."

Hansel pointed to a spot beyond the dilapidated stable.

Benjamiah walked through the trees. Snow flurried and drifted. Moths fluttered, including the violet-patterned moths visible only to Benjamiah. They continued to pull in a different direction, trying to lead him elsewhere. Nuisance was a dormouse, peeking out of Benjamiah's breast pocket. Ariadne was beside her, head poking out like an inquisitive snake.

Benjamiah's stomach roiled. Nerves spread through him like reaching tendrils. Somewhere ahead was Elizabella. He'd missed her every day, every moment, since leaving Wreathenwold. But what should he say? More worrying still, what if she hadn't missed him in return? What if she didn't care he was back? What if, in the months apart, Elizabella had made other friends and forgotten all about him?

The first Benjamiah saw was a midnight-blue bear with marbled eyes, slightly bulkier than a large dog, meandering along the forest floor, dragging her snout through the snow. Emba—Elizabella's poppet. Stomach lurching, Benjamiah kept his distance and followed.

Emba came to a clearing. Sitting cross-legged on a tree stump, her back to Benjamiah, was Elizabella. She was throwing stones into an icy pond, each punching through the glassy ice with a small crack.

Benjamiah took a deep, fearful breath. "Hi," was all he could manage.

Elizabella stiffened mid-throw. Emba the bear turned,

marble eyes fixed on Benjamiah. She sniffed the air, then looked to Elizabella for guidance.

Elizabella turned her head as she clambered up, a little clumsily. She wore a bonnet, out of which tumbled strings of pale hair. Her eyes were big and dazzlingly green, freckles scattered across her face, her teeth a little crooked. Her mouth gaped.

"It's me, Benjamiah," he said stupidly.

Elizabella planted her hands on her hips. Her eyes narrowed, her stare sharpening as though surprise had given way to . . . was it anger? Benjamiah's stomach plummeted. Maybe he had misjudged it, just as he'd feared—maybe Elizabella had meant more to Benjamiah than Benjamiah had ever meant to Elizabella.

Sadness flexed its wings, but never took flight. Elizabella began walking toward him. Halfway she broke into a run, kicking up spouts of snow. Before Benjamiah could say another word, Elizabella had flung herself upon him and wrapped him in the tightest and best hug of his entire life.

SIX
WITH THE WITCHSTONE TREE

"Agatha Drake, Agatha Drake,
Beneath the witchstone tree,
I am good and true and worth your grace,
So play your game with me."
—*The Book of Barely Believable Stories*,
Mildred Fogge

THE EMBRACE LASTED a few seconds before embarrassment took over. The children sprang apart, Benjamiah staring down at his feet and Elizabella fiddling with her bonnet. It was then that she took a closer look at the stone looped round Benjamiah's eye.

"Benjamiah, what is . . ." she gasped, covering her mouth.

"It's how I got back," he said, before describing the specter in the mirror and the magical moths.

When he was finished, Elizabella only gawped, wide-eyed and mouth agape.

"Stop staring," he said, blushing.

"Do you have *any* idea what that thing is?" replied Elizabella, voice trembling.

Benjamiah shook his head. "Do you?"

"I think so." Elizabella looked both pensive and spooked. "It's easier if I show you. Come on."

They set off in the direction of the manor, crunching through the snow. Elizabella's reaction to the stone had been even less comforting than Hansel's. Dread gathered in the pit of Benjamiah's stomach.

"How did you find us?" said Elizabella.

By this time, Emba the bear was playing delightedly with Nuisance the capuchin. They'd clearly missed each other too. Then Ariadne spidered her way out of Benjamiah's breast pocket and joined in with the fun. Elizabella smiled.

"I wondered where Ariadne had got to," she said. "How did she find you, though? She can't find people."

Benjamiah had wondered the same thing. It made no sense, and Ariadne, for all her brilliance, was helpless to explain herself.

"I met Clover," said Benjamiah. "He's . . . interesting?"

Elizabella smiled. "Hansel says being cooped up here all his life has made him a bit *off*," she said. "He took us in, at least. But he can't wait for us to leave. Believe me, we're only here because we have to be."

"Because of the Viper?"

She nodded. They walked toward the manor, through the flickering snow and the wiry bonewoods, their branches cross-hatched against the milky sky. Emba, now a capuchin with midnight-blue fur, was wrestling and hooting with Nuisance. Poor Ariadne struggled to keep up as they rolled and scampered and leaped. Being with Elizabella again had Benjamiah feeling jittery with excitement, unsure how close to stand, how quickly to walk.

"We knew she wouldn't forget," said Elizabella through gritted teeth.

Benjamiah nodded. He had left Wreathenwold, out of the Viper's reach. But Elizabella and Hansel remained in the crosshairs. Elizabella and Benjamiah had enraged the Viper by breaking into her home, at the forbidding Magimmaculum, in search of one of Edwid's whisperwicks. They'd found it, but not before getting into a scrape with Odith's repugnant daughter, Gertrid. The Viper had vowed revenge for her daughter's injuries, despite the fact that Gertrid had brought them upon herself.

"She couldn't take the revenge she wanted," said Elizabella, referring to the Viper's desire to extract Elizabella and Benjamiah's eye colors. "But that only made her change approach. Instead, she increased Hansel's taxes.

She's Captain of the Company of Colornomics, after all. She can do what she likes. She kept demanding more and more money until Hansel was ruined. Fighting it was useless. Finally, the Hanged Men came, dragged us out of Follynook, and bolted the door."

Fury swept through Benjamiah. How could the Viper be so cruel, so vindictive? The image of Hansel and Elizabella rooted out of their beloved bookshop—their home—was crushingly sad.

"I have money," he said. "Five whole packs of playing cards. We could . . ."

Elizabella smiled sadly. "It isn't enough," she said. "Follynook will be auctioned, for a price we'll never be able to afford. Anyway, she'd only find another way to punish us afterward. It's just a house. An old bookshop. We had time to grab Edwid and Ada's soulblooms. A few important belongings. That's it. The rest is gone, and so is Follynook."

Elizabella was doing her best to show acceptance, but Benjamiah didn't buy it. Beneath the surface, he sensed how Elizabella seethed and flamed—like magma under a stony crust. It was contagious, too. Benjamiah felt it: a hot, living fury at the Viper's cruelty. Follynook was more than a house and an old bookshop. It was *home*. Benjamiah knew it, and Elizabella and Hansel must know it too.

"How was your journey?" asked Elizabella.

Despite herself, she couldn't help looking like

Benjamiah's arrival was the best thing that had happened to her in a long time, biting her lip to trap an enormous smile that seemed determined to escape.

As they walked, Benjamiah described how the door had led to the impossible library, kept by the creepy Chained Monks—Elizabella was enthralled by the story. Then he described encountering Silas, Ariadne's arrival, their journey here.

"And another thing," he said, swallowing nervously, "I told Silas he could have Ariadne back."

Elizabella looked briefly cross, but took a deep breath before replying.

"I guess that's the right thing to do," she said, sounding like it was completely the wrong thing to do. "Edwid stole her from the Mapmakers, after all."

"What about getting back to Follynook?" said Benjamiah.

"Follynook is gone. We don't need to find our way back."

Benjamiah was about to reply—to tell her she was wrong and that there must be something they could do—when he was interrupted.

"Dinner soon."

It was Clover, peering out from behind a bonewood tree. As before, he looked alarmed and dismayed at the very sight of children on his property, remaining half-hidden behind the tree.

"Yes, Uncle," said Elizabella, a picture of perfect sweetness.

Clover drifted away, as silently as he'd approached, and Elizabella's extravagant smile dissolved.

"He's so *weird*," she whispered. "I'd never met him before."

Elizabella led Benjamiah back to Ogbo's Rest, past greenhouses full of strange plants with drooping leaves and thorny stems. Inside, the manor was shadowy and bitterly cold, lit by a few trembling oil lamps, with high ceilings and rafters lashed with cobwebs and a cloying dustiness. It might once have been grand, but was now run-down and drafty, the floorboards creaky and the walls empty of decorations.

As they climbed a creaky, splintery staircase, Elizabella said, "I've only got one book with color illustrations now. They're too expensive. But this one is special. That's how I know—that's how I *think* I know—what that thing on your face is."

Despite Elizabella's obvious worry, Benjamiah detected a music in her voice that he felt in himself: the familiar, intoxicating thrill of a mystery to be chased down and unraveled together. Alongside Elizabella, Benjamiah thought, danger and darkness became merely the promise of adventure.

Stomach fluttering, he followed Elizabella into her

temporary bedroom. It had no real character, much like Benjamiah's new bedroom at Mum's flat. Seeing it, he felt a stab of sympathy for Elizabella—she'd been uprooted, just like him. There was a messy bed, and a ratty old armchair by the window, and a traveling chest full of tangled clothes. Another chest was absolutely crammed with books. From it, Elizabella grabbed one and handed it to Benjamiah.

It was a large illustrated edition of *The Book of Barely Believable Stories* by Mildred Fogge. Benjamiah flicked through the faded pages, examining the ornate, colorful sketches and the names of stories: "Bolly Pondwater," "The Imp and the Lamp," "The Other-Way-Ups."

Elizabella took it back and leafed through frantically.

"Here," she said, biting her bottom lip. "Read."

It was a story called "The Witchstone Tree." In the middle of the first two pages was an elaborately sketched tree, deathly white with ribbons of faint violet spread throughout its trunk and boughs. The colors matched the stone clamped round Benjamiah's eye.

With a lurch in his stomach, Benjamiah read on.

The Witchstone Tree
Once upon a time, there was a deep and wild forest. It was a gnarled, barbed, sprawling expanse, alive with mutters and whispers, flooded with damp shadow and

stubborn mist. Gossipy locals claimed it was haunted, home to all manner of tricksy and malevolent wraiths who would lure unsuspecting travelers to their demise.

At the very heart of the forest was a cottage where there lived a young woman named Agatha Drake. Here she had always lived, alongside her poppet, Dusk, and her plumpkin patch and her smokeberry orchard, and the witchstone tree.

It was Agatha's task, as it had been her mother's before her, and her grandmother's before that, to guard the witchstone tree. It was a great stone thing, chalky white and coursing with strands of pale purple, looming over the cottage. Only during the month of Midsommer, when the sun hung high and true, would the witchstone tree soften. Its trunk would temper and its leaves would tremble and the violet veins, snaking throughout the stone, would sharpen and glimmer.

During Midsommer, the witchstone was alive, a source of great and strange magic determined to spread its roots throughout Wreathenwold. It was the task of the Drakes to protect the people from this fount of ungovernable sorcery, which might otherwise consume all of the land. This troubled the good-hearted Agatha, who wished she could use the witchstone tree's power for good.

One Midsommer morning, a child came to Agatha's cottage in the forest.

"Miss," said the trembling little boy, "I have come to ask for help."

"I cannot," replied Agatha, though it saddened her.

"Me and Ma live by a deep lake," continued the boy desperately. "We are very poor. At the bottom of this lake grows the finest deepweed, which we could gather up and sell to put food on the table. Only, the deepweed is too far down and my lungs are scarred from ouroboros flu. Can you help me?"

Moved by the boy's struggles, Agatha, beneath the warm Midsommer sun, peeled a length of witchstone from the tree, and wove it into a mask. Before the witchstone set, she carved glyphs into its surface with a daggered fingernail—investing the mask with the desired magical property.

"Wear this when you dive," said Agatha. "You will breathe underwater and swim as the river serpents do. But be warned: should you use this witchstone for any reason other than to gather deepweed, it will fix upon your face, become unbearably heavy, and drown you. And the witchstone tree will worm its roots deeper into my soul, for it longs to grow."

The boy took the mask, thanked Agatha, and ran back to his ma.

At first, he used the mask as he'd promised, gathering deepweed to sell from a barrow in town. Soon they had plenty of food on the table, and a warm hearth, and fine clothes. Then one day Ma heard that a merchant's ship, loaded with flasks of pure color, had sunk in a nearby river.

"Why not use the witchstone to claim a little treasure?" said the boy. "Why should we not be a little richer? The witch will never know."

Ma agreed. The boy traveled swiftly to the river. He plunged into the murky deep as a river serpent would. Finding the shipwreck, the boy gathered as many flasks of color as he could carry. Then he set off toward the surface.

Before he reached it, the witchstone mask gripped his face. It became unbearably heavy, dragging him back to the depths where he surely drowned.

Far away, beneath the witchstone tree, Agatha Drake gasped—as the tree's roots corkscrewed deeper into her soul.

The next Midsommer, another child came to the woods.

"Miss," said the shaking little girl, "I have come to beg for aid."

"You'll find none here," said Agatha as she watered her plumpkin patch.

"There is a deep cave in the mountain above our village," said the little girl. "It's Father's job to go into this cave and gather goblin-moss. Only, Father has a bad back and now I have to go instead, otherwise we'll starve. I'm dreadfully afraid of the dark and my poppet fire isn't bright enough. Can you help me?"

Agatha sighed. Against her better judgment, she tore a strip of witchstone from the tree and spun it into a mask.

Into its surface she engraved the spell.

"Wear this when you enter the cave," said Agatha. "You will see as the cave wraiths see. But mark my words: Should you use this witchstone for any reason other than to gather goblin-moss, you will live in darkness for the rest of your days. And the witchstone tree will reach further into my soul."

The girl nodded, thanked Agatha, and left the forest.

Initially, the girl used the mask just as she'd promised, venturing into the cave to scrape goblin-moss from the jagged rocks. With the mask upon her eyes, the darkness was lit up in greenish light and she became the most prolific gatherer in the village.

"With this witchstone," said the girl, "I could venture even deeper into the caves where the ore sparkles with seams of fiery riches. We could be wealthy, Father. The witch would never know."

Father agreed, so the girl pushed deeper into the network of caverns with a pickaxe and sack. She mined as much of the fabulous ore as she could carry, then set off for home.

She had not made it very far before an impenetrable darkness fell. The witchstone mask became fixed upon her face, and no matter how she struggled she could not pry it loose. She never saw another thing, and never made it out of the caves.

Far away, beneath the witchstone tree, Agatha Drake felt a stab of pain as the tree reached further into her soul.

Three more Midsommers brought three more children, all of them pleading for the witchstone tree's magic. One child asked to sing, another to always know the truth, the third to save her friends. Each time, they betrayed the magic they'd been given, and a little more of Agatha was lost, a little more of her goodness eaten away by the tree's hungry tendrils.

The following Midsommer, a boy named Bo came to Agatha's cottage. By now, Agatha was much changed, the witchstone tree's roots coiled fast round what remained of her soul. Her skin was ghoulish white, her blood vessels lit an unearthly purple.

"Miss," said Bo, "I have come to ask for help."

"Ask for it, then," croaked Agatha.

"I would like to live forever as a child."

"And why should I help? All children are false. They are foolish, and unkind, and cowardly, and disloyal, and incurious. And, for their falseness, it is I who pays the price."

"I will not fail you," declared Bo.

So Agatha stripped a length of witchstone from the tree and wove it into a mask. Then she carved her magic into its surface.

"Now we shall play a game," said Agatha. "Wear this. I will challenge you five times this Midsommer. Prove to me you are good, that you are clever, kind, brave, loyal, and curious—everything a child ought to be. Should you succeed, you will live forever as a child. Should you fail, it is you will pay the price. The witchstone will claim you, as it has me."

Bo took the mask, assured Agatha he would not let her down, and left the forest.

Over the coming weeks, Agatha tested Bo. Bo failed every challenge, proving himself the opposite of all those things—foolish and cruel, cowardly and disloyal, interested only in himself. With the witchstone mask upon his face, a delighted Bo boasted he had fooled the stupid witch of the forest into granting him immortality.

But, as Midsommer wore on, Bo began to change. The witchstone mask clasped his face and could not be removed. With every day that passed, Bo's memories began to slip away. Before long, he could barely remember the facts of his own life, nor could he sleep, eat, or recognize his own family.

Then, when Midsommer was over, Bo vanished. Though people searched for days and weeks, no trace of him could be found.

It so happened that Bo's father was a very powerful man called Cecyl Greaves, Captain of the Company of Strangities. When no sign of his beloved son could be found, Cecyl commanded that Agatha Drake be hunted down and forced to reveal Bo's fate.

A procession of Hanged Men thus marched through the ancient and wild forest in search of Agatha's cottage. Many were lost on the way, lured into ravines and marshes and pits by ravenous spirits. A number made it to Agatha's cottage, however, among them Cecyl Greaves.

Agatha was promptly captured and interrogated. When she would reveal nothing, a noose was drawn around her throat and tied to a bough of the witchstone tree.

"You have one final chance, witch!" said a furious Cecyl. "Reveal where you have taken my son, or you shall hang!"

"Your son asked to live forever," said Agatha. "And so he shall."

And, though a despairing Cecyl demanded further explanation, Agatha said no more. She only sang softly to herself, with her eyes closed, as Cecyl gave the order for the stool beneath her feet to be kicked away.

Though this was done, Agatha did not hang.

Warm Midsommer sunshine fell from the clouds and the violet veins of the witchstone tree blazed. Before gravity could claim Agatha, the great tree changed shape and became an enormous bird. Upon its back, Agatha was ferried far away from the frenzied

Cecyl Greaves and the baffled Hanged Men.

Though the truth of what happened to Bo Greaves can never truly be known, whispers have carried throughout the ages. They say Bo spends all year in a woodland no other can reach, only free to wander Wreathenwold during the month of Midsommer—with the witchstone mask upon his face, no memory of who he ever was, and a heart warped by spite and malice.

The great witchstone bird took Agatha far across Wreathenwold where she found a lonely tower upon a snowy hill. Here she lived a simple, solitary life—with the witchstone tree standing tall and beautiful in her courtyard. Now a slave to the tree, it is said that Agatha Drake can still be called upon at Midsommer. A child must stand in front of a mirror, cover one eye with their hand, and recite:

"Agatha Drake, Agatha Drake,
Beneath the witchstone tree,
I am good and true and worth your grace,
So play your game with me."

Agatha will appear and give the child witchstone to wear upon their eye. This witchstone will present the child with five trials in order to test the values Bo Greaves lacked. Should the child succeed, Agatha will grant that child a wish.

Should the child fail, they will join the wicked Bo as another lost child of Midsommer—as another snatchling of Agatha Drake, memoryless and undying, condemned to the most bleak and unhappy eternity.

Benjamiah finished and found Elizabella pink in the cheeks, eyes lit up with excitement.

"You can't be serious," he said, knowing she was. "This is a fairy tale. It's a morality tale, about children not doing as they'd promised."

"Look at the illustrations, Benjamiah," said Elizabella. "The colors. The story is true. Every child in Wreathenwold knows it. It's always been a bit of fun to stand in the mirror and chant the rhyme. Edwid and I used to do it. Not that anything ever happened."

"But I didn't," said Benjamiah. "I . . ."

Panic lodged in his throat. He may not have said the rhyme, but he had agreed to play the specter's game, such was his desperation to return to Wreathenwold. What had he done? He read again: *condemned to the most bleak and unhappy eternity.*

"I didn't call Agatha Drake!" he cried.

"No," said a voice from the doorway. "Your mother did."

It was Hansel, looking tiny and troubled as he crossed the creaking floorboards, staring at the witchstone upon Benjamiah's eye.

"It was Midsommer when the fire happened," said a weary Hansel, not taking his eyes from the witchstone, "and your mother fled Wreathenwold. Before that, I woke one morning to find that in the night Eyla had been given that stone. In the night, Eyla had stood before the mirror and called upon the fabled Witch of Midsommer. And Agatha had responded."

"Well, we have no choice, then," said Elizabella. "Benjamiah has to play the game."

"We always have a choice," said Hansel gravely. "I told your mother the same thing, Benjamiah. Whatever the story says, we cannot possibly be sure of the truth of it, nor the danger it presents. There is foul magic in Wreathenwold, Benjamiah. We cannot trust in fairy tales. Your mother saw sense and never placed that thing upon her eye, though she wanted to with every fiber of her being. She still had it when she left Wreathenwold. And now you have found it, and have done what Eyla did not."

Heat traveled up Benjamiah's neck, the prickly discomfort that rises when being told off.

"I didn't know!" he said.

Hansel smiled sadly, propping a frail hand on Benjamiah's shoulder.

"How could you?" he said kindly. "I only ask as, I hope, somebody you trust that you be sensible now. The witchstone is likely a mechanism to lure children toward peril and worse. We will find another way to wrest the stone from your eye. I forbid you from pursuing this. Your mother would never, ever allow it. Is that clear?"

It was the sternest Benjamiah had ever seen Hansel, the gentle and soft man overcome by a quiet anger more frightening than if he had screamed. Benjamiah gave the smallest nod.

"You too, Elizabella Cotton," said Hansel. "You are not to leave Ogbo's Rest. You are not to fill Benjamiah's head with any more of this nonsense. Agreed?"

"I wouldn't dream of it," said Elizabella with the sweetest and falsest of smiles.

Hansel studied them both carefully, perhaps considering whether to reinforce his dire warnings. Eventually, he decided against it, gave a watery smile, and left to prepare Benjamiah's room.

"He's wrong," whispered Elizabella. "He knows exactly

what you have to do. There isn't any other way. You don't have a choice, Benjamiah."

Despite Hansel's warnings, Benjamiah couldn't help but agree with Elizabella. It was mortal fear that compelled Hansel, but it wasn't him with the witchstone clamped upon his eye—nor was it Hansel who might end up like Bo Greaves.

Elizabella stood, eyes narrowed, straightening her hat.

"You came with me to bring Edwid's soulbloom back," she said.

"I know, but it doesn't mean . . ."

"You think I'm letting you go alone?" she said crossly.

Then she smiled radiantly. The clot of fear in Benjamiah's breast loosened a little. At least Elizabella would be by his side. The relief was so intense that for a moment he forgot the dangers that lay ahead.

"We leave tonight," she whispered.

Despite himself, Benjamiah felt a spark of nervous excitement. It seemed they were going on another adventure.

SEVEN
WITH THE TOADSTOOL CASSEROLE

> Archscholar Omelia had a great many important letters to send, but found her inkwell empty whenever she sat down to write them. Before long, she discovered that a troop of minuscule monkeys, no larger than a fingernail, were slurping up the ink whenever her back was turned.
> —*The Book of Barely Believable Stories*,
> Mildred Fogge

THE CHILDREN FOUND Hansel on the second floor, making up a bedroom for Benjamiah and Silas. Silas was nattering proudly away about the importance and virtues of the Company of Mapmakers—and how the Viper had committed a grievous crime against Wreathenwold in disbanding them. Hansel nodded solemnly along as he prepared beds with hairy blankets and misshapen feather pillows.

"Ah, here they are!" he said, spotting Elizabella and Benjamiah.

While Elizabella and Silas were reacquainted, Hansel finished the beds and lit oil lamps. The room was poky, with a single murky window overlooking the tangle of bonewood branches outside. In one corner was a hulk of indeterminate furniture, encased in a yellowed sheet. The dust was so thick it stung Benjamiah's eyes and left him coughing.

"Not much, I'm afraid," said Hansel. "My brother seems not to have had guests for the last thousand years or so. Now, Benjamiah, I suspect it will upset him to hear about your . . . Well, about where you're from. The same goes for that thing on your eye. Let's just call it a Midsommer mask."

Benjamiah nodded. Hansel patted him on the back, his colorless eyes twinkling.

"What a delight to have you back," he said, meaning it. "Dinner shortly, which I shall cook myself. Guests must be spared, at all costs, the unique suffering of Clover's cooking."

The children laughed and then Hansel and Elizabella left Benjamiah and Silas to settle into their new room. Shamed by the thought of letting Hansel down so badly, Benjamiah stood wracked by doubts and second thoughts. But what choice did he have? Through the witchstone, he spied the violet-patterned moths fluttering among the snowy trees outside, eager to lead him on. To where, he wondered?

"I wanted to ask about our agreement," said Silas, perched on the edge of his bed. He tested the mattress, looking awkward.

"Of course," said Benjamiah. "Thanks for coming with me. I didn't want to travel alone. Ariadne is yours. Elizabella already knows."

Silas broke into a relieved smile, then recovered himself and nodded formally.

"You're doing Wreathenwold a great service," he said grandly. "The Mapmakers thank you."

Then, a little embarrassed, Silas hurried off in search of Ariadne. Benjamiah suspected he would have a hard time finding her.

While waiting for dinner, Benjamiah and Nuisance explored Ogbo's Rest. Featureless corridors and staircases rambled one way and another, everything much the same—dark and cold, dusty, with the floorboards worn and splintery and the windows grimy. It was fiercely cold, Benjamiah's breath smoking before him. Even Nuisance the capuchin made a point of shivering, her hairy little arms wrapped tightly round her torso. Poking his head into various rooms, Benjamiah saw the same things over and over: sheeted furniture, gutted fireplaces, floods of dust and darkness.

On the first floor, Benjamiah spied Clover sitting at a desk, hammering away at a typewriter that didn't seem to be loaded with any paper. There were a row of them along the bench.

"No blasted ink again," Clover muttered, despairing over a nearby inkwell. "Ever since Hansel arrived, no ink!"

Benjamiah crept back downstairs where he found Elizabella and Silas standing over a closed, dust-soaked piano.

On the lid was Ariadne—absolutely still. Silas was wide-eyed, seemingly on the brink of tears. Briefly, Benjamiah feared something had happened to Ariadne. Then he saw Elizabella doing her very best not to laugh.

"What's going on?" asked Benjamiah.

With feigned gravity, Elizabella said, "We told Ariadne it's time for her to leave. And, well, she's come over a little *faint*...."

Now it was Benjamiah's turn to swallow down a laugh. Ariadne was playing dead to avoid going with Silas.

"I can't understand it!" he wailed. "Why would she not want to fulfil her destiny? The cause of the Mapmakers is the truest and noblest of all causes. We were the best of companions before she was *stolen*."

The implication erased all trace of humor from Elizabella's face. Technically, Edwid had stolen her from the House of Mapmakers, but Benjamiah feared for anybody who impugned him in front of Elizabella.

"Careful," was all she said, hand on her doll.

After that, Silas was more circumspect—if no less distraught.

"Please, Ariadne . . . ," he begged.

Ariadne didn't move.

"Ariadne?" said Benjamiah, leaning down. "It's time for you to go home."

Nothing.

"We've had some great adventures," said Elizabella. "But you belong with the Mapmakers. They need you."

Nothing.

"I refuse to leave without her!" howled Silas before storming off.

Only when he was gone did Ariadne show signs of life, lifting her head to make sure he had left.

"I know you like being with us," said Elizabella, holding out her hand. "We'll miss you so much. But Benjamiah said you could go with Silas."

Ariadne coiled round Elizabella's fingers, venturing a reproachful flick of her tail in Benjamiah's direction as she laced through her knuckles. Worry nagged at Benjamiah. Would Ariadne let Benjamiah and Elizabella leave without her? In truth, having Ariadne join them as they cast themselves out into the labyrinth would be an enormous comfort and help. But what did that mean for Silas?

Dinner with Clover was an unusual experience.

Every moment throughout the meal, a long glassy smile lay fixed across his face, his eyes big and froglike and blinking incessantly as he glanced round the table. He seemed utterly terrified by the presence of children in his home, as though somebody had told him that, should he stop smiling for a single instant, they would eat him alive.

The dining room was completely without charm, high-ceilinged and drafty with not a single painting or ornament in sight. A measly fire spluttered and gasped in the hearth.

"The Honorable Company of Mapmakers thanks you heartily for your hospitality, sir," said Silas importantly.

Clover would have looked less baffled had Silas been a talking teapot. Elizabella and Benjamiah caught each other's eye and covered their mouths to mask their giggling.

Mercifully, Hansel bustled into the dining room then with an enormous dish shaped like a tagine, trailing tails of delicious-smelling vapor as it was delivered to the table. It looked as good as it smelled—an array of tender vegetables in thick reddish sauce with swirls of cream, dusted with strange herbs and spices. Hansel also brought sides of crispy phantom leaf and loaves of perfectly baked sweetdough.

"My famous toadstool casserole," he declared, a little breathless and red in the face. "The *real* reason you boys came, I don't doubt."

Benjamiah beamed as Hansel dished up, ladling generous helpings for the children and a slightly less generous helping for his brother. With nobody talking and the atmosphere dense, Benjamiah focused on eating. The casserole was every bit as delicious as he'd hoped: the toadstool was tender and juicy, flavored like magic itself.

For a time, there was only the clanking of cutlery to be heard. Hansel sipped a tumbler of clear, smoking liquid, which Benjamiah knew to be poppysyrup. The children had milk punch.

Clover ate what little he could stomach and then excused himself, fleeing the dining room as though it were infested with cockroaches. The mood improved considerably, with Silas telling wild and boastful tales of famous Mapmakers. He lauded the peerless heroics of Ernold Lacer, who slew a fire-breathing wyrm with only his poppet and a fire poker, and the genius of Cathy Faulker, who built a compass out of silver and griffin bone that mapped Wreathenwold as she traveled. A morose Silas did add that Cathy was ultimately tracked down by the Widow and murdered by her fearsome poppet, Grief.

Hansel was politely rapt, though grew increasingly bleary-eyed as he worked through the bottle of poppysyrup. Meanwhile, Elizabella and Benjamiah created an obstacle course from candelabras and had Nuisance and Emba race, controlled by their owners. Unsurprisingly, Elizabella won every time—though she was forced to cheat in the last race, transforming Emba from a dormouse to a hare in order to bolt over the finish line ahead of Nuisance.

A sulking Benjamiah gave up and joined Hansel by the fire, while Silas and Griffyn took a turn racing Elizabella and Emba. Hansel sucked a pipe giving off trails of chocolate-smelling smoke, staring into the crackling flames.

"I'm sorry about Follynook," said Benjamiah, taking Silas's chair.

Hansel waved a hand, smiling in a way that never reached his eyes.

"It's my fault," continued Benjamiah. "I should have let the Viper take my eye colors. I should have—"

"Never," said Hansel firmly. "You will never do so. Anything before that, dear boy. Houses, books, money—all can be replaced. But not that color in your eyes. That is yours and yours alone. Well, your mother's, too. Is she well?"

Benjamiah gave a brief—but painful—description of Mum's separation from Dad. He also told Hansel how much she clearly missed Wreathenwold, though she'd chided Benjamiah for feeling the same.

"I imagine that was difficult to take," said Hansel gently. "But parents protect us with a ferocity that would outdo the most menacing of monsters. They feel their children's pain as though it were happening to them instead. No doubt it kills Eyla to see you suffering."

Benjamiah considered this, wishing he could find fault with it. The guilt at their impending departure cranked up another notch.

"How can the Viper rule Wreathenwold?" he said. "I met the Minotaur and he'd never have chosen her."

"I agree," said Hansel. "There's something amiss. The rumors say the Minotaur is unwell, not long for this world. The decree granting the Viper temporary rule of Wreathenwold was hung all over the labyrinth, and there can be no doubt as to the authenticity of the Minotaur's seal on it. But whether he has made this choice willingly—or under duress—is another matter."

Benjamiah's blood simmered. That somehow Odith Murdstone had coerced the ailing Minotaur into this decision seemed far more likely.

"What about," said Benjamiah quietly, "the Widow?"

The Widow, Osmeralda, was a dark figure from Wreathenwold's past—perhaps the darkest and cruelest ruler this world had ever known. It was widely believed that the Widow was dead, but Benjamiah, Elizabella, and Hansel knew differently. Her spirit was in fact imprisoned somewhere—it was in attempting to hide this grave secret that Edwid had lost his life.

"No word, my boy," said Hansel, taking a long puff from his pipe.

"But Manfred must know where she is now," said Benjamiah.

Manfred Tarr was a magus who desperately strived for the restoration of the Widow—no matter the cost to Wreathenwold or any who stood in his way. He had also learned the secret, despite Edwid's efforts to hide it from him.

"One must suspect," said Hansel solemnly, "that there is more to freeing the Widow than merely knowing where she is. The Minotaur is no fool. She will be sealed away tightly, I don't doubt. Think no more about it, Benjamiah. Do not let her darken a bright night."

Benjamiah nodded, gazing into the white, ashen heart of the fire.

"It brings me such joy to see you and Elizabella reunited," said Hansel. "On top of losing Edwid, your going home was quite a blow to her. I doubt she'll ever admit it, though."

"She hasn't." Benjamiah smiled. "Not with words, anyway."

"Between you and me," whispered Hansel, leaning in conspiratorially, "I have it on good authority that she has spent the last few months writing you letters. Though I fear for anyone who tries to read them."

Benjamiah laughed, warmth swarming his chest. Elizabella really had missed him as much as he'd missed her, though Hansel was, of course, correct—she'd never admit it.

Just then, Benjamiah's attention was drawn to a tiny chattering sound rising from the other side of Hansel's chair. Hansel leaned down and lifted a threadbare top hat, which he held upside down very carefully. Having set it upon his lap, he beckoned for Benjamiah to look inside with a mischievous smile.

Inside was a tiny woodland formed from shredded bonewood leaves, matchsticks, and popped smokeberries. Inhabiting the miniature forest was a troop of minuscule monkeys, smaller than a fingernail. Two were wrestling, one was sipping from a thimble of dark fluid, another dangling from a matchstick tree by its tiny tail. Their mottled fur was daubed with ink, of which the entire top hat smelled.

"Monkeys-of-the-inkpot," said Benjamiah, grinning.

Hansel nodded. "The troop from Follynook," he whispered. "I couldn't leave them behind. Took me hours to catch them, let me tell you."

Benjamiah recalled what he'd overheard earlier. *Ever since Hansel arrived, no ink,* Clover had wailed. When Benjamiah told Hansel, he laughed heartily.

"I might have forgotten to mention I'd brought the little fellows along," he said, and they shared another laugh.

Shortly afterward, Hansel ordered everybody to bed.

"What a lovely evening," he said, sighing happily as the children headed for the door. "I needed that. Goodness, I needed it."

The children ascended the creaky staircase together. Silas went straight into their room, mumbling that it was so cold he feared losing toes to frostbite—a grim fate that had befallen many brave Mapmakers, he added.

At the door, Elizabella made Benjamiah wait while she retrieved something from her room along the hallway.

"Here," she said, pushing *The Book of Barely Believable Stories* into Benjamiah's hands. "You can't spend Midsommer in Wreathenwold without reading this."

"Thanks," said Benjamiah. "And it's good to, you know . . ."

"Yes," said Elizabella stiffly. "I'm glad you're . . ."

Benjamiah nodded. Then Elizabella mouthed: *Wait for my signal.*

After a garbled goodnight, Elizabella strutted off and Benjamiah closed the door.

By the oil lamp above his bed, he began Mildred Fogge's collection of illustrated fairy tales. On the inside page was a dedication from Mildred Fogge:

> *To my beautiful daughter, Rosa,*
> *claimed by the cruel coils of this labyrinth.*
> *These stories are yours; I pray they reach you.*

Shaking off this stab of sadness, Benjamiah read a story at random—"The Soul Snatcher." It was the tale of Ciaen the Lesser, a rogue magus from long ago who, with help from the Company of What Cannot Be Explained, learned a means of extracting the souls of children and imprisoning them within his cane. Wielding this weapon, Ciaen's powers grew. The soul of a child, the story claimed, is one of the most powerful and untamable essences in all of nature, a spring-loaded ball of goodness and color capable of almost anything.

With this vile weapon, Mildred wrote, *the cowardly Ciaen could control people, compel them to speak the truth, even bind them to his will.* But the magus grew too greedy, incapable of dominion over all those souls, and was soon destroyed by his own cane.

By the time Benjamiah had finished, Silas had lapsed into a deep sleep, snoring away on the other bed with one leg dangling off the edge.

Before long, Benjamiah's eyes began to prickle with exhaustion. Setting the book down, he blew out the oil lamp and lay in the darkness. He thought of Mum, Dad, and Grandma. A wave of terrible guilt washed over him at what he was putting them through all over again. Maybe he should have left a note. Mum would have explained everything to the others, he felt sure. But would they have believed her?

I'm safe, Benjamiah thought, willing the sentiment to reach them somehow. *And I'm sorry. I just had to go back.*

Sleep took a while to come, given the knot of emotions he felt. Excitement to be in Wreathenwold once more, fury at the Viper, worry for Hansel and Elizabella, guilt about his family. And a certain stubborn terror in the pit of his stomach at the witchstone stuck over his eye, and what Benjamiah might have to do in order to be free of it. What had Mum wanted so badly in the first place? Was it worth this risk?

Silas's snoring kept Benjamiah awake for some time. As did the sound of a soft but definite ticking, seemingly coming from just outside the window. Benjamiah was too tired to investigate, instead drifting off to the peculiar sound, wondering what on earth it could be.

Tick. Tick. Tick.

EIGHT
WITH THE SPELLBOOKS

The poppet battle raged. Our Hero, on the brink of defeat, cast her poppet as the mighty earthworm. Though the Enemy chased furiously with all manner of fell creatures, the earthworm eluded her. Only then, when exhaustion and rage had diminished the Enemy, did our Hero strike the fatal blow.

—*The Book of Barely Believable Stories*,
Mildred Fogge

ELIZABELLA'S SIGNAL CAME in the dead of night, a gentle tapping on the bedroom window. Emba, a sparrow, was perched on the ledge outside. It was time: the great labyrinth, its many spirals of wonder and peril, was calling.

Quietly, Benjamiah slipped out of bed, pulled on some clothes, and grabbed his knapsack. Inside were the playing cards, *The Book of Barely Believable Stories*, one of Clover's smaller flat caps, and Benjamiah's school planner and pencil case. He'd need to buy more clothes on the journey—at the moment, he only had those in which he'd arrived.

Ariadne had been snoozing on the oil-lamp bracket above Benjamiah's bed. Now she was awake, unfurling happily toward Benjamiah.

"No, you have to stay with Silas," he whispered. "I promised."

"What's going on?"

Silas was sitting upright in his bed, wearing a mesh undershirt and an expression of bleary confusion.

"Nothing," said Benjamiah.

Silas clearly didn't believe him. To add further offense, Ariadne—the moment Silas spoke—let herself drop on to Benjamiah's pillow and resumed playing dead. Nuisance the capuchin tittered with laughter.

Silas's shoulders slumped, a picture of gloom. His eyes pivoted moodily to Benjamiah.

"Where are you going?" demanded the Mapmaker.

"Nowhere," said Benjamiah. When Silas kept staring, looking increasingly hurt, Benjamiah said, "Okay, *somewhere*."

Deciding upon honesty, he explained about the witch-stone, the story, and the need to win Agatha Drake's game.

"It's a big chance to take on the basis of a fairy tale," said Silas grumpily.

"You're not the one with this thing stuck on your face," replied Benjamiah.

"You can't take Ariadne."

"I know," said Benjamiah. "That's what I was telling her when you woke up. Only . . . I'm worried she'll follow us."

"Ariadne goes nowhere without me," said Silas, inflating his chest.

This was heading in only one direction, so Benjamiah came right out and said it: "Then you'll have to come too."

That seemed to spook Silas. Not for the first time, Benjamiah detected a soft, fearful center beneath his bravado.

"Decide quickly," said Benjamiah. "I have to go."

"Do you want me to come?" said Silas, biting his nails.

"I . . . Do you want to come?"

"Are you *asking* me to come?"

Benjamiah smiled. It seemed what had hurt Silas the most was not being invited. Feeling lonely—and left out—was an experience all too familiar to Benjamiah. And, despite his almost maddening pomposity, Silas had grown on him.

"Yes, I'm asking you to come," he said.

"Of course you are!" said Silas grandly. "Who would dare brave this dreadful labyrinth without the company of a fearless Mapmaker? You wouldn't stand a chance."

While Benjamiah did his best not to roll his eyes, Silas hopped out of bed and got dressed. Ariadne, deciding it was safe to abandon playing dead, sprang to life and slithered up Benjamiah's sleeve. Nuisance hooted impatiently.

When Silas was ready, they snuck through the house. No journey was ever creakier. The floorboards were a piano of groans and rasps, but thankfully the boys spilled out into the cold night without incident and followed Emba. Trees formed ghostly strands encircling the house, as the snow swooped and the icy wind speared. Crouched behind the woodshed was Elizabella, beckoning them over.

"What are you doing here?" she hissed at Silas when the three of them were united.

"He's coming, too," said Benjamiah.

"You'll be far safer traveling with a Mapmaker," declared Silas, nose turned up rather ridiculously.

Elizabella rolled her eyes, shook her head, and led the way. They crunched through the grounds, at once dark and glossy with snow. Strange birds hooted and shivered in the canopy. Their breath smoked. The magical moths, dazzling and dreamy in the darkness as they left behind long trails of violet dust, led them to the gate of Ogbo's Rest and beyond.

They traveled until night gave way to morning, putting a healthy distance between themselves and Hansel; whenever Benjamiah thought of him, despairing and bereft and let down, his stomach roiled. Elizabella had brought the despectacles she and Benjamiah wore on their previous journey through the labyrinth, which Benjamiah could just about fit over the witchstone. When worn, they made eyes appear colorless—color-poachers were everywhere and Elizabella's and Benjamiah's bright eyes were bound to attract danger.

They walked down a rainy street of taverns and pipe-smoking lounges and town houses lost to ivy. They rode a hansom along a windy street of allotments and cottages, where scarecrows were adorned with Midsommer masks and ballgowns. Along another street, plumpkin-shaped paper lanterns of black and white hung from bonewood branches—another Midsommer tradition, according to Elizabella.

The children had breakfast in a sunlit courtyard. Benjamiah had given Elizabella her own pack of playing cards, so they all had money now. While a waiter delivered plates of opple pastries, toasted sweetdough, and a jug of smokeberry juice, Elizabella consoled Ariadne.

"You know how much we love you," she said, leaning down.

Ariadne was coiled sulkily in an empty teacup. Upon discovering the children had another guide for this journey—the magical moths visible only to Benjamiah—Ariadne had been mortally affronted.

"It's just that even *we* don't know where we're going,"

continued Elizabella, picking up the teacup. "So we can't ask you to take us there. Do you understand?"

Judging by Elizabella's face, Ariadne had made some gesture that suggested she very much did *not* understand. Sensing an opportunity to get into Ariadne's good graces, Silas seized the teacup and crooned gently into it.

"Nobody understands you like I do, Ariadne," he said. "Let's leave together, you and I. I'll let you lead me anywhere."

Elizabella jabbed a finger into her mouth, pretending to gag. Benjamiah laughed suddenly, choking on his toast. Silas looked furious, setting the teacup down and folding his arms.

"I have something for you," said Elizabella to Benjamiah.

From her satchel, she withdrew a stack of slender, battered books. Excitement fluttered in Benjamiah's breast before his brain had even caught up. He recalled seeing similar books in Follynook last year.

"Spellbooks," said Elizabella.

There were seven or eight in her hands. Every one corresponded to a form a poppet could assume. A dollcaster needed to understand everything about the animal they were casting—their anatomy, behavior, habitat—in order to perform the spell. Benjamiah hustled the books out of Elizabella's hands and examined the titles: *Red Squirrel*; *Fruit Bat*; *Shire Horse*.

"But how do I . . . I don't know how to do it," he said.

"I'm going to teach you, of course," said Elizabella.

"Really?" Benjamiah felt excitement swelling within him.

"Of course. It would be preferable if you and Nuisance weren't a *complete* liability along the way."

Then cast as a nightjar, Nuisance squawked angrily at Elizabella from her perch on Benjamiah's shoulder. Benjamiah decided against reminding Elizabella that he and Nuisance had more than held their own on their previous adventure.

"I'm not sure how much we'll cover in the time we have," said Elizabella, "but we'll do our best. Try not to be slow, though."

Ignoring this latest jibe, Benjamiah said, "I'll start with this one."

He showed Elizabella the spellbook—on the front it said *Gray Wolf*.

"You will *not* start with a wolf," said Elizabella, snatching it away. "That's ludicrous. You'll start where we all start. Though admittedly most of us start when we're three years old."

She dropped a tattered old spellbook in Benjamiah's lap: *Earthworm*.

"Very funny," said Benjamiah. "Where do I really start?"

Elizabella's expression was fixed and humorless. Even Silas, still sulking, managed a somber smile.

"You can't be serious . . . ," said Benjamiah. "What use is an *earthworm*?"

"It's not about use," said Elizabella. "It's about taking one step at a time. The earthworm spell is one of the most basic. You master that one first, then we move on. Believe me, gray wolf is a *long way* down the list."

Still, when Elizabella wasn't looking, Benjamiah smuggled the *Gray Wolf* spellbook into his knapsack.

"So you're telling me you know all this stuff about every animal you cast?" he said.

"Ask me anything," said Elizabella, steely-eyed.

So Benjamiah did. Flicking through various spellbooks, he tested her on random facts until it was abundantly clear that she did indeed have all this information filed away in her brain.

"Show-off," mumbled Benjamiah.

"Hard work makes the magic happen," said Elizabella smugly, like a particularly irritating schoolteacher. "First things first: read the *Earthworm* book. As many times as you can. I'll test you until you know it back to front. Only then will we practice the spell with Nuisance."

Elizabella smiled and Benjamiah returned it. Magic, it seemed, was even more delightful than he had realized: it was reading, absorbing facts, all lovely and orderly and precise.

And so the day passed. The moths led Benjamiah, and Benjamiah led the others. Silas did all he could to charm Ariadne, though no breakthrough was made. Elizabella flitted between noisy impatience, whether at the pace of the magical moths or at the various Midsommer festivities slowing them down, and pensive silence in which Benjamiah suspected she fretted about poor Hansel.

"He'll understand," said Benjamiah.

"Who will?"

"Hansel."

"Hm," was all Elizabella said.

Whenever he could, whether in hansoms or when they stopped to rest, Benjamiah read the *Earthworm* book. Though not as dense as anatomy books back home, Wreathenwold spellbooks were nonetheless exacting in detail. All day he read and memorized, absorbed and recited, shooting excited glances toward Nuisance—changing between dormouse, nightjar, and capuchin of her own volition—thrilled at the prospect of performing more complicated magic.

Night saw the children cramped in another hansom, rattling along a weaving strip of cobblestones bordered on both sides by stone cottages with thatched roofs and smoking chimneys. Streetlamps blazed in the rainy sky.

Either side of Benjamiah, Elizabella and Silas were working their way through a paper bag of smokeberry melts—round, fizzy sweets that dissolved on the tongue.

"Are we being stupid?" said Benjamiah suddenly.

The others looked at him, mouths full of sweets.

"The witchstone," he said. "Agatha Drake. The game. What if we're wrong? If she really has been consumed by the tree, who says the game is even winnable? And what will these trials be, exactly? What if I have to face them alone? What if I'm supposed to do magic?"

"Stop worrying," said Elizabella. "We'll do this all together or not at all. You're overthinking it, as usual."

It was some comfort, but not much. Outside, the cottages fell away and now the hansom rocked and shuddered beneath overhanging bonewoods, the clockwork horse clip-clopping through the thrumming rain. The streetlamps had grown more sporadic, the darkness denser.

"And *you're* underthinking it, as usual," replied Benjamiah moodily.

For once, Elizabella was caught off guard.

"Have a sweet," was all she said, offering him the paper bag.

Before Benjamiah could reach inside, the horse at the front of the hansom broke into a chorus of distressed whinnying. Through the front window, Benjamiah saw it rearing.

"What on earth—" began Silas.

He never finished his sentence because the hansom was dragged abruptly to the left by the spooked horse. They were hauled up a muddy bank before—witnessed helplessly by the children—a bonewood rose from the blackness and smashed into the hansom. The children were hurled forward, the world itself seeming to career as the window imploded and glass and rain lashed inward.

Then everything was still and quiet, save for the pattering rain and the muted crying of the horse.

Having escaped with only cuts and bumps, the children wrestled open the hansom door and clambered gingerly out into the night. The hansom was wrecked, pitched upward into the monolithic tree trunk. There was no sign of whatever had distressed the horse. Regardless, it continued to thrash in the harness, stomping and snorting and throwing its head from side to side.

"Look," said Silas.

He was pointing at the driver, who remained in his seat behind the carriage. He had fallen to the side, grip slack on the reins.

"Is he dead?" whispered Elizabella.

While Silas bemoaned the miserable labyrinth—which, he claimed, would do all it could to impede any Mapmaker—Benjamiah climbed up for a closer look. Relieved, he found the driver's eyelids flickering, saw the faintest rise and fall of breath. Some kind of yellowish powder dusted the bristles of his beard.

"Just unconscious," said Benjamiah. "That must have been what upset the horse. He fell to his left and dragged the reins."

But how? Benjamiah could see no obvious reason for the driver's sudden collapse. There was nobody around to help—the lane twisted through walls of throttling, dripping woodland. Rain fell in freezing veils. With the adrenaline fading, pain began to throb all over Benjamiah. He shivered, already soaked.

Then they heard it, carrying from the trees, unmistakable amid the hiss of rain.

Tick. Tick. Tick.

"Do you hear that?" breathed Silas.

It grew louder. Then something else began ticking from the other direction, so that the sounds overlapped, snicking through the rainy blackness.

Tick tick. Tick tick. Tick tick.

Benjamiah whirled, casting around for the source.

"I heard that sound before," he mumbled, "back at Ogbo's Rest."

Beside him, Elizabella had unhitched Emba from her noose and now gripped her tightly. Likewise, Silas held Griffyn, though his hand trembled as he spun round.

"A single one of you moves," said a small voice, "and you all die."

It was then that several ghostly figures unsheathed themselves from the gloom. There were two girls and two boys, Benjamiah's age or even younger. They wore rags, an assembly of frayed and patched garments, with gloves and boots that didn't match and fitted poorly. Two of them were pointing crossbows loaded with bone-tipped bolts.

It was their faces that absorbed all attention, though. Fused with the skin were masks of chalky-white stone threaded with pale purple, a material that Benjamiah—with a plunge of horror—recognized as witchstone. The masks had fixed round the real eyes of the children, giving the horrendous effect of living eyes socketed in stone. The stone mouths were lipless, lined with long, nightmarish teeth like the wicked grins of skeletons.

Benjamiah turned to Elizabella for help, terror turning through him like a corkscrew. She mouthed, with a stunned expression: *The snatchlings*. Benjamiah realized with horror that it was the snatchlings who were ticking.

"Three for the price of one," said the snatchling who'd told them not to move.

He was mousy and bony, dressed in an ancient, half-disintegrated tunic, a fancy and unlikely bowler hat perched on his head. He was most distinguishable from the others because of the claw marks scored into his witchstone mask, running diagonally from high to low.

"What do you want with us?" shouted Elizabella.

She stood poised for trouble, her fists clenched and her eyes flashing warily between the crossbow bolts.

The scarred snatchling approached, ticking away. He had the rheumy, bloodshot eyes of a hundred-year-old man. What did that mean? What did the snatchlings want with them? This wasn't part of the "Witchstone Tree" story.

"Touch us and you'll regret it," said Elizabella.

"You're tired," said the scarred snatchling. Then, to the girl on his right, he added: "Help them rest."

The girl came forward, ragged chestnut hair falling out of the sides of her witchstone mask. Her eyes were younger than the others', amber and opalescent. Her poppet was hitched to her hip, fern green and dismally frayed, with a rodent skull clamped over its head—a feature of all the snatchlings' dolls.

In her hands was a small corked vial filled with a yellowish powder that flurried and swam like fireflies. Benjamiah recognized it as drowsipowder—a dash of it upon their faces and they'd be out like a light. That explained what had happened to the driver. . . .

"Do it," snarled the scarred snatchling, and the girl did it.

Except, in one continuous and lightning-fast movement, she cast drowsipowder—not into the faces of Benjamiah, Elizabella, and Silas but into the hideous masks of her fellow snatchlings. The powder flurried like pollen, leaving yellow splashes over the witchstone.

For a moment, the snatchlings stared, baffled. Then they staggered, falling one by one to the cobbles.

The snatchling girl froze, momentarily stunned. Then she looked from Elizabella to Silas to Benjamiah, her amber eyes moonlike with terror.

"We have to run!" she said, a tear traveling down the witchstone mask. "*He'll* already know. More will be coming. Many more. We have to run!"

"He?" said Benjamiah, not liking the way the girl had shuddered.

"*Run!*" screamed the girl.

They ran, bolting through the slippery woods, feet sliding on muddy inclines and mossy roots, their breathing wild and blind panic snapping at their heels like a hungry dog. Nuisance swooped above as a nightjar. Elizabella had cast Emba as a bear; Griffyn was a lion. Both bounded among them as they slalomed through trees and ravines. Rain pelted and sinister voices howled through the darkness. The girl was right—more snatchlings had come. Nobody ran with greater fervor than the snatchling girl, her gangly limbs crashing through the undergrowth, disoriented by a kind of mindless horror.

Mercifully, they threaded out of the trees and onto a cobbled street of narrow town houses. The group slowed to a shaky-legged, breathless canter, winding through passageways and alleyways and beneath archways until Benjamiah could bear it no longer.

He folded forward, hands on his knees, heaving in oxygen. White spots dazzled in his eyes. The bumps and cuts from the crash throbbed and stung. He was drenched to the bone and sick to the stomach. They'd stopped in an alleyway, a bright moon suspended in the starry sky above.

As the children caught their breath, all eyes traveled to the snatchling girl. Unlike the others, she continued to breathe sharp and fast, her eyes huge. She'd backed against the stone wall and lifted a hand to her chest, breathing quicker and shallower until suddenly she was hyperventilating.

"What have I done . . . ," she gasped. "What have I done . . ."

It was Benjamiah who went to help, laying a hand on her shoulder. She flinched at his touch. It sent Benjamiah's mind hurtling back to the very first night after Mum had moved out. He'd sat in the corner of his bedroom, in the dark, sobbing until his breathing rampaged and he'd fallen into the grasp of a panic attack. Dad had come to his aid. It was a terrifying experience, one Benjamiah wouldn't wish on anybody.

"It's okay," he said, exactly as Dad had said. "Just breathe. Long breaths in through the nose, slow breaths out through the mouth. Just breathe. All the way to your center."

Steadily, the snatchling girl fought down the panic attack. Behind Benjamiah, Elizabella stared with narrow eyes and Silas stood hunched in the shadows. In the moonlight, the girl's mask glowed eerily.

"Explain," said Elizabella, standing in front of the snatchling.

With her breathing under control, the girl kept a hand over her heart and spoke.

"I didn't want them to take you," she said, "like they're taking all the others."

"Others?" said Benjamiah.

"Other children. We have orders to snatch as many children as we can. As soon as Midsommer began, we left the Witch Wood with instructions to take children and . . ."

Benjamiah recalled the evidence he'd already seen, in just a few short days, of missing children—the posters, the bereft guardians in the streets.

"Orders from who?" demanded Elizabella.

"From . . . from . . . *him*."

With Elizabella staring flintily, the girl wilted, curling up closer round herself, dropping her voice to the faintest and palest of whispers.

"From Bo."

"Bo?" said Benjamiah. "The boy from the 'Witchstone Tree' story?"

Benjamiah repeating the name summoned another

wave of panic. She straightened up, looking wildly from side to side, apparently considering running off. Her breathing quickened again.

"It's okay," said Benjamiah. "Nobody's here but us. Just try to explain."

"The story is true," she said, deathly quiet. "It began with Bo. The first snatchling. That was hundreds of years ago. The witchstone fixed itself to his face and erased his memories. All year except Midsommer, Bo lived alone in what he calls the Witch Wood. There's no way out, no way to escape. Except at Midsommer when he's free to walk Wreathenwold again.

"And every Midsommer, just like in the story, Agatha Drake would gift fragments of witchstone to some of the children who called upon her. A fragment just like yours, that would let them play her game."

This last part was for Benjamiah. Fear twisted in his stomach.

"It leads to Agatha's trials, with the promise of a wish for the winner. But nobody ever wins. And if you lose you become . . . like us. Forever under Bo's rule."

"Is that what happened to you?" said Benjamiah.

The girl's amber eyes, sparkling in the moonlight, bubbled with tears.

"I . . . I don't remember," she said. "It must be. I . . . All I know is the Witch Wood. And doing what Bo tells me. This poisonous thing upon my face. I . . . I . . ."

Sensing the girl was on the cusp of another panic attack, Benjamiah patted her on the shoulder and helped smooth out her breathing again.

"I still don't understand," said Elizabella. "You said Bo had ordered you and the other snatchlings to take as many children as possible this Midsommer. Why? What's different this year?"

"Bo . . . He has a new master. Somebody with great power, who has promised him something that has Bo very excited."

"Who?" said Elizabella.

"None of us know," said the girl. "Only Bo."

"What would anybody want with children?" asked Benjamiah.

"Only Bo knows," said the girl. "We just capture them and keep them prisoner in the Witch Wood. But . . . I *know* it's something awful. Absolutely awful."

Benjamiah's mind raced.

"Bo says all the children deserve it, anyway," continued the snatchling. "That's the kind of thing he always says. He's so spiteful. He makes us all feel worthless. We hear him in our heads, talking through the witchstone. He taunts us, tells us that nobody ever missed us, that nobody ever wanted us or came looking for us. He . . ."

Benjamiah had to calm her down again before she continued.

"I saved you because you have a chance to win the game and make a wish," she breathed. "We've been tracking you. Watching you at that house. I saw the witchstone on your eye. And I thought . . . maybe you could win and ask Agatha to put an end to this whole thing. To stop Bo. To set us free, even if being free means . . ."

Benjamiah grasped the sentiment, finding it terribly sad: being a snatchling was so nightmarish that the girl saw death as a mercy. It was a fate that might well be Benjamiah's before Midsommer was over, he realized with horror.

"Come with us," he said. "Let's ask her together. And if I get to make a wish, I'll choose to set you all free."

Elizabella studied Benjamiah, before giving a small nod of agreement. Silas didn't looked pleased. A moment's pause followed before the girl sobbed into her hands.

"What's your name?" said Elizabella.

The girl's eyes expanded, wobbling. Fresh sadness shot through Benjamiah's chest: she couldn't remember.

"Me? Uh . . ."

"Mea? Delightful," said Elizabella. "Lovely to meet you, Mea."

Benjamiah was about to point out that Elizabella had misheard, before catching the snatchling's expression. Her eyes had widened, luminescent in the moonlight, as though Elizabella had offered her the most rare and precious of gifts.

So Benjamiah stayed quiet, and the snatchling girl was called Mea from that moment onward. Only later did he suspect that Elizabella had heard perfectly well to begin with.

NINE
WITH THE PYRATE QUEENE

In the cabin of her famed ship, Moggie Blueheart kept a veritable allotment of exotic plants and flowers. Among them was deadly demon-lace, which fruited during Midsommer. It was these berries that Moggie fed to the poppets of the great pirate lords who had betrayed her, thus sealing their doom.

—*The Book of Barely Believable Stories*,
Mildred Fogge

GIVEN THE WITCHSTONE mask was not entirely inconspicuous, traveling with Mea required some adjustments. Benjamiah gave Mea her own pack of playing cards, which caused her great confusion—she'd held no money, nor bought new things, for however long she'd been a snatchling. When the shock had passed, Elizabella helped her choose some new clothes: an apron dress, neat black shoes, a bonnet, and a smart brown coat. Emerging from the shop, Mea was, save for the ghoulish witchstone blight upon her face, almost unrecognizable—particularly because of the uncertain giddiness she showed at having new things.

With the bonnet drawn round her cheeks, the seam between Mea's mask and her face was hidden. Thus the witchstone could just about pass for another Midsommer mask, albeit a particularly fearsome one. To help further, Elizabella and Silas sought the most frightening and unusual masks to wear, alongside Benjamiah and his witchstone eye.

To compound Mea's conspicuousness, she was perhaps the clumsiest person Benjamiah had ever met. Whether because of anxiety, her willowy limbs, or because the mask and bonnet impaired her vision, barely a moment would pass without Mea tripping over something, crashing into something else, poking somebody in the eye, or knocking something off a table, or otherwise contriving, in quite remarkable fashion, to draw attention when it seemed otherwise impossible to do so.

"I'm so sorry," she'd say, her eyes big and glassy.

Silas would grumble about it, mistrustful of Mea. Privately to Benjamiah and Elizabella, he'd made his feelings clear about the snatchling joining them.

"If you don't mind me saying, it was a terrible idea

inviting her along," he moaned. "Now we'll have those crazy children on our tails every step of the way."

"What should we have done instead?" replied Elizabella, eyes narrowed. "Leave her behind after she saved us?"

In reply to Elizabella, Silas mumbled under his breath.

"I didn't catch that," she said loudly. "Can you speak up?"

Silas was sensible enough not to repeat whatever he'd muttered, though he did say, "Ariadne and I must fulfil our destiny and save this wretched city!"

Elizabella snorted and Silas scowled.

"It's not the primary concern right now," she replied dismissively.

"It's the only concern!" wailed Silas dramatically. "Nothing else matters! *Nothing.*"

"So we should have left poor Mea behind so the Mapmakers can fail to map Wreathenwold *again*?" said Elizabella.

Silas actually teetered where he stood, such was his offense at Elizabella's slight—though Benjamiah didn't think it was entirely unfair. With Silas unable to string together an appropriately mortified response, Elizabella continued.

"We'll be patient with Mea," she said, "and kind. And if you don't like it, nobody is making *you* come."

After that, Silas kept his doubts to himself, stewing and muttering a few steps behind the others. True to her word, Elizabella was about as patient with Mea as she could manage, given that she wasn't famously tolerant. For Benjamiah, he had all the sympathy in the world for the snatchling. What she had been through was utterly nightmarish. And a fate that, before long, could well be his own.

At night, they stayed at inns, the girls in one room and the boys another. Safely in bed, with Silas snoring away, Benjamiah would study the *Earthworm* spellbook, committing details about its skin and its mouth and its internal organs to memory, ready for when Elizabella would begin testing him. The notion of performing more magic was a constant tonic for the stubborn dread brought on by Agatha Drake's game.

Two days passed without incident. During that time, Mea barely said a word. Nobody could coax much out of her, except that she knew nothing about herself and that any thought of her fellow snatchlings—and Bo in particular—left her almost catatonic with terror. Of the snatchlings, thankfully there had been no sign since the ambush. That didn't stop Benjamiah flinching at the slightest flash of sudden movement, particularly after dark.

"Why do some of the snatchlings tick?" Benjamiah had asked Mea.

"The older ones have started to fall apart," said Mea, keeping her voice low as if they might be lurking right behind them. "They use clockwork parts to hold themselves together."

Benjamiah shuddered at this abhorrent news.

Their journey ground to a halt at an embankment on a wide strand of the Smeath, the great river of Wreathenwold that crisscrossed the labyrinth like the filaments of a spiderweb. Beneath a high, bright sun, the dock was a maelstrom of noise and motion. Boats—merchant ships and rowing boats and gondolas—were moored on either side of the choppy water, while sailors loaded and unloaded ships, or sat smoking pipes, or hammered and sawed at damaged vessels.

Along the wharves were stalls selling food and treacle tea and poppysyrup, and shops of all kinds, and bards telling stories, and musicians playing instruments with upturned hats for donations.

"Let's wait awhile," said Benjamiah, fearful of how busy it was.

So the children killed some time in a quiet spot beneath a great blossomy bonewood, on a knoll overlooking the frantic dock. Naturally, to pass the time, Elizabella thought they should have some sweets. She slipped down to the hectic market and returned with a bulging paper bag of wyrm's eggs. Benjamiah and Silas dived in, setting the sugary orbs on their tongues and letting them hatch in a rush of delicious fizz.

"Try one," said Elizabella, holding the bag out to Mea.

The snatchling regarded the bag with mistrust. She'd told them that the only food she could ever remember eating was the dry, flavorless follyweed of the Witch Wood. With great caution, she finally dipped in her long fingers and withdrew a sweet, before putting it between the stone teeth of her mask.

Something happened then that nobody was expecting. When the wyrm's egg hatched on Mea's tongue, she lit up with the most joyous and uncontrolled giggle, her eyes blazing with color. Benjamiah and Elizabella joined in with the laughter, the most infectious of sounds. Afterward, Mea looked embarrassed, covering her mouth with her hands, which only made it funnier.

Then she took the bag of wyrm's eggs, leaned against the trunk of the bonewood, and worked her way through the entire thing, a picture of absolute happiness.

From the edge of the knoll, Silas watched Mea intently with his arms crossed.

"If you want to talk to her, go and talk to her," said Elizabella.

"Why would I want to talk to her?" snapped Silas.

Elizabella shrugged. "Maybe if you got to know her, you'd have more sympathy."

Silas grumbled, puffed himself up, and sidled over to sit with Mea, presumably to recite various valiant deeds of the Company of Mapmakers. Benjamiah smiled.

He and Elizabella sat together, overlooking the manic dock below.

"Why would somebody ask Bo to kidnap children?" said Benjamiah.

They'd seen more missing posters in recent days, more desperate parents begging for help finding their children.

"I don't know," said Elizabella, looking grim. "Nothing good, though. Mildred Fogge says Midsommer is the most magical time of year. *Magic forged at Midsommer is the strongest and truest of all magic—both fair and foul.* If somebody is planning sorcery, Midsommer would be the time to do it."

Wrestling with this dark thought, Benjamiah lapsed into silence. They waited until afternoon became evening, then continued on their way.

The following morning, Benjamiah's witchstone delivered the children to an archway. A flight of mossy steps fell downward between old rock and creeping vines. Given the frantic fluttering of the moths, he suspected they'd arrived at Agatha Drake's first trial. The impending challenge had made a fisherman's knot of Benjamiah's stomach. What horror would they find here? Only Elizabella, calm and supportive and determined, kept his legs moving.

At the bottom, they found not horror but beauty. It was a waterfall tumbling from a cliff above into a picturesque pool bordered by boulders and overhanging bonewoods swollen with blossom. Most striking was a gloriously bright Midsommer sun, suspended between the trees where the river trailed off from the waterfall. Its rays made a fiery jewel of every waterdrop.

"Wow," said Elizabella.

The children, slightly dazed, drifted to the edge of the pool, basking in the sunshine and watching the foamy strands of the waterfall as they unspooled upon the rocks. It was Mea who kicked her shoes off first, setting them aside before dipping her feet into the clear water, a smile in her eyes. Elizabella followed, wading in up to her calves. Even Silas had a gruff smile as he picked up a pebble and tossed it into the pond.

Benjamiah watched the moths. They wreathed and spiraled, weaving their dusty trails, before settling upon a gnarly old bonewood near the waterfall. From a knot midway up, a chalky-white branch extended, lit with veins of effervescent purple. Then, on the breeze, Benjamiah heard a faint, childlike chanting, a shadow of a sound: *Agatha Drake, Agatha Drake, beneath the witchstone tree . . . I am good and true and worth your grace, so play your game with me . . .*

"Is that . . . ," said Elizabella, eyes on the branch.

"A branch of the witchstone tree," breathed Mea.

Its leaves trembled. The violet strands gleamed. Benjamiah felt the hairs on the back of his neck prickle. Dangling from the branch was a wooden sign engraved with a rhyme. Sunlight poked through the branches.

Benjamiah swapped a glance with Elizabella, finding reassurance in her steely eyes. He approached the sign and read:

BETRAYED BY THOSE WHO SWORE TO SHARE,

THE PYRATE QUEENE DECREED

THAT EACH WHO BROKE THEIR VOW SHOULD LOSE

THEIR POPPET FOR THEIR GREED.

SO GRASP THE WITCHSTONE BRANCH AND SWIM

INTO THE MURKY DEEP,

AND FIND THE TREASURE IN THE WRECK

WHERE MORE THAN DARKNESS SLEEPS.

"'The Pyrate Queene,'" said Elizabella, enthralled. "That's a Mildred Fogge story. Have you read it yet?"

Benjamiah shook his head. Elizabella opened her mouth to explain but was promptly interrupted.

"Oh, it's brilliant!" said Mea excitably. "It's about Moggie Blueheart. Moggie was a fearsome pirate who battled four other pirate lords for supremacy of Wreathenwold. After a lot of bloodshed, the five of them made an oath to share power. Each was to gift one-tenth of any plunder to the other four as part of the pact. Moggie made them all sign a treaty that said that any who broke their vow would forfeit their soul."

Benjamiah had never seen Mea so animated, rattling breathlessly through the story.

"But the other pirate lords betrayed Moggie," continued Mea. "Because she was a woman, most likely. They ambushed her ship. But, when they attacked, the poppets of the other pirate lords turned against them. Breaking the treaty meant they lost their poppets—their *souls*—to Moggie. Apparently, she fed them magical berries from a special plant, which severed the connection between the pirates and their poppets. She destroyed the other lords, took their poppets, and sailed away, never to be seen again."

Though there was little in the story to comfort Benjamiah, Mea's exuberance was heartwarming. Finding everybody staring, she drew back into her shell.

"I just . . . ," she said. "I love those stories. They're all that kept me going. B-Bo burned my copy a long time ago, but luckily I knew them all by heart. . . ."

Elizabella gave Mea a reassuring smile. Benjamiah's mind circled back to the task at hand.

"I'm supposed to swim down," he said, "where *more than darkness sleeps*. What does that mean? It's just like the first child in 'The Witchstone Tree' who had to dive underwater and ended up drowning. I'm a terrible swimmer. How will I breathe? And how will I protect myself? I can't do it. I can't . . ."

A formidable panic gathered steam in Benjamiah's breast. This was absurd. The witchstone wasn't meant for him—it was meant for a dollcaster capable of magic. Around him, as his mind reeled, the others closed ranks.

"It's okay," said Elizabella. "We'll help. Our poppets will go with you. As for swimming down, let's find out. The rhyme says to grasp the branch."

Being accompanied by the others' poppets was something, at least. Mea nodded encouragingly. Taking a deep breath, Benjamiah approached the witchstone branch spearing crookedly out of the bonewood tree. He reached up and gripped the pale wood.

Every hair on his body prickled and shivered, the violet veins flaring. Heat charged through him before—to his great shock—the witchstone upon his eye *moved*. He gasped, releasing the branch, as the witchstone slid down his face—watched in mute shock by the others—and settled in a new shape upon his mouth and nose.

"What's happened?" he shouted, wild with panic, fingers clawing at the witchstone.

But it wouldn't budge. When Benjamiah was satisfied he could still breathe, he looked to Elizabella for help.

"It...," said Elizabella, inspecting it closer. "Benjamiah, I think this will let you breathe underwater!"

"I can't do it," he said.

It was Elizabella who could do this sort of thing. Benjamiah was just Benjamiah, short and bookish and a magical dunce. Elizabella stepped closer, resting her hands on his upper arms.

"You can," she said. "Remember the Magimmaculum? And the raven? And Manfred's monster? You can do anything. Emba will be there. She'll guard you with her life. And Griffyn and Hope, too, right?"

Silas and Mea nodded emphatically. Hope was the name Mea had chosen for her poppet—like everything else, she couldn't recall the doll's original name.

Benjamiah took a deep, shaky breath. Their support fortified him—and so did the witchstone mask clamped on Mea's face. That would be his own fate if he couldn't win Agatha's wicked game. And Mea, and all the other snatchlings, would never be freed.

"Okay," said Benjamiah, feeling mildly faint, "let's go."

They stood at the edge of the pool, Benjamiah's heart frantic. What was he even looking for down there? The rhyme suggested he'd find Moggie Blueheart's wrecked ship, but what else lurked in the depths? Fear plugged his throat, preventing him from asking the others.

Nuisance the capuchin hooted encouragement.

Benjamiah wished Nuisance could join him, but the poppet could only take three forms of her own volition and none were marine animals. Benjamiah would have to learn those himself.

After one final, reassuring nod from Elizabella, Benjamiah waded into the water. When it lapped up to his waist—cuttingly cold despite the warm sun—the others threw their poppets. The dolls transformed before they hit the water: Emba into a midnight-blue eel; Griffyn into a pale blue turtle; Hope into a fern-green carp, with a skull for a head.

Benjamiah took a deep breath, heart charged with fear, and plunged forward into the water.

The cold was stunning and total, driving all the way to his bones. In the clear water, he found Emba, Griffyn, and Hope nearby. When the shock of the cold began to pass, Benjamiah emptied his lungs through his nose in a stream of bubbles. Then, fully expecting to immediately drown, he inhaled.

The witchstone filtered out the water and it was only air that threaded down Benjamiah's windpipe. He could breathe underwater. For a moment, he forgot the trial entirely, such was the elation he felt.

Then he set off downward. The pool was far deeper than it had seemed, tumbling away into a deep trench of dark blue water. The eel, turtle, and carp accompanied him.

Swimming deeper, Benjamiah passed corals and phosphorescent flowers, and fish and serpents of ludicrous shapes and colors, and crabs with four claws and shells patterned like butterflies.

A little deeper and Benjamiah reached a jut of sparkling rock—robed in trailing cherry-colored weeds—which afforded him a view of the basin of the trench.

Wedged there was a shipwreck, tilted forlornly to one side. It must once have been a magnificent, imposing vessel; now timber had fallen from its hull, and its masts were snapped, and its sails had been stripped to ribbons by the elements. Dark water and sand drifted through its carcass.

Emba, Griffyn, and Hope hovered beside Benjamiah, providing a fresh dose of courage. Just as he detached himself from the rocky outcrop, something monstrous drove him back into the weeds.

It looked like a tremendous vine snaking upward over the ledge. Then Benjamiah saw how it was studded with suckers, pulsing and flexing and slimy—saw how one tentacle became two, then four, as a monumental poppet octopus hauled itself upward, churning water and clumps of loosened rock, all played out in the unearthly pulsing silence of the deep.

Benjamiah was paralyzed. The monstrous octopus climbed, slippery and vaguely translucent, eerie eyes throbbing menacingly either side of its head. It clambered beyond where Benjamiah hid in the weeds, continuing up the wall of the trench. It had spotted neither Benjamiah nor his poppet companions, who had swiftly darted into hiding.

Benjamiah's heart thumped. When the octopus had vanished from view, he peered out and studied the shipwreck, waiting. Then he saw it. A large poppet tiger shark came undulating from behind the hull, patrolling the waters with bladed flint for teeth and pearls for eyes.

To whom did the poppets belong? Benjamiah could make no sense of it. Mea had said the Pyrate Queene somehow stole the other pirate lords' poppets, but Moggie—if she had ever lived—was surely dead now.

With little choice but to go on, Benjamiah waited for the shark to swim out of sight. Then, heart galloping, he loosened himself from the ledge and swam downward, escorted by Emba, Griffyn, and Hope. Plunging through the open water toward the shipwreck was one of the longest and most frightening moments in Benjamiah's life. He was fully expecting the shark to come spearing out of the murk with its mouth wide and ruinous.

With the shipwreck almost in touching distance, Benjamiah froze. What he had assumed to be a long flank of shell-encrusted timber in the sand suddenly moved, throwing up a tendril of sand. An eye opened. A tail shivered.

Basking in the murk beside the ship was a poppet crocodile. Benjamiah floundered, hopelessly vulnerable, as the beast stirred. Before it fully turned its head, the poppets spurred themselves into action. Emba the eel went first, falling like a javelin toward the crocodile. Then Griffyn and Hope followed, darting at the beast, demanding its attention. It snapped its monstrous jaws and flailed in pursuit, lifting from the bed in a plume of disturbed sand.

The poppets drew the crocodile away. Likewise, Benjamiah saw the shark come stabbing out of the darkness, joining the chase. It was all Benjamiah could do not to follow—if a poppet died, so too did its owner. Elizabella, Silas, and Mea were risking their lives to save him.

Benjamiah made to move, but found himself trapped. Then he felt his chest being wrung of air. Looking down brought a wave of dull terror. A tentacle, slimy and muscular, lined with suckers, had enlaced him. Flailing wildly, his mind a confused, chaotic horror, he knew there was no escape. Another tentacle came, and another. While struggling, Benjamiah got a view of the abominable octopus, all legs and eyes and a wide, clammy mouth, toward which the snared Benjamiah was being helplessly drawn by its raft of mighty limbs.

And then, from nowhere, came Emba. The eel was back, stabbing at the octopus's eyes. Benjamiah felt the tentacles' grip slacken. Emba was a pointed fury, pecking and spearing, which gave Benjamiah his chance to scramble clear.

Emba lured the beast away. Benjamiah, hoping desperately that she would escape, reached the shipwreck. He floundered through a tear in the hull.

What happened next was bewildering. Where a moment before he'd been swimming, once inside he was snatched by gravity and hauled to the floor. Sopping wet, he looked around. He was no longer underwater, instead inside the perfectly dry—and absolutely opulent—belly of a pirate ship.

From within, the shipwreck was not a shipwreck at all. Benjamiah had swum in through a hole in the hull that seemed to pin back the flood of water. He was in a cabin below deck cluttered with coiled rope, cannonballs, and what appeared to be a bulging treasure chest.

Somewhere nearby, Benjamiah could hear music. And he could smell cooking. Somebody was *living* here. And, judging by the story Mea had told and the presence of the multiple poppets outside, Benjamiah had a good idea who.

Dripping wet, bruised and reeling from his encounter with the octopus, Benjamiah eased open the cabin door and peered along a thin corridor bordered by bulkheads. Gleaming treasure adorned the walls, and maps, and the bones of enormous marine animals. Music and light and the smell of food spilled from a cabin up ahead. Benjamiah crept toward it, dripping water as he went.

He eased the door open a fraction and peeked inside. It was a huge cabin, with a wide window overlooking the submerged bow. There was a bed, and a table and chair, and bookshelves and cabinets. Everything was rendered in chestnut mahogany and plush red velvet, a bafflingly lavish captain's hold at the heart of a shipwreck. Scratchy music drifted from a gramophone in the corner. Some kind of fishy broth hissed and spilled from a warped pot on the stove.

Hunched over the stove was an ancient, owlish woman. Her hair was white and fell in long ropes to the floor. Her arms and hands were all bones; even the weight of the ladle seemed to trouble her. She had a peg leg which looked very much like whalebone. Her face was wrinkled, her nose small and sharp, and when she tilted her head to taste the soup her eyes were milky and unfocused—she was blind.

Benjamiah stayed hidden. Somewhere here was *something* he needed to find, some particular treasure. Moggie might have been hundreds of years old, but she still commanded a family of terrifying poppets, two of which he'd yet to encounter. How was he to search the cabin without being discovered? Especially when he didn't even know what he was looking for.

Then—as Benjamiah looked closer round the cabin, at

the bed in disarray and the books and paper fallen to the floor, at the unwashed goblets and plates by the stove, at the membrane of grime covering everything and the overflowing laundry by the window—he recalled the values from the "Witchstone Tree" story, those values that Agatha had demanded of Bo.

They are foolish, and unkind, and cowardly, and disloyal, and incurious, Agatha had said in the story.

Unkind . . .

"Can I help you?" said Benjamiah.

Moggie Blueheart froze, teetering with the weight of the ladle. Then her mouth twisted into a wry smile.

"Aye," said the Pyrate Queene. "That you can."

Benjamiah smiled. Having helped Moggie settle in a rickety rocking chair by the window, he cleaned and tidied and swept. By this time, all five of her poppets had entered the cabin—not as octopuses or sharks or crocodiles, but as pudgy little dogs gathered round Moggie's feet, eyeing Benjamiah curiously as he tended to the cabin the old pirate could no longer manage.

After bringing Moggie a bowl of broth, Benjamiah stroked the dogs and waited for Moggie to speak.

"You think I didn't know you were here, lad?" said the Pyrate Queene, her voice raspy.

Though her eyes were unseeing, they glimmered and settled directly upon Benjamiah.

"Heard you the moment you came in," said Moggie. "Crashing, dripping, *breathing*. You'd better have mopped up all that water, or I'll have your guts for rigging. I may be small, but I'm quick as a bonefish."

Benjamiah smiled, saying, "I mopped up all the water."

"Well then," said Moggie Blueheart, "ask for it."

"I don't know what it is," said Benjamiah.

"Aye, that's about Agatha's way," she replied. "No wonder the poor beggars always fail."

"Have other children come?"

"Aye, that they have. Most Midsommers she would leave a fragment with me. Almost none of 'em worked out that they were supposed to help me, not steal from me. Been a while since she left this one, though. And she ain't been back since. I reckon she's given up, so she has."

One of Moggie's dogs pottered over to the bookshelf. It transformed into a spider monkey, climbed up, opened a small tin box, and withdrew something. The creature dropped down and offered it to Benjamiah.

He took it. It was a crooked slither of witchstone, no bigger than a matchstick.

"When you get back up," said Moggie, "fit it to the fragment around your eye. It will lead you on, lad. There's more ahead of you, and worse. You're lucky I'm a thousand years old or I might have sprung upon you and stuffed you into my cannon."

Benjamiah pocketed the witchstone fragment, then sat cross-legged on the cabin floor.

"How can you be a thousand years old?" he asked. "And live down here..."

Moggie, grinning toothily, only said, "Midsommer is a mighty magical time, lad. Me endin' up down here is one of my duller tales. Aye, I could tell you some stories."

"I'd love to hear them," said Benjamiah, smiling.

Moggie looked a little taken aback. Then she leaned back in her rocking chair and talked and talked, regaling Benjamiah with outlandish tales of plundering, pillaging, and warring, all told against the backdrop of the ghostly depths outside the window.

TEN
WITH BOLLY PONDWATER

"There's no magic like goodness, my sweet girl," said Bolly's mother with almost her last breath. "Be good if nothing else. A child's soul is just about the best and most magical thing in the universe—don't be afraid to show it."

—*The Book of Barely Believable Stories*,
Mildred Fogge

BENJAMIAH'S RETURN was an altogether more pleasant swim, rising toward the glittering sunlight with Moggie's fantastical tales still ringing through his head. Breaking the surface and stumbling up the bank, he was accosted by a jubilant Nuisance before he'd even cleared his eyes of water.

"Okay, okay!" said Benjamiah, peeling the exuberant monkey from his face.

Benjamiah was helped onto dry land by Elizabella

and Silas, water streaming from his clothes. The sunlight warmed his skin and the sound of the waterfall fluting upon the rocks was blissful after the uncanny, throbbing silence of the deep.

Elizabella, looking frazzled, snapped, "What took so long?"

Benjamiah knew this was Elizabella's way of demonstrating how worried she had been. Before he could respond, he felt the witchstone on his mouth move. As before, it shifted of its own accord—climbing up his face and resettling in a loop round his eye.

Elizabella tried her hardest to remain cross, but her expression twisted into something else.

"What's wrong?" said Benjamiah.

"Mea," said Elizabella, worried. "She ran off. She suddenly got upset about something. We tried talking to her, but . . ."

Silas chewed his fingernails, his expression inscrutable.

"Where is she?" said Benjamiah.

They found Mea behind a mossy boulder, knees drawn up to her chin and tears weaving down the witchstone mask. Her eyes were enormous and she whispered to herself, shaking her head from side to side. Hope, now a rabbit with a skull for a head, nuzzled her foot.

"What happened, Mea?" said Benjamiah, crouching.

She flinched, unaware the children had approached.

She regarded them as though they were more confusing apparitions in a nightmare from which she couldn't wake.

Elizabella crouched, too. Silas hung back, kicking the dirt with his shoes.

"It was . . . It was . . . It was . . ."

As before, Mea careered breathlessly toward a panic attack. And, as before, Benjamiah put a hand on her shoulder and helped steady her breathing.

Finally, tearfully, Mea composed herself and said, "It was . . . *him*."

The way Mea delivered the word—shivering, scanning around—meant it could only have referred to Bo. Benjamiah looked to Elizabella, who shook her head.

"Bo wasn't here," said Elizabella.

"No," said Mea. "He was *here*." And she jabbed the forehead of the witchstone mask.

"What do you mean?" said Benjamiah gently.

"I heard him in my head!" cried Mea. "Through the witchstone. He . . . He . . ."

"What did he say?" asked Benjamiah.

It took Mea an age to gather her strength.

"He said, 'Coming for you . . . Coming for you . . .' And he said that I'm a d-disgrace, that we were a f-f-family and I . . . and I . . ."

Then Mea burst into tears, burying the witchstone mask

in her hands. Silas's face was drawn, troubled. Elizabella put her hand on Mea's other shoulder, her eyes full of fire and danger.

"You tell him," said Elizabella, "that he'll have to come through me first. I *dare* him. Tell him I can't *wait* to meet him."

Mea sniffed loudly, looking up with wobbling eyes.

"Me too," said Benjamiah.

"You don't want me here," said Mea. "That's what Bo says. And he's right, isn't he? I'm nothing but a burden. Silas knows it."

All eyes swiveled to Silas, who chewed his bottom lip and kicked at the undergrowth sulkily.

"Tell Mea she's wrong, Silas," said Elizabella.

It would have been less threatening had Elizabella unsheathed a dagger.

Silas only said, "Of course."

"You're not a burden, Mea," added Benjamiah. "You're one of us now."

Though Mea still looked unconvinced, she nodded and hauled herself up, somehow tripping over her own poppet as she did so.

"Come on," said Benjamiah. "I can tell you all about meeting Moggie Blueheart."

Joy and envy ignited in Mea's eyes and chased away all thoughts of Bo. The four children went back to the water's edge, basking in the sun while Benjamiah regaled his audience with his encounter with the fabled pirate.

Nobody wanted to leave the idyllic waterfall behind, but inevitably the time came. Before setting off, Benjamiah withdrew the fragment of witchstone he'd received from Moggie and, using the water as a mirror, connected the two pieces. A seam of fiery violet light flashed. When Benjamiah removed his hand, the new fragment had merged with the old. The magical moths had returned, looping and frantic, trailing luminescent dust.

Returning to the cobbled streets, Benjamiah felt exhaustion catch up with him. The swim and the tension had taken their toll, not to mention the pain of being wrung by a gigantic octopus. The others suggested they find a nice inn and resume their journey tomorrow, which Benjamiah thought was an excellent idea.

Soon the children arrived on a particular street and shared a smile. It was a tight, twisty lane of thatched cottages, the sky a latticework of cloud and pale sunlight. The entire road was ablaze with splendid Midsommer fun. An old man in a flowery tunic played a pretzel-shaped fiddle while masked men, women, and children danced. Neighbors had set up tables with treacle tea and pastries, sweetdough sandwiches, and poppysyrup. Blossom fluttered and paper lanterns of black and white hung from bonewoods.

Weaving through the dancing throng, Benjamiah spotted a big-bellied man standing over a smoking barrel. Masked, exhilarated children were gathered round it, chittering and hopping like unfed birds.

"Treacle opples!" said Elizabella.

On cue, the large man dipped an opple on a stick into the barrel, swirled it around, and withdrew it—now coated in oozing, steamy treacle. Benjamiah found his mouth watering.

"Let's find an inn," said Elizabella. "Then we're coming back for one."

They found a place called the Gremlin's Nest, a tall, crooked town house with low-beamed ceilings and log fires in every room. The innkeeper was a short, bespectacled woman named Oleanor, her eyes bleary from too much poppysyrup. After booking the children in, she demanded they join the party outside.

Upstairs, Benjamiah and Silas washed and changed before there came a knock on the door. It was Elizabella and Mea.

"I wondered if maybe we should go to the party," said Mea meekly, trying to hide how keen she was. "It might seem rude otherwise...."

Benjamiah smiled.

"You and Silas go," said Elizabella. "Benjamiah and I have some work to do first."

She'd crossed the room and picked up the *Earthworm* spellbook from Benjamiah's side table. Excitement flurried in his stomach.

Silas looked stiff, unable to meet Mea's eye. Mea finally bit her lip and spoke up.

"Will you come with me?" she said nervously. "I'd . . . feel much safer with a famous Mapmaker there. To make sure I don't wander off and get lost. . . ."

This, just as Mea had intended, more than did the trick. Silas visibly puffed up, like a peacock showing off its plumage.

"You're quite right," he declared grandly. "It's absolutely my duty to ensure your safety. Shall we?"

He and Mea, smiling coyly, hurried off. Somehow Mea contrived to bang her head on the door before closing it.

Elizabella sat on the edge of the bed, staring out of the window. Benjamiah joined her and found her eyes glassy, full of light from the street outside.

"Are you okay?" he asked.

"Fine," said Elizabella stiffly.

"Are you thinking about Hansel?"

"No."

"Follynook."

"No."

"Do you miss Clover?"

Elizabella laughed, despite herself. Then melancholy renewed itself upon her face.

"Sometimes I think the world is just *bad*," she said. "Full of bad people doing bad things. Who always win, one way or another. Bad people get all the stupid things they want—like power and money—at the expense of good people who want real things, like safety and family and . . ."

"A home?" suggested Benjamiah.

Elizabella stiffened again. "It's just a place we lived," she said, "and now we don't."

"It isn't, though," said Benjamiah gently. "It's *home*."

For a moment, Elizabella's eyes narrowed, hands balling. Then the moment passed and she sighed.

"Yes, Follynook is home," she said. "It's worth less than nothing to the Viper. Worth very little to anybody else. But for Hansel and me it means a lot. It's where Edwid and I grew up. It was the first place Hansel and Ada lived. It's where me, Edwid, and Hansel made forts out of books on stormy nights, reading stories and toasting marshfruits."

"We'll get it back," said Benjamiah.

Elizabella shook her head, resigned to defeat.

"What about your home?" she said.

So far, he'd only told her that Mum and Dad had separated, and that he sometimes stayed at Mum's and other times stayed at Once Upon A Time. But describing the bare facts of the situation belied its complexities and difficulties, the way it made Benjamiah feel—rootless, becalmed between two places, frustration eating him from the inside.

"I miss the way things used to be," he said eventually. "I know you're not supposed to do that. But I can't help it."

"That's normal," said Elizabella. "I wish every day that Edwid was alive. And Ada."

Benjamiah nodded, wishing with every fiber of his being that he could make it so for Elizabella. Her words also gave him an uncomfortable dose of perspective. What right did he have to complain compared with what Elizabella had lost?

"If all that wasn't enough to worry about, then *this* had to happen," said Benjamiah, touching the witchstone upon his face. "Maybe soon I'll be a snatchling and will have forgotten all about Mum and Dad, anyway."

"Which would be a terrible thing, wouldn't it?" said Elizabella.

Benjamiah paused, arriving late to the point Elizabella was making—that what had happened with his mum and dad was a part of him now, a part of his story, and to forget or undo it would be to unmake a part of himself.

"Right," said Elizabella. "Time to test you."

They sat cross-legged on the lumpy bed, facing each

other. Elizabella held the *Earthworm* spellbook, hair tied up and regarding Benjamiah patiently as though he were a three-year-old chewing on his own shoe.

"Now, it's okay if you don't know everything yet," she said. "Don't be too hard on yourself. It's difficult. Just try your best, okay?"

"Shall we just get on with it?" snapped Benjamiah.

With a grin, Elizabella leafed through the tattered spellbook at random, cleared her throat, and began.

"Of approximately how many segments is an earthworm—"

"—between one hundred and one hundred and fifty," said Benjamiah confidently.

Elizabella made a "hmph" noise, then added, "Started with an easy one. Okay . . ."

No matter what Elizabella tried, though, she couldn't catch Benjamiah out. Whether quizzing him about the earthworm's closed circulatory system, or that they don't have lungs and breathe through their skin, or the fact that their tunnels aerate the soil to the benefit of plants, animals, and even humans, Benjamiah had the answer.

"Are you cheating?" said Elizabella, looking increasingly cross.

Benjamiah shrugged. "Only if cheating means studying hard."

"Fine," said Elizabella. "Learning the spellbook is the

easy bit, anyway. Let's see how you get on with actually *doing* some magic."

A tingle traveled through Benjamiah, a rush of excitement that made him bite his lip.

"Bring Nuisance over here," said Elizabella.

Nuisance was cast as a dormouse. Benjamiah reached out with his mind and assumed agency of his poppet, feeling every muscle as though it were connected to his own mind. It was like nothing else in the world, a splendid, rapturous experience that he'd grieved for in those long months back home. Instantly, the dormouse—who until then had been nibbling happily on a chair leg—fell completely still. Benjamiah had her run across the rug, up the side of the bed, and crouch obediently between him and Elizabella.

"First we have to test your control," she said.

This entailed Elizabella instructing Benjamiah to do one thing while making Nuisance do another. Initially, Benjamiah thought this a legitimate part of the preparation, but soon began to wonder if Elizabella was doing it simply to humiliate him. By the end, she had Benjamiah standing on one foot and scratching his nose, while making Nuisance the dormouse balance on her opposite paw on the top of his head.

"I think we've covered this now," said Benjamiah grumpily.

Elizabella scratched her nose to mask her amusement, which only made Benjamiah more annoyed.

"Very good," she said, trying not to laugh. "Okay, it's time."

They sat cross-legged once again, the music from outside pressing against the window.

"Take deep breaths and clear your mind."

"Are we dollcasting or meditating?" said Benjamiah with a groan.

"Do as I say," said Elizabella, eyes narrowed.

So Benjamiah did as he was told. Though what exactly did it mean to clear his mind? The act of clearing his mind inherently required *something* going on in his mind. Was his mind clear? Asking the question seemed to be a *thing* of which his mind wasn't clear. The music from outside didn't help, nor the hot and intoxicating drift of treacle-opple scent.

"Now occupy Nuisance," said Elizabella. "Forget about yourself. You're now the dormouse. Think about her little limbs. Her fur. Her tiny heart. When you breathe in, breathe through Nuisance's nostrils."

With his eyes closed, Benjamiah did as he was told. It was hard to separate his imagination from reality, but he did his best nonetheless.

"Now visualize the change," said Elizabella, "but don't do anything. Just prepare yourself. The dormouse becoming the earthworm. Think about everything you know now. Its skin and the way it moves. Its size and shape. Have it in mind all at once, confidently and clearly. Like music, all the instruments playing in harmony, a whole rather than its parts."

What did that mean? Nothing as far as Benjamiah could tell. Nonsense. Still, he did as he was told, eyes closed, breathing slowly and arranging every detail about earthworms in his mind.

"Are you ready?" said Elizabella, and Benjamiah nodded.

"On the count of three, seize every part of Nuisance and transform her into an earthworm."

Benjamiah took a deep breath, charged with nervous energy.

"Three . . . two . . . one . . . go!"

Benjamiah gave it his best shot, trying to simultaneously map every part of Nuisance into the parts of an earthworm all at once, like a great well of anatomical detail falling instantly into place—like dashing a hundred jigsaw pieces to the floor and hoping they fell into a perfect picture.

Instead of transforming, Nuisance the dormouse gave a horrible, agonized squeal, her body contorting and shifting uncomfortably while a fierce pain cleaved down the center of Benjamiah's skull. He gasped. Nuisance was still a dormouse and Benjamiah's head throbbed, eyes watering.

"That was a miscast," said Elizabella. "Talk me through what you did."

Benjamiah did his best to explain, while his head pounded and Nuisance eyed him fearfully. The last thing Benjamiah wanted to do was hurt his poppet—her tormented squeak had been like a knife to the heart. When Elizabella had given him some advice on doing it correctly—some of it useful and some of it hopelessly vague—they tried again.

Three times, then four, then five. Each time, Benjamiah miscast. Each failure brought more writhing and squealing from Nuisance and more brutal pain inside Benjamiah's head.

"I can't anymore," he said, head in his hands. "It hurts too much."

Nuisance the dormouse crept up Benjamiah's chest. He cupped her in his hands.

"I'm sorry. I'm trying."

Nuisance squeaked reproachfully.

"Okay, let's leave it for today," said Elizabella. "But we need to keep practicing. It's harder to start dollcasting the older you are. You're probably overthinking it. It isn't about a particular process as much as *feeling* and *believing* the spell."

Benjamiah's head throbbed too hard to demand further explanation. He was desperate to perform magic, but couldn't bear putting Nuisance through more pain.

Joined by his headache, Benjamiah followed Elizabella to the street party. The scene was as jubilant as before. Mea and Silas were together, watching the fiddler play; Mea swayed happily, eyes full of life, with Silas seeming to find more joy in Mea's happiness than the music. Benjamiah set a course for the treacle-opple barrel, but was waylaid en route by Oleanor the innkeeper, who took Benjamiah on a wild waltz round the cobbles until he was finally able to squirm loose. The fiddler played and people sang along, a chorus of well-known Midsommer songs about Lyly Well-I-Never and the Wyrm of the Well and Bolly Pondwater.

"Bolly's story is my absolute favorite!" said an overexcited Mea.

She was on her third treacle opple by the time Benjamiah caught up with her, sticky sauce smeared round her witchstone mouth and her eyes wild and charged with sugar.

"Tell me about it," said Benjamiah.

So Mea did. It wasn't the story itself that cheered Benjamiah, but rather the gleeful way in which she told it. Bolly Pondwater, according to Mea, was a young girl whose kind mother died, leaving her as a servant to her wicked stepfather. Bolly ran away from him, traveling all of Wreathenwold during Midsommer, helping people who needed help, for no reason other than kindness. But the stepfather, a vindictive sorcerer, put a curse upon her so that at Midsommer's end Bolly would die.

"And she did," said Mea. "But you won't believe what happened next! All the good things Bolly did brought her back. All the people she'd helped wept and summoned up the memories of her goodness, and she came back to life, and the wicked stepfather was sent to the deepest cell of Loomgate Prison."

Benjamiah agreed it was a lovely story. While Mea dashed off for another treacle opple, Benjamiah found Silas telling bold tales of Mapmaker daring to a group of rapt, masked toddlers. Elizabella came bustling over to Benjamiah with his very own treacle opple, which tasted as mesmerizing as it smelled—sweet and crunchy and perfect.

Looking around at the dancing and singing, the clapping and hugging, neighbors eating and drinking—with his best friend beside him—Benjamiah thought that there was no way the world was fundamentally *bad*, neither this one nor any other. There were good people everywhere enjoying good things. Maybe those things just seemed smaller and quieter than the terrible things people did.

Much later, the party dwindled and the exhausted children filed back to the inn. After saying good night to the girls, Benjamiah read *The Book of Barely Believable Stories* until his eyelids became too heavy. He blew out the oil lamp and sank happily toward sleep—only possible after he had got out of bed and undone the mechanism of the mantelpiece clock. Ticking had never seemed so creepy.

ELEVEN
WITH THE OTHER-WAY-UPS

> The Van Craggs haunt Crokerley to this day, stalking the ceilings with long arms trailing downward, fingernails like barbed wire and teeth like wild dogs—scampering as quick and deadly as spiders to snatch up any who dare enter.
> —*The Book of Barely Believable Stories*,
> Mildred Fogge

They traveled for two days, threading the vast and unguessable labyrinth one street at a time. Roads weaved, and bridges crested, and staircases climbed and fell. Tunnels burrowed, lanes twisted, paths looped. Sun sparkled and rain whipped. Starlight and music, fog and smoke, bards and Hanged Men and color-poachers—every strand of Wreathenwold shivered with fun and danger. Onward they drove through the immense tangle of streets and forests, the path behind them forgotten and the path ahead ominously unknowable. Every step cranked up Benjamiah's fear of what lay ahead; likewise, every glance toward the friends, right there beside him on the journey, soothed his fidgety heart.

Following the moths, they navigated a racecourse where jockeys rode their own poppets, a jostling and jeering crowd baying for their champions. In an ancient valley of trees and chalky slopes, a toothless Root Folk woman bid them beware of the Weird Wood, where a blight that would consume all of Wreathenwold was gathering in strength. Another street speared into a maze of black walls and shadow and dead ends, in which they grew increasingly bewildered and panic-stricken, before Ariadne—still irked at being overlooked as a guide—led them begrudgingly to safety. Wherever they went, Silas sketched maps and made notes—belligerently rejecting the pointlessness of it.

They saw more posters for missing children. Midsommer grew in noise and color around them, now over a week into the monthlong festival. Everywhere were masks and costumes and street theaters. Blossom fluttered. The air smelled sweet and smoky and seemed charged with some trembling anticipation—though whether for anything good or bad, Benjamiah had no idea.

As twists became turns, as back became forth, as they traveled Wreathenwold as though caught in the gyrations of an endless whirlpool, Benjamiah fretted. These worries were varied, scuttling about within him like an infestation of mice in an old house—so that often he was unaware of their presence until one of them scratched in the darkness, or darted suddenly from the shadows of his mind.

Benjamiah worried about the witchstone upon his eye and where the moths were leading them next. Benjamiah worried about losing Agatha's game and ending up as another snatchling. And what about the children being taken by Bo and his horde? Benjamiah worried about Mea and Bo, about Elizabella and Hansel, about Mum, Dad, and Grandma. What had Mum asked of Agatha Drake all those years ago? Would Benjamiah ever find out?

Mea was skittish and clumsy, gorging on every sweet thing for sale. Silas, having still made no breakthrough with Ariadne, grew increasingly exasperated with her.

"We are absolutely doomed," moaned the Mapmaker when yet another heart-to-heart with Ariadne had failed to stop her playing dead. "The Mapmakers and all of Wreathenwold with us. Why can't she *see* it?"

Ariadne remained unmoved. Silas spent the rest of the afternoon skulking behind the others, scuffing his shoes and grumbling about the weather, his unrelenting misfortune, and the utter misery of the labyrinth. Mea tried to cheer Silas up, but ended up poking him in the eye, which only worsened his mood.

The following afternoon, the moths delivered them to a street that trailed upward toward a turreted house on a hill—a crooked and spindly silhouette against a backdrop of ashen cloud, wrapped in a thin shawl of mist. On either side were abandoned houses, gnarled trees, and the kind of stillness and deadness that might easily harbor all manner of horrors.

"I don't like the look of this place," said Benjamiah.

"Nothing to worry about," said Elizabella. "Just some old houses and a dab of mist. Where are the moths heading?"

Benjamiah pointed toward the creepy house on the hill.

"Of course," muttered Silas behind them.

"Let's go, then," said Elizabella, striding forward.

There was a dampness in the air, a chill that traveled to Benjamiah's center with every inward breath. They passed an old boarded-up well, and a swing hanging from a bonewood branch, creaking in the soft breeze.

The lane climbed toward the house. Again, just as he had at the waterfall, Benjamiah caught a snatch of childish chanting on the breeze: *Agatha Drake, Agatha Drake, beneath the witchstone tree . . . good and true and worth your grace, so play your game with me.* The house was clad in miserable gray timber, with steep gabled roofs and spires and turrets, and myriad windows that were thin and arched and boarded up from the inside. Its many dark points pierced the white sky. The garden had sprawled and swelled, a mass of trees and weeds and bracken that rose as high as the railings.

They reached the forbidding front gate. On a bronze plaque, barely legible, was a single word: CROKERLEY.

"It can't be . . . ," said Mea, eyes wide.

Unlike "The Pyrate Queene," Benjamiah *had* read this one. It was called "The Other-Way-Ups," another tale from *The Book of Barely Believable Stories* that he'd read two nights ago while Silas snored away in the next bed.

It was about a family called the Ravendales, who were Other-Way-Ups—that is, according to Mildred Fogge, an upside-down race of people for whom gravity worked in the opposite way. The earth was their up and the sky was their down. The only way the Ravendales could avoid plunging upward into the sky was to live on the ceilings of an old manor house called Crokerley.

This they did for many years, hiding in secret panels in the ceilings during the day and only venturing out at night—when the actual residents of Crokerley were in bed. The Ravendales were a sweet and gentle family, content with their small, and very quiet, life. At night, the mother and father would waltz silently across the ceilings, while the son and daughter would play silent rounds of hide-and-seek.

Naturally, there were times when the Ravendales were nearly discovered. Various Crokerley residents throughout the years came across strange things on the ceiling as though held there by glue: a tumbler of poppysyrup; the sketch of an imp; a ball. Others complained about the faint sound of snoring emanating from beneath the upstairs floors, or the creaking of ceilings in the dead of night. Gradually, Crokerley developed a reputation for being haunted, and was ultimately left derelict.

Then came the Van Craggs. They were a family of monster hunters, infamous throughout Wreathenwold for their bloodlust and brutality. There was the father, Olbert, the mother, Luella, and their vicious children, Marfa and Feo. A single purpose had lured the Van Craggs to Crokerley—to catch and destroy the Ravendales.

Thus the Van Craggs set about hunting them. They bored holes in the floorboards, and hammered their way into the walls, and held flaming rags in the cavities to smoke the Ravendales out. Eventually, the Ravendales were driven all the way to the top of Crokerley, to the attic ceiling, where the ruthless Van Craggs had them cornered.

Here there was an immense struggle, the Ravendales on the ceiling tangling with the Van Craggs on the floor. It was during this fateful brawl that something very peculiar happened, according to Mildred Fogge:

> Then—perhaps because of some condi-
> tion of magic or science not then known,

or perhaps because the universe, despite all claims to the contrary, does in fact have an admirable sense of humor—the Van Craggs hauled the Ravendales downward just as the Ravendales hauled the Van Craggs upward. Down the Ravendales tumbled just as upward the Van Craggs fell, crashing on to the underside of the roof in a snarling, baffled heap.

The Ravendales and Van Craggs swapped places. The Ravendales escaped Crokerley, no longer upside down and free to live their lives normally. As for the Van Craggs, they became the very monsters they had hunted—the Other-Way-Ups, confined to the ceilings of Crokerley.

Benjamiah looked at the others, stomach tied up with fear. Rising above them, dark and silent, was Crokerley. The violet moths soared through the gate, navigated the snarl of bracken and weeds, and crept beneath the front door of the manor.

"Over here," said Elizabella.

She'd slipped through the gate and turned the corner. The others followed, battling the overgrowth until they found her. She was standing beneath a dead tree, except one of its branches was different and very much alive—bone white and lined with strands of faintly pulsing purple.

A wooden sign hung from the witchstone branch, twisting in the breeze.

Composing himself, Benjamiah read:

> CONDEMNED TO LIVE AS THOSE THEY LOATHED,
> THE HUNTERS WERE UPTURNED,
> THEIR UP NOW DOWN AND DOWN NOW UP,
> A DOOM THEY TRULY EARNED.
>
> SO GRASP THE WITCHSTONE BOUGH AND CREEP
> INTO THE PERILOUS GLOOM,
> AND WREST THE PRIZE FROM THOSE WHO HAUNT
> THE HEIGHTS OF EVERY ROOM.

Benjamiah found himself shaking. Even Elizabella looked pale and troubled.

"I suppose this must be the 'bravery' trial," she said. "In 'The Witchstone Tree,' the second girl asked for help navigating the dark caves. Before . . ."

"She was lost in the darkness forever," croaked Benjamiah.

The prospect of searching Crokerley while the awful Van Craggs stalked them from above was truly terrifying. Benjamiah buried his face in his hands. Nuisance the nightjar crooned soberly—even she was afraid.

"Grab the branch, Benjamiah," said Mea kindly, putting a hand on his shoulder.

His mind a menagerie of snatching hands and razor-sharp nails, Benjamiah reached up and grasped it. As before, the violet threads blazed with color. Again the witchstone came to life upon Benjamiah's eye—and, though he was prepared for it this time, the feeling was no less uncomfortable. Finally, it settled in a new shape, a vague figure of eight looping round his eyes, like a pair of witchstone spectacles.

"Great, now it's wrapped round both my eyes!" he said.

"How is that going to help?" moaned Silas.

"I know how," said Elizabella. "It will help you see in the dark. It's the only thing that makes sense."

Which was some comfort to Benjamiah, but not much. He looked again at the manor house—crooked and bleak, every window blanked out by boards and timber. He opened his mouth to tell the others not to come, but was stopped by Elizabella's raised hand.

"Save your breath," she said. "We're coming. Let's go."

"Well, let's hear him out," said a clearly terrified Silas. "Maybe it would be better if, you know, some of us waited outside. . . ."

A withering stare from Elizabella silenced him. Silas slumped. Led by Elizabella, the children snaked through the Crokerley wilderness and onto the porch. The timber was mildewy and had fallen away in places. The front door was wide, the paint flaked away, the lock broken.

"Maybe we should make a plan," suggested Benjamiah. Elizabella tutted. "We don't need a *plan*. We stick together, stay low, look for the witchstone. And, obviously, keep an eye out for people on the ceiling."

Was that supposed to be funny? It was typical that Elizabella was making jokes when it was all Benjamiah could do not to curl up in a ball on the ground.

"Let's light our poppets," said Elizabella. "The Van Craggs will be able to see us, anyway. At least it gives us a chance of spotting them."

All four children gripped their dolls. As one, the poppets ignited—a ball of fire encasing their hands, burning hot to all but themselves. This was one spell Benjamiah knew.

With Elizabella at the front and Silas at the back, the children entered Crokerley.

When the front door opened, grayish light splashed about six feet across the hallway. Beyond that—and above—was a darkness so deep and immaculate that it defied belief. Benjamiah only knew it was darkness because, peering through the witchstone spectacles, everything was cast in a ghoulish green light. As for the others, he could tell by their faces that they were effectively blind.

Above was a high ceiling. All kinds of furniture were piled upon it—chairs, bureaus, tables—arranged in stalactites that reached downward. It was as though some alternative gravity were pulling things toward the ceiling.

To test this, Benjamiah picked up an old coin from the floor. He threw it in the air, not very far, and it fell back into the palm of his hand. Then he threw it again, harder this time. When the coin passed the midpoint, the ceiling's mass took over—the coin plummeted upward, hitting the ceiling with a resounding din and remaining there.

"What can you see?" whispered Elizabella.

Benjamiah described the stacks of furniture.

"They've made towers so they can reach us from up there," wailed Silas. "We're going to die in here!"

"Stay low," whispered Elizabella. "Stick together. We'll be fine."

Unusually, Benjamiah found himself agreeing with Silas. But what choice did he have? Fail and he'd never tear the wretched witchstone from his face. It would spread, sink into his skin, erase all trace of him, and make him another mindless underling of Bo Greaves.

While the house above was an almighty tangle of furniture and objects, on the ground Crokerley was bereft. It seemed the Van Craggs had systematically gathered everything from below to build their nefarious towers on the ceilings. There were floorboards, rotted rugs, a few stray objects: an empty poppysyrup bottle, a pile of rags, a fire poker.

Huddled together, their breathing ragged, the children edged into the darkness. Benjamiah described what he saw above—settees and drinks cabinets and bookcases arranged upside down on the ceiling—and ahead, which tended to be more empty rooms: a sitting room with a grand fireplace, a parlor with the remnants of a piano, a kitchen. There was no sign of witchstone anywhere, nor any glimpse of the Van Craggs.

Then the front door slammed shut.

The sound went through the house like the boom of a cannon, causing the children to flinch. They stood completely still, fearing even to breathe, listening while their blood thundered and their hands shook. Silence reigned. The Other-Way-Ups were here somewhere—now there was no doubt.

"We need to go upstairs," said Elizabella. "There's nothing down here."

The four of them, crouched in the darkness with their faces lit up by the poppet fire, were resolute. Despite betraying varying degrees of fear—from Elizabella's stiff-jawed denial to Mea's outright shuddering—nobody left.

So they crept on, keeping low, Benjamiah desperately scanning for signs of sudden movement above. None came. Nothing stirred in the bewildering upside-down scene. Together they came to the foot of the stairwell and fell still.

Only Benjamiah could track it all the way to the top—for the others, it traveled upward into a perilous throat of total blackness. In hushed, shaky tones, Benjamiah described what he saw: a horribly narrow staircase, with the sloping ceiling above absolutely crammed with furniture so that the space between above and below was not much taller than Mea, who was the tallest among them.

"It's a trap," she whispered. "The perfect place to catch us."

Benjamiah's stomach churned. She was right. If the Van Craggs were lurking in the mess of dilapidated furniture here, they'd be able to reach the children.

"Then we run," said Elizabella.

Benjamiah looked at her, horrified. Her expression was unmoved.

"They already know we're here," she said. "Sneaking around won't do any good. It just prolongs the danger. If this is the most dangerous part, then let's get through it as quickly as possible."

Though Benjamiah couldn't fault her logic, it was typical of Elizabella to push for something so maddeningly reckless. He wobbled, not at all sure he could face this. Returning to Wreathenwold was something he'd ached for intently, but right then he'd have given everything to be bored and miserable on the Wyvern-on-the-Water pier.

"Agreed?" whispered Elizabella.

One by one—first Mea, then Benjamiah, and finally Silas—the children nodded. What choice did they have?

"I'll go first," said Elizabella. "Be quick. Keep low. *We can do this.*"

Benjamiah's head spun, heart thumping. In front, Elizabella counted with her fingers, ghostly pale in Emba's firelight. *One, two, three . . .*

Elizabella bolted up the stairs, followed by Benjamiah. Every step brought an almighty din, carrying through Crokerley. Benjamiah was about halfway up, Elizabella ahead, and Mea and Silas behind, when it all went horribly wrong.

Springing from the clutter above came monsters: screaming and hair flailing, arms long and rubbery and ending in yellowish, curling, razor-sharp fingernails. Their ropey limbs swung as the world above seemed to crash downward and Benjamiah was grabbed, flailing one way and then the other, while his friends likewise were attacked, floundering in darkness. Amid the carnage, Benjamiah glimpsed other poppets—presumably belonging to the Van Craggs—cast as great fanged bats. All was chaos.

Benjamiah wriggled onto his back, feeling blood run warmly down the side of his face and from a dull, throbbing spot under his arm. Above him, he saw Luella van Cragg reaching downward from the bird's nest of furniture—tall, hair tumbling down the sides of her waxy face, her eyes wild. Her arm swung, nails missing Benjamiah's face by inches.

Poppets fought while the Van Craggs swiped and grabbed for the children. Somewhere Benjamiah heard Mea moan in horror and Silas yelp. Bodies went crashing down the stairs. One of the enormous bats swooped upon Benjamiah before he could turn to help. Nuisance the nightjar charged it, pecking its reddish eyes, the two creatures grappling in the air.

Hands grabbed Benjamiah and he flailed. But they were small, friendly hands. Elizabella had reached the landing above. Cast in greenish light, her hair was a mess and a nasty lump was forming beneath her eye.

While Luella van Cragg swiped and snarled from above, Benjamiah wriggled upward, back against the stairs, until he thrashed breathlessly on to the landing. From here, Luella couldn't reach them.

"Run!" whimpered Elizabella, helping Benjamiah to his feet.

"What about Mea and Silas?"

"They fell downward," said Elizabella, "and two of them followed. We have to find the witchstone, Benjamiah!"

Luella van Cragg screamed from above, now joined by another figure—a plump, balding, veiny-faced man. This had to be Olbert. Like his wife, his arms were unfathomably long and ropey, tipped with ruinous barbs. On the ceiling of the landing, the two Van Craggs circled, licking their lips.

"Stay low and they can't reach us," said Elizabella.

Their poppets could, though. Shrieking out of the gloom came two enormous bats. Benjamiah grabbed

Elizabella's wrist and hauled her onward, hurrying through the warren of rooms while the Van Craggs chased.

Finally, Benjamiah spotted somewhere to hide—a fireplace. He dragged Elizabella inside and there the two of them crouched, the walls sticky with soot, breathing carefully and trying not to cough. They trembled together. Benjamiah held Elizabella's hand—she must have seen absolutely nothing. After the horror on the staircase, everything was deathly quiet.

Then they heard footsteps. Slow, patient creaks traveling across the ceiling. Benjamiah dared not peek out from the fireplace.

"Children," came a scratchy, smoky, half-dead voice. "Do not be afraid. Come out and play. We've had such fun already. Let's have some *more*."

"There's no way out now, little ones," came Luella's voice, rasping and inhuman. "Better make a dash for it. Give yourselves a chance."

The Van Craggs, unable to see them, creaked out of the room. Luella crooned and threatened and taunted as she went.

"Are you okay?" whispered Benjamiah, perhaps the quietest he'd ever spoken.

"Yes," said Elizabella. Then, after a few sharp, fearful breaths, she said: "We have to find the witchstone."

It took all the strength Benjamiah had to lean out of

the fireplace and look around. On the ceiling was another chaos of objects and furniture: torn books, a rocking horse, a stack of crates. There was an old telescope and a box of cutlery and what looked like the wheel of a wagon. Then, incredibly, Benjamiah saw it.

A strand of strobing violet in the greenish blackness.

The fragment of witchstone glimmered from the upside-down drawer of an upside-down writing desk, filled otherwise with a mess of necklaces and pins and ribbons. Benjamiah eased back inside the fireplace and reported what he'd found.

"Use Nuisance," said Elizabella.

Nuisance, a nightjar, flexed her wings. Benjamiah assumed control of his poppet. With two minds, and two pairs of eyes, Benjamiah leaned out of the fireplace and scanned the top of the room again. Nothing moved. Somewhere below there was a thump and a muffled shout. Were Mea and Silas okay? The only thing Benjamiah could do was grab the witchstone and get everybody out of Crokerley.

Controlled by Benjamiah, Nuisance took flight. Benjamiah saw with his own eyes—and felt from within Nuisance—how gravity turned on its head halfway up. One moment Nuisance was fluttering up; the next she was fluttering down, landing on the edge of the open drawer. Something creaked, but Benjamiah had to focus.

Nuisance dropped into the drawer and wrapped her

tiny claws round the witchstone. Then two hands flashed out from behind the desk, closing upon Nuisance like the jaws of a bear trap.

Benjamiah felt the pain as if the nails were digging into his own flesh. He lurched out, gasping, as the portly figure of Olbert van Cragg unfolded from his hiding place. Nuisance cheeped and thrashed in his grip, shaking feathers loose. Olbert only grinned, his gums big and gruesome and his teeth filed down to wolfish points.

He smiled. "Pretty little birdy," said the dreadful Other-Way-Up. "A pretty, tasty little morsel . . ."

Benjamiah twisted in pain, begging for Nuisance to be freed. Luella van Cragg stalked back into the room, licking her lips. No matter what Benjamiah tried, Nuisance couldn't escape.

Emba speared out from the fireplace, cast as a bat. She soared upward, but was chased away by Luella's raking arms and the Van Craggs' poppet bats.

Olbert drew the helpless Nuisance toward his mouth, drool sliding down his chin.

Somewhere, amid the devastating panic, Benjamiah pounced upon a single lucid thought. He grasped it as though it were the last vine overhanging an abyss. Nuisance thrashed, drawing ever closer to Olbert's ghastly mouth. Benjamiah pulled at the thought, at the only way out, at his very last chance to save himself.

The skin, the mouth, the organs. The aortic arches, the bristles, the vessels, dorsal and subneural and ventral. The muscles, both circular and longitudinal, which lengthen and shrink the body. Benjamiah thought it all at once, precisely and confidently, not just an array of facts in his head but something whole and precise, like a symphony of information.

Nuisance shrank in Olbert's hands. For a moment, he was baffled. Then, as his fingers parted, something small and thin slipped loose and tumbled toward the floor.

Benjamiah caught Nuisance. In the palm of his hands was an earthworm, mostly black but for a red tint to some of her segments. Her eyes were white buttons.

Olbert and Luella howled. They leaped, flailing their ropey arms. Benjamiah felt the lash of air as he fell backward. The Van Craggs frothed and snarled, piling up furniture in order to extend their reach. Much closer and their sawing fingernails would reach Benjamiah.

Elizabella dashed out from the fireplace. Emba battled valiantly against the Van Craggs' much larger poppets.

"Get back, you monsters!" screamed Elizabella, hurling a billiard ball that struck Olbert in the temple.

Though it incensed Olbert further, it didn't slow him down. By now, the frenzied Van Craggs had assembled a mountain of ransacked furniture in the center of the ceiling and begun scrabbling up it. They crawled downward.

Benjamiah and Elizabella were on the ground, wriggling too slowly toward the door. The Van Craggs were nearly upon them.

And then the Van Craggs screamed. Something had flared through the darkness and into their faces. Upward Luella and Olbert tumbled, crashing back down the mound they'd built. Reeling, Benjamiah saw Mea and Silas stumbling into the room, bloody and bruised and wild-eyed. Their poppets had waylaid Olbert and Luella.

"We need to get out of here!" roared Silas.

Scampering into the room—across the ceiling—came the Van Cragg children, Marfa and Feo. They were every bit as rabid and terrifying as their parents, licking their lips and whirling their hands.

"The witchstone!" said Benjamiah, pointing upward.

Emba tried but was flung aside. Hope was chased away by Feo. Nuisance was still an earthworm and Benjamiah didn't know how to transform her back. In the end, it was Griffyn, cast as a barn owl, who soared upward and snatched up the witchstone fragment.

By now, the deranged Olbert and Luella had reassembled their heap of furniture and begun climbing again. But the children were already on the move. Benjamiah was helped up by Elizabella and Mea. He then led the way, Griffyn fluttering above with the witchstone in his talons. Each child held the hand of the one in front, led by Benjamiah.

Though the Van Craggs screamed and snatched and slashed, the children bolted as fast as their wobbling legs would carry them—down the stairs, along the hallway, out into the blissful, dizzying daylight.

TWELVE
WITH THE RIVER WOLVES

The great pack of wolves, hunted for their fur, took to the water. There they thrived, remaining to this day—preying on the very boats once used to transport their pelts.
—*The Book of Barely Believable Stories,*
Mildred Fogge

THE CHILDREN DIDN'T stop until they'd dragged themselves through the wilderness of Crokerley's grounds and stumbled out of the gate. Then they breathed fiercely, bent double. Benjamiah looked back at the looming, spindly house—all was silent, as though nothing had ever happened.

The adrenaline sapped and pain spiked. There was a gash near his temple that had left the right side of his face sticky with blood. Beneath his arm was a slash, from the scrape of a Van Cragg fingernail. The others had suffered too: the lump beneath Elizabella's eye was round and purple like a plum; Silas was holding up his right arm as though his shoulder were damaged; Mea's fingers were cut and it looked like she had a nosebleed beneath her mask.

The poppets, too, were wounded. All four had tears from which plumed thin streams of rippling air—this was aether, their primordial substance, and unless they were fixed by a dollmender the result would be fatal for both the doll and its owner.

"Just when I thought Clover was the worst host in Wreathenwold," said Benjamiah.

Elizabella smiled. Then Mea giggled, slightly hysterical. That set the others off. As with Mea, there was an undercurrent of hysteria to it. Events inside Crokerley had shaken Benjamiah to the core. And it was all his fault. *He* was putting them through this, all because he had placed the stupid witchstone on his eye in the first place.

"Thanks for coming back," Benjamiah said to Mea and Silas.

"It was Silas," said Mea. "Feo and Marfa had us trapped downstairs, but Silas said we couldn't leave you behind."

That was a surprise. Benjamiah felt certain it would have been Mea leading the return upstairs.

"Why did you do that?" Elizabella demanded, hands on hips.

Silas, still cradling his arm and wincing slightly, looked bashful.

"You'd have come for me," he said. "Not for any *reason*, except that it would have been the right thing to do. I've been so obsessed with the Mapmakers' mission for all these years that I never stopped to think about *why* we want to save Wreathenwold. Which is to have more of the good things in this world, like . . . friends."

It was the most open Silas had ever been, the most vulnerable. As though he'd betrayed too much of himself, he looked suddenly aghast. It was a fear Benjamiah knew all too well.

"Friends," agreed Benjamiah.

Elizabella nodded too.

"Friends?" said Mea.

They all said it, smiling at Mea and nodding their heads emphatically, desperate to make her believe it. Mea smiled, though she didn't look entirely convinced.

Together they limped and groaned their way to a doctor's office, then to a dollmender's—led to both by Ariadne, briefly delighted to resume her role as their guide. Here their poppets were stitched and repaired. During Nuisance's turn, Elizabella leaned over to Benjamiah, her eye now partially closed by the angry lump on her cheek.

"Don't think I didn't see," she said. "You did it. The earthworm. *Told you* you could do it."

Benjamiah couldn't help but smile, wildly happy. He *had* done it. And it had only required the threat of Nuisance being eaten by an upside-down monster.

They rested that day before continuing the following morning—somewhat delicate, impeded by their bruises and sprains and cuts. The moths swirled and eddied and flashed, urgent and excitable. Benjamiah wouldn't let them be rushed, though. Hurrying to Agatha's next trial when the last had been so brutal was not an appealing prospect. What if they got increasingly dangerous as the game went on?

Instead, Benjamiah put time into perfecting the earthworm spell. Before long, he could transform Nuisance into the wriggly worm as quickly and seamlessly as Elizabella could cast Emba. Seeing the earthworm take form—black and red, squirming happily with her eyes white buttons—was a source of unrivaled delight for him.

"Time to move on," Elizabella had said when she'd caught Benjamiah yet again admiring Nuisance the earthworm. She dropped three new spellbooks into his lap. "Get studying."

The new books were *Cellar Spider*, *Dormouse*, and *Sparrow*.

"Now the hard work *really* begins," said Elizabella in

her annoying schoolteacher voice. "Our next test I set you will include all three. So make sure you put the work in."

Benjamiah rolled his eyes and smiled privately: if there was one thing Benjamiah Creek could do well, it was study.

So, as the children traveled, Benjamiah read, wringing every drop of information from the new spellbooks. He read in hansoms, read as they stopped to eat or rest, read at night by the oil lamp of whichever inn they were staying in. Thinking and dreaming about dormouse hearts, or how a cellar spider's eight eyes were arranged, was better than worrying about Agatha Drake's deadly game.

After the breakthrough at Crokerley, Mea seemed more comfortable, still gorging on every sugary treat Wreathenwold had to offer and chattering away about random tales from *The Book of Barely Believable Stories*, imbued with that singular confidence that comes only in the company of those you trust.

Silas, too, was a different person, now a much more agreeable companion. His pompous, selfish shell had cracked and fallen away. This paved the way for his first successful conversation with Ariadne since their journey had begun. While the foursome read books in a tearoom (and Silas consulted his notebook, trying fruitlessly to link up two different maps), Ariadne unexpectedly climbed out of Benjamiah's pocket and eyed Silas. The Mapmaker stared back, swallowing nervously.

"Um . . . ," said Silas.

Ariadne fidgeted, a little shy.

"How are you today?" he asked, rather formally.

Elizabella snorted. Benjamiah raised his spellbook to mask his own silent laughter.

"Lovely weather, isn't it?" continued Silas.

It wasn't. Tendrils of rain crawled down the window, the sky a sweep of curdled, murky gray. Benjamiah was unable to look at Elizabella for fear of a full-blown laughing fit.

"Well, I'm pleased we could have this chat," said Silas. "Perhaps we should do it again sometime?"

Finally, it was too much for Elizabella and Benjamiah, who laughed so hard and loudly that Ariadne ran for cover. Silas might have sworn at them were it not for Mea patting him kindly on the arm and telling him he did very well.

Later they found themselves on the bank of a wide river splitting two halves of a Root Folk wood. The water was blackish and slithered across rocks and through clumps of crooked pale bulrushes. Bunched at the base of trees were fat toadstools patterned like exotic snakes, which Root Folk children picked and stowed in wicker baskets.

On a jetty, a boatman was lounging in a hammock beside a peculiar-looking rowing boat. From its flanks extended a battalion of iron tusks, festooned with thick, razor-sharp brambles. The hull was scored with claw and bite marks.

"Wanting to cross, my friends?" he said.

He was short and bald, dressed in various shawls with bracelets and bangles jostling on his wrists. Glyphs covered his cheekbones and neck, something slightly labyrinthine about the symbols. His left arm had grown into the branch of a tree, which had then been carved into a large oar. Root Folk became parts of the natural world as they aged, eventually planting themselves as trees, flowers, or shrubbery.

Elizabella cocked an eye at Benjamiah, checking if they needed to cross. The moths fluttered toward the opposite bank and Benjamiah nodded.

"Keep your arms tucked in if you like having them," said the boatman, untying the boat from the mooring post. "River wolves. Half wolf, half fish. A whole pack of them in these here waters."

Before Benjamiah could check if this was a joke, the children were hustled on board and huddled together in the middle, facing the boatman. He used his arm, alongside a real oar, to row. Only Elizabella peered over the edge, apparently irked by the lack of carnivorous creatures.

"Probably a load of rubbish," she said grumpily.

Then they heard a mournful, threatening howl—not from the trees but from the depths. The boatman grinned. Benjamiah shuddered, praying the iron tusks and brambles round the boat's hull were sufficient. They heard another howl, a cross between a wolf's call and a whale's mournful moan.

"I see them!" said Elizabella, leaning far over the edge. "Benjamiah, you have to look!"

"No, thank you."

"Oh, come on . . . They can't possibly reach us."

Dragged by Elizabella, Benjamiah found himself peering over the side. There, among the murky whorls of water, swam a pair of river wolves—their heads and shoulders lupine, their lower half more like that of a seal. Their eyes glared yellowish and famished as their bodies undulated alongside the boat.

Benjamiah scrambled away from the edge and the boatman grinned. Elizabella continued studying the river wolves as though they were no more dangerous than goldfish in a bowl.

The boatman ferried them further along the river, through a tunnel of willowlike trees trailing their branches in the water. Then, along one bank, the woodland was suddenly gone. For a mile or so there were only scorched slopes and the blackened stumps of trees. Planted in the soil were row upon row of small stone trees engraved with labyrinthine characters and darkened by ash and moss. Benjamiah recognized it as some kind of graveyard or memorial before the boatman even opened his mouth.

"This used to be Tyger Myle," he said. "Before the Widow burned it to cinders."

Sadness skewered Benjamiah. The sight of the graves stretching far into the distance, the absolute deadness of it all, smothered him.

"Why?" he asked.

"For no reason at all," said the boatman solemnly. "This world has never been short of tyrants. Mad magi, evil sorcerers, pirate kings. But there weren't none like her. She didn't dream of power and wealth like the others. She only dreamed of pain and suffering."

Benjamiah felt cold, forgetting about the river wolves for the rest of the journey.

Several days of traveling passed without incident, until one evening they came to a mask market, a canopied, mazelike bazaar selling every mask imaginable. Elizabella had told Benjamiah that the Grand Masquerade was approaching, which was a famed masked ball attended by only Wreathenwold's elite. Ordinary folk held their own balls, too, galas and parties in which they dressed glamorously and wore masquerade masks. Benjamiah recalled, with a cold somersault in his stomach, that the Grand Masquerade also marked High Dusk, the midpoint of Midsommer. Time was running out.

Elizabella also said that the night of the Grand Masquerade was typically when Midsommer gifts were given: between parents and children, friends and family. Benjamiah detected a sadness in her voice as she said it. Though she'd never admit it, Benjamiah knew how much Elizabella missed Hansel.

"I've never had a Midsommer gift before," said Mea. "Well, not any I can remember."

Silas and Elizabella likewise made small, incomprehensible noises. For both the Mapmakers and the Cottons, Benjamiah expected, any kind of pricey Midsommer gift was out of the question.

"Let's get presents for each other, then," he suggested.

The idea generated immediate excitement, though not without a hint of worry. Earlier that day, they realized that they were burning through their playing cards at an alarming rate—staying in fancy inns and dining extravagantly and splashing out on sweets, treacle tea, and new clothes.

"I know we need to save money," said Benjamiah, "but it's a special time of year. How about we all buy one present? Like Secret Santa back home."

This, to the children of Wreathenwold, meant absolutely nothing. So Benjamiah explained: they'd draw names from a hat and each of them would buy a present for only one other person. They'd all buy and receive one present. Everybody agreed.

Benjamiah wrote all their names on a scrap of paper, threw them into his flat cap, and commenced the lottery. Mea went first, then Silas, then Elizabella, before Benjamiah took the last scrap. Nobody was giving anything away.

Smiling, Benjamiah read his: *Silas*. The Mapmaker didn't strike him as the easiest person to buy a gift for. Very little made him happy, after all. Still, Benjamiah had a few days to find something. The other children likewise seemed lost in thought for the rest of the evening.

In the early hours of the morning, Benjamiah was shaken awake by a terror-stricken Mea.

To save money, all four children shared a room that night. Elizabella and Mea were in one bed and Silas and Benjamiah in the other.

Benjamiah thought at first that he was dreaming—Mea's witchstone mask above him, her eyes huge with silent horror and hemmed in by the dreamy darkness, seemed thoroughly unreal. Then she hissed his name, as sharp as a dagger.

"We have to go!" she moaned.

"Why?" mumbled Benjamiah.

"It's Bo! He's *here*!"

Benjamiah shot up. Elizabella and Silas were already awake, Elizabella trying to calm Mea, and Silas peering nervously out of the window.

"Please . . . ," begged Mea, a tear tumbling down her mask. "We have to run. *Now.*"

Everything felt surreal in the early-morning darkness. Nuisance was a capuchin, Ariadne looped sleepily round her neck like a scarf.

"Mea, there's nobody here," said Elizabella, trying to settle her.

But Mea wriggled away, despairing, dragging at Benjamiah to get up and shoving bags into their hands before bolting to the door.

"They're here!" she whimpered. "Why won't any of you listen! Please, please listen to me. Bo is here. *They're coming!*"

Benjamiah opened his mouth, planning to soothe Mea. He thought perhaps she'd had a nightmare, until something creaked outside the door.

Everybody froze. Mea teetered, covering the mouth of her mask with both hands. Benjamiah's heart grew stormy. The silence was heavy and cloying, dense as smoke.

Another creak of the floorboards from the hallway beyond the door. Mea's eyes looked as though they might pop. Benjamiah turned to Elizabella for guidance. Even she had paled.

Then they heard it.

Tick. Tick. Tick.

Panic traveled between them. Elizabella cast Emba as a bear. Silas likewise cast Griffyn as a lion. The two poppets neared the door, as from the other side there was another creak, a hushed whisper, that faint but certain ticking.

Mea ran to the window and threw it open. Then she dragged them all toward it, hauling them silently and desperately away from any confrontation. Elizabella looked determined to fight, but Mea's blind panic persuaded Benjamiah that it would be a bad idea. He urged Elizabella with his eyes. Her mouth formed a thin, defiant line.

Somebody tried the doorknob. Fortunately, they'd locked it before bed. A creak, a tick. A whisper.

Next something heavy smashed into the door, throwing out puffs of dust.

"*We have to run!*" begged Mea.

Finally, as somebody threw themselves against the door again, Elizabella nodded. Mea clambered out of the window, followed quickly by Silas. Beneath it was a ledge, occupied by a grotesque, and then a jump down to an empty cart on the street. By the time Benjamiah was climbing through the window, the door was on the verge of buckling.

Elizabella clambered onto the ledge as Benjamiah dropped down to the cart. Something thin and sharp thrummed through the blackness, flashing murderously past Benjamiah's face. It was a crossbow bolt, now buried in the wood barely an inch from his eye.

On the roof above were three snatchlings, aiming their

crossbows, their witchstone masks moonlike and terrible against the black clouds.

"They're out here!" one of them screamed.

"Come on!" wailed Mea.

More crossbow bolts pinged as the four children staggered away from the inn, still in their nightclothes and just about clinging to their half-packed bags. From everywhere, snatchlings howled and screamed. Two more dropped from a tree and chased. Bone-tipped crossbow bolts speared through the darkness.

The children ran into the mask market, now closed. The stalls were folded away, covered with cloth. The canopy above offered cover from the crossbow bolts, but Benjamiah felt fear clog his throat—they were running into a maze in which they might easily be trapped.

Mea led the way, turning down one street and another. Nuisance fluttered as a nightjar above them. They heard snatchlings behind and ahead and from every side, shrieking and taunting like a pack of hyenas. Benjamiah was sure there was nowhere to go, no exit not covered by the snatchlings. Mea stopped, turning to the others, spinning and spinning as she came to the same realization. The children bunched, pressing against each other.

"I told you I'd come for you," a voice called through the stalls.

It sounded both like and unlike a boy's voice:

high-pitched but croaky and dusty and hoarse. The voice of a boy who'd lived forever.

At its first syllable, Mea almost fainted. Silas helped steady her. Then Benjamiah lifted the cloth of a nearby stall and ushered the others beneath it. One by one, they scrambled underneath and huddled—all heartbeats and quivers and fractured breathing.

The other snatchlings had fallen quiet.

"Come on out," called Bo, "and I'll let your friends go!"

Mea verged on a panic attack. She looked wild-eyed at Benjamiah, but he shook his head.

"They don't want you, anyway!" shouted Bo. Was he behind them or in front? It was impossible to tell. Ticking sounded from somewhere, as well as the crunching of boots on the grit. "How could you do this to me? I took you in when you had no home. Welcomed you when you had no family. Cared for you when nobody else did."

The ticking grew louder. Bo's croaky, venomous voice was growing more prominent, too. From wherever he was approaching, he was getting closer.

"And this is how you repay me?" he spat.

Tick. Tick. Tick.

"You are *pitiful*," Bo called out to Mea. "You have betrayed *me*—betrayed *us*—when we are all you have in the world."

Mea was vibrating between Benjamiah and Elizabella.

Benjamiah held her hand, squeezing it—trying to tell her that Bo was wrong and vile, and she was worth a thousand of him.

"We are your family!" screamed Bo.

Now he was very close. The ticking was thick and noisy. Beneath the cloth, Benjamiah spied Bo's clunky boots. He was walking slowly, almost level with them. Dragging along the ground was the tip of a curved bone sword. And traveling alongside Bo was the snout, paws, and tusks of what seemed to be a monstrous wolf. But what kind of wolf had *tusks*?

"Come out now," croaked Bo. "Save the others. They don't care for you, anyway. Don't ever believe they do. You're only a burden. They want to be rid of you. They talk about you when you're not there. Laugh when your back is turned."

Bo stopped. As did the tusked wolf. Benjamiah's chest locked up, his head swimming. He glimpsed Elizabella, who was clasping Emba and looked livid and ready to fight. Benjamiah shook his head, begging her with his eyes.

Bo's poppet growled and snarled. Benjamiah saw slobber fall to the ground. Then Bo took another step forward, and another. He was passing them. . . .

"There's no way out, you coward!" he screamed.

A hand fell on Benjamiah's shoulder and he almost yelped in fright. It was Silas, who had cleared some of the crates behind them. A gap revealed a path away. The slowest he had ever moved, trembling from top to toe, Benjamiah crawled behind Silas, with Mea behind him and Elizabella at the rear.

Bo kept on taunting. Other snatchlings patrolled the market, armed with crossbows, bone-headed poppets prowling and baying. The children crept and crawled. Nearing an exit, Elizabella mouthed an order to the others: on her signal, they'd cast their poppets, cause a racket in the opposite direction, and then run for their lives.

"I will find you," snarled Bo from somewhere. "You have my word, girlie. Your time is almost up!"

Elizabella gave the signal. Nuisance, Emba, Hope, and Griffyn soared and galloped and scampered, crashing through stalls and ripping down cloth and smashing through posts. It proved an effective din. They sensed the swell of howling and screaming snatchlings rushing toward it. The children ran the other way—out of the bazaar, back onto the street, hurtling away. Distantly, the four of them recalled their poppets, by then cast as birds. The dolls joined them at the other end of the street and from there they kept on running.

THIRTEEN
WITH THE GHOUL BALL

> It is a little-known fact that the dead attend the Grand Masquerade. Dancing keeps one young, after all. They waltz with the healthy and vibrant and absorb a little of their vitality— at least enough to keep them going for another year.
> —*The Book of Barely Believable Stories*,
> Mildred Fogge

AN ABANDONED TOWN house proved to be the setting of Agatha's third trial. They'd fled from Bo and the snatchlings for hours in the end. Even with dozens of streets between them, Mea hadn't stopped shivering and had barely uttered a word. The others had done all they could to persuade her that Bo was completely wrong in everything he'd said, but Mea seemed not to hear them. Given how long she'd spent in Bo's grip, Benjamiah wasn't wholly surprised.

"How did they even find us?" said an irritated Elizabella.

"Because they're everywhere," replied Mea, bereft. "Watching."

The ground floor of the town house was a boarded-up dress shop, inhabited only by spooky mannequins standing among broken crates and scraps of ribbon and fabric. The house above was deserted, dust splashed over the moth-eaten furniture and shredded drapes. Daylight punched through the broken windows.

In the attic room, a witchstone branch curved out of the stone wall. Hanging from it was another wooden sign with another rhyme. Also in the room were two dresses and two evening suits, glamorous and incongruous in the forsaken house.

"Are those for us?" said Elizabella.

They certainly looked made to measure. Benjamiah read the rhyme:

> TONIGHT THE DEAD WILL COME TO DANCE
> BENEATH THE GHOSTLY SUN,
> AND POSE A MYSTERY YOU MUST SOLVE
> BEFORE THE NIGHT IS DONE.
>
> SO GRASP THE WITCHSTONE LIMB AND WALTZ
> ABOUT THE MASQUERADE,
> AND DRAW THE TRUTH FROM THOSE WHO COME
> FOR ONE NIGHT FROM THE SHADE.

"The masquerade?" said Benjamiah. "Does that mean..."

"The Grand Masquerade," said Silas. "That would explain the clothes."

"And we're supposed to learn something there from the *dead*?"

"It's another one from *The Book of Barely Believable Stories*," said Elizabella. "Mildred Fogge says some of the dead attend the dance. *They* call it the Ghoul Ball. This must be the 'curiosity' trial."

"It gets better and better," muttered Benjamiah.

"How will we get to the Resplenda, though?" mused Silas before explaining that was where the Grand Masquerade was held. "We could consult my maps, but is there time?"

Elizabella snorted.

Just then, a breeze swept through the room. Casting around for the source, Benjamiah discovered a dark slash in the wall—tall and wide enough for a child to squeeze through. Above it, crude dancing figures in dresses and frock coats had been scratched into the stone.

"I think we go through here," he said, poking his head into the gap.

He found only darkness and a coldness that made his breath smoke, a thin passage twisting out of sight. The idea of climbing into a crack in the wall was deeply unpleasant to Benjamiah, who recalled all too well that last year Edwid,

Elizabella's brother, had inadvertently freed the evil magus Manfred Tarr from inside a wall.

Meanwhile, Mea and Elizabella were inspecting the dresses. Tucked in the collars of the outfits were invitations—ornate, shimmering slips of silver, on which was written:

The honor of your presence is requested at the 551st Grand Masquerade.

After a nervous breath, Benjamiah gripped the witchstone branch. The veins flared and the witchstone mask upon his face slithered again, moving itself from the left eye and cheek to span the upper half of his face. When it was finished, Benjamiah looked at the others for explanation.

"It's a masquerade mask," said Elizabella, smiling. "Not bad."

"We'll all need one if we're going to the ball," said Silas, sounding a lot like he'd rather go swimming with river wolves.

"You'll have to go without me," said Mea.

Everybody looked at her. Though Benjamiah wanted to argue, he couldn't see any other option. It was one thing traveling through Wreathenwold, but Mea's mask would not survive scrutiny at the Masquerade. Hers was not a mask anyone would choose for a ball. She sighed, fiddling with the dress, eyes wistful.

"I'll stay with you," said Silas, a little nervously.

"No, you don't have to do that," replied Mea.

"I want to," said Silas. "I hate dances, anyway."

"But you'll miss out!"

"I'd rather stay with . . . ," said Silas.

Silence fell. Silas stuffed his hands in his pockets and scuffed his shoe, clearly embarrassed. Finally, Mea smiled.

"Thank you," she said.

With that settled, a new worry squirmed in Benjamiah's stomach.

"The rhyme makes it sound like I'm supposed to waltz with the dead," he mumbled. "I don't know how to dance!"

Silas wore a look of genuine sympathy. Elizabella, meanwhile, snorted. Benjamiah resisted the urge to throw something at her. Before he could, she sidled over.

"I'll teach you some steps," she said.

"Thanks," he said, smiling.

She smiled back.

For the rest of the day, Elizabella taught him how to waltz—which essentially involved Benjamiah stepping on Elizabella's toes for several hours, while Mea clapped happily and Silas mumbled sympathetic encouragement.

Elizabella wore a dark green gown with black gloves and a silver masquerade mask. Benjamiah had a dark blue dinner suit with an extravagant bow tie (Elizabella had had to tie it) and a stiff shirt with a winged collar. Needless to say, he felt ridiculous.

"Ready?" said Elizabella.

Benjamiah nodded, tugging unhappily on the rigid collar. Silas and Mea wished them luck.

"We'll be back as soon as we can," said Benjamiah.

Then Elizabella led the way, slipping into the peculiar slash in the wall, quickly absorbed by the darkness. Benjamiah followed, hoping desperately they wouldn't be ambushed by more unpleasant criminals imprisoned in Wreathenwold's walls. The passage was perishingly cold and blindingly dark. Before panic truly bloomed, Benjamiah saw illumination ahead—a similar gap to the one he'd entered, except filled with light. He was helped out by Elizabella's gloved hands.

They'd emerged in an entirely different part of Wreathenwold. Looming above them had to be the Resplenda. It was a castle whipped straight from a fairy tale, built into a mountainside with towers and turrets of pinkish stone and a series of threading waterfalls tumbling downward through gardens of immaculate hedges and blankets of resplendent flowers. Above it, the high, bright Midsommer sun was suspended, teasing a gleaming majesty out of every color and surface. The water sparkled and the flowers sang and the warmth had a magic all its own.

Everywhere—all around them, across the flowery grounds, upon every balcony and gatehouse, within every tower and keep, peering from crenellations and turrets and bridges—were people. It was a carnival of opulence and extravagance. The colors told Benjamiah as much. The gowns and dinner jackets, the hats and coronets, the jewels and pearls of the Masquerade attendees—all gleamed with color only the very wealthiest in Wreathenwold could afford. Everybody wore masquerade masks decorated with patterns or precious stones or flamboyant feathers.

The breeze carried music, and laughter, and the clinking of glasses, and the smells of woodsmoke and flowers and sweet and delicious roasting food.

"The Viper will be here," said Elizabella, clenching her fists.

Benjamiah hadn't thought about that—the presence of the dead at the Masquerade had posed enough anxiety.

"We need to stay away from her," he said, worried Elizabella's emotions might get the better of her. "She'll remember us. She'll take our eye colors. Or worse."

Elizabella said nothing. Which was no kind of comfort for Benjamiah.

Ahead of them, a bridge arched over a moat scattered with fallen bonewood blossom and lily pads as large as cartwheels. They crossed it, then wandered through the gardens, weaving between clusters of chatting and laughing revelers, and waiters with platters of confusing canapés and tumblers of poppysyrup and rosewater, among the flowers and magnificent bonewoods showering blossom upon the party. Chains of small glass bulbs were strung round the trees, filled with floating specks that glimmered like fireflies of all colors in the Midsommer sun.

As they walked, Elizabella spotted attendees from various Honorable Companies.

"That's the insignia of the Company of Stargazers!"

"That woman there wears the livery of the Company of Alchemists."

"He's from the Company of the Gaps Between Things," declared Elizabella, pointing at a fussy, hunchbacked man sipping poppysyrup by himself.

"That woman there is . . . ," said Benjamiah, then trailed off.

It was impossible—and yet there was no mistaking it. Benjamiah was looking at a dead woman. Though she wore an elegant mauve dress and flapped a silken fan, the woman only had flesh on half her face. Her left jawline was skinless bone, her left eye a hollow socket. Her left hand, too, was bone and nothing else, while her right hand was perfectly ordinary. Bushy orange hair grew from the living half of her head, the other half bald as an egg.

"What about her?" said Elizabella, following Benjamiah's gaze.

"What do you think! She's half skeleton!"

"I . . . ," said Elizabella, looking baffled. "She looks normal to me."

It dawned on Benjamiah then. The witchstone mask allowed him—and him alone—to spy the dead among the living. He explained as much to Elizabella. While she expressed envy, Benjamiah shivered.

"Let's talk to her," said Elizabella.

The prospect didn't appeal, but what choice did he have? Elizabella hurried in pursuit of the woman and Benjamiah followed. The dead woman strode purposefully through a huge castle door leading into the most magnificent courtyard—a stone square hemmed in by the castle walls, with fountains bubbling in little ponds and flowers swaying and blossom fluttering. There were long trestle tables loaded with flutes and tumblers and platters of exotic food.

It was jammed with people. Already the dead woman had vanished into the crowd. Before Elizabella and Benjamiah could give chase, a cheer spread through the guests—a few whoops and claps at first, building to a roar. All heads pivoted to the left. Benjamiah, with a dropping sensation in his stomach, found the source of the commotion.

Coming down a winding staircase, arm in arm, were Odith Murdstone and Manfred Tarr.

The Viper wore a long trailing dress of deep purple, a tiara on her head studded with an array of jewels incandescent in the Midsommer sun. Her mouth was wide and coated in purple lipstick, her reddish hair tied into complicated plaits round the side of her head. Stretching from her hands to her elbows were snakeskin gloves. A purple masquerade mask looped round her eyes.

Beside her, the magus Manfred Tarr wore a black evening suit beset with silver specks that flashed like starlight. Even from this distance, Benjamiah recognized the eyes: they were oblivion itself, a living, swirling inkiness. His skin was waxy, hair slicked back, tailcoats flapping, and his cane long and dark and topped with a silvery masquerade mask for a handle. In the crook of his collar was a bright pink flower. Dangling at his hip was a yellow doll that was nothing but a ruse—Manfred was a magus, and magi did not need poppets. Their magic was far greater and more dangerous. Manfred too wore a masquerade mask—black, to match his heart.

Beside Benjamiah, Elizabella tensed up, her fists clenched. The Viper had ruined Hansel and driven her family from Follynook. Manfred had caused the death of her brother. Seeing the two of them, resplendent and beloved and slimy with self-importance, ignited fury in Benjamiah; he could only imagine how it made Elizabella feel.

"Forget about them," Benjamiah whispered. "They're not worth it. Let's do what we came to do and get out of here."

Elizabella didn't respond, shaking with anger, her eyes small and knifelike. Benjamiah pulled her away, casting around for the dead woman as the crowd continued whooping their adulation.

". . . hear they're to be wed," Benjamiah heard a man say.

"But which will come first? The wedding or the funeral?" replied a woman, smirking.

"I hear Mr. Tarr is personally funding an elixir to keep the Minotaur alive," responded the man gravely. "Grygor from the Company of What Cannot Be Explained told me so. He has been a regular visitor to the palace in recent months. Mr. Tarr has Grygor scouring the Company archives, no doubt in search of some more permanent cure. If you ask me, we should let nature take its course. . . ."

It was at this point that Benjamiah and Elizabella were caught gawking. The couple cranked their noses up and scuttled off into the crowd as though fleeing vermin.

"Why would Manfred want to keep the Minotaur *alive*?" said Benjamiah.

"They're going to get married!" fumed Elizabella. "But he loves the Widow!"

She shook her head, as confused as Benjamiah. Though Benjamiah couldn't piece it together, he knew it meant nothing good for Wreathenwold. Across the courtyard, he spotted Gertrid Murdstone—Odith's twelve-year-old daughter. She wore a ballgown dyed with eye colors, even more extravagant and vile than the last dress Benjamiah had seen her wearing. Right then, she was scolding a harried, teary-eyed waiter.

"Let's find the dead woman," said Benjamiah.

They turned to find Manfred Tarr looming over them.

"I do love these parties," he said. "One runs into all kinds of *old friends*."

Horror washed through Benjamiah, cold and dizzying. Manfred's eyes were swarms of blackness, bloodless lips pressed into a false smile. Benjamiah wanted to run, but seemed unable to function. Elizabella looked like Elizabella: defiant and dangerous and as if she would surely be the death of Benjamiah. The only comfort was the very busy Masquerade. Surely Manfred wouldn't try to harm them here?

"You two have quite the talent for upsetting dangerous people," he said.

Something banged and Benjamiah jumped out of his skin. But it was only an eruption of blossom from a cannon on the castle wall, followed by rapturous applause. Elizabella's fists were still clenched.

"One day you'll pay for the people *you've* upset," she replied.

Manfred laughed, showing off rows of gleaming teeth.

"You are a treasure, Miss Cotton," he said. "Though I wasn't referring to myself on this occasion. I mean our mutual friend, Bo Greaves."

Elizabella's mouth fell open. Benjamiah's breath hitched in his throat. Of course, he thought. Why hadn't they considered it before?

"*You're* Bo's new master," hissed Benjamiah.

"Nothing so formal," said Manfred. "A business arrangement, nothing more."

"But what do you want with all those children?" said Elizabella in disgust.

"That is my concern," said Manfred. "Your concern should be to keep your noses out of places they do not belong. My friend is angry that one of his underlings has betrayed him. It consumes him. So much so that it's distracting him from the task at hand. And what should I discover when I ask him to describe the children with whom the snatchling girl has fled? That it can only, surely, be Miss Cotton and Master Creek. The strange gravities of fate seem determined to throw us together, wouldn't you say?"

Manfred stepped forward and Benjamiah flinched. Elizabella's hand drifted toward Emba. Manfred only smiled, eyes flashing, black and bottomless. Around them, revelers chattered and drank and giggled.

"You live only because I did not put enough care into your dying," said Manfred in a low voice. "Do not think you survive because you have any means to match me. A wave of my cane and you will be finished. Indeed, you would be if we were not surrounded by witnesses. I ask only—politely and just once—that you do not interfere with my affairs. Concern yourselves with yourselves. Go back to your families and your homes. Give Master Greaves the snatchling girl, who is quite beyond saving. Do not make me intervene, children. You play a game in which the prospect of victory is vanishingly small and the price of defeat irreversible."

"How can you marry the Viper when it's the Widow you care about?" demanded Elizabella.

"And what do you want with the Minotaur?" blurted Benjamiah. "And the children you're stealing?"

Manfred lifted his cane, fingers lacing round it. A humming filled Benjamiah's ears, the air about them suddenly rippling, the emptiness curdling inward as though an invisible fist were clenching him. Benjamiah gasped, feeling himself being compressed, squeezed, while around them the revelers continued, utterly oblivious. It was aether, all of it at Manfred's command—a threat. All the while, Manfred's eyes swam with a deep, dismal blackness. Benjamiah whimpered and Elizabella spluttered, panicking.

"Careful," said Manfred, his voice a guillotine. *"Careful."*

Then it was over. Everything slackened and Benjamiah breathed hungrily. Manfred straightened his jacket and the flower in the crook of his collar.

"Enjoy the party, children," he said, smiling. "It would be best if this were the last time we met."

Off he strode, back through the adoring throng. Benjamiah's knees trembled. Elizabella looked grave, breathing shakily.

"The witchstone," she said finally.

By now, the courtyard had begun to empty. Guests swarmed in their hundreds up the grand staircases into the belly of the castle. Benjamiah and Elizabella joined the flow, still shaken by their encounter with Manfred. Fear coursed through Benjamiah—fear for the Minotaur and Mea, for themselves and Wreathenwold, for the children caught up in Manfred's wicked scheming.

"Focus," said Elizabella, sensing Benjamiah's distraction. "Nothing else matters if we don't win Agatha's game."

She was right, of course. Benjamiah had seen no sign of the dead since the woman earlier. Not that he could see much of anything at the moment, swept up in the crowd.

They emerged in a ballroom of peerless splendor. A vast dance floor spilled beneath a dome of glass, the High Dusk sun hanging in the center like a chandelier, its light striking a spiderweb of glass threads teeming with the same fiery, colorful flecks as the glass bulbs outside. This set them glowing in magnificent colors, spiraling down the dome, curling round enormous marble bonewood trees that encircled the dance floor. On the far side of the ballroom was a stage lined with empty chairs and music stands and a bizarre array of instruments that must have constituted a Wreathenwold orchestra. Along the edges of the room were tables and chairs, candles glowing in plumpkin-shaped lamps. Balconies overlooked from every side.

Applause rippled as the orchestra emerged and began to play. A clearing formed in the middle of the ballroom and couples commenced dancing, including Manfred and the Viper. Blossom erupted from above, the petals twisting like snowflakes.

"The dead must be around somewhere," said Elizabella, having to shout in Benjamiah's ear. "Let's find them and get out of here."

It didn't take Benjamiah long. Sitting at a table on her own, watching the dance, was the half-skeletal woman from earlier. She had a tumbler of smoking poppysyrup in her hand.

"There," said Benjamiah, pointing her out.

"Let's go."

Dodging exuberant couples, Benjamiah and Elizabella reached the table. The woman looked up: one pale blue eye, the other an empty socket; a smile that started as lips and ended in the naked leer of a skull.

"It's rude to stare," she said primly. "Sit or scuttle off."

The children sat. Now that Benjamiah was here, he had no idea what he was expected to do. They'd surmised that this trial concerned curiosity, but curiosity about what? The woman smelled of florid perfume and dust.

"What's your name?" said Benjamiah.

"Jem," said the woman. "You flatter me, young man, but I fear I'm a little old for you. And a little dead."

Benjamiah blushed while Elizabella grinned.

"I'm looking for something," said Benjamiah.

"Living people always are. It never gets found, let me tell you."

"It's a fragment of stone that looks like my mask," said Benjamiah.

"No idea about that," said Jem dismissively.

The way she said it, though, made Benjamiah think otherwise. She sipped her poppysyrup.

"Can you still taste it?" asked Elizabella.

"It tastes of something," replied Jem. "Whether the right thing, I couldn't possibly say."

"What's it like being dead?" asked Benjamiah.

"Less interesting than being alive, and mighty longer."

Benjamiah and Elizabella exchanged a glance. This wasn't going to be straightforward.

"How many of you are there?" said Benjamiah.

"Of the dead? Good heavens, young man. Numberless. All the world is built on fallen bones."

"I meant *here*," said Benjamiah.

"Oh, I know what you meant," said Jem, dabbing a trickle of poppysyrup from the skull side of her mouth. "Well, let's see. . . ."

She proceeded to point out various dead attendees in the ballroom. There was Pollus the Eager, who had died rushing to open a door for his betrothed. Dancing with the Captain of the Company of Wheelers was Osme 'Undred, the heiress of a powerful family who apparently died of boredom when being talked through her future responsibilities. Jem also showed them a large, bearlike man and a cheery-eyed woman on opposite sides of the ballroom, whom she identified as the Count and Countess of Hollyrock.

"They lost their son, you know," said Jem. "Very sad. Something no parent should have to face."

"You mean he . . . ," began Benjamiah before realizing he had no idea what she meant. "Can you die again? Die more?"

"What are you, a simpleton? Of course you cannot die *again* or die *more*! Why should dead parents mourn a dead son? I mean to say he went and *lived*. Imagine the horror of it! A cruel, wicked fate. Their grief drove them apart, you know. They have not spoken to one another in nearly three hundred years."

Benjamiah glanced between the various dead—sitting,

standing, dancing, chatting. How was he to find the witchstone? Where was he to begin? He looked at Elizabella, but she seemed equally confused. Benjamiah thought back to Agatha's rhyme. *Waltz about the Masquerade* . . . With no other inspiration forthcoming, Benjamiah took the plunge.

"Would you like to dance?" he asked Jem.

"Young man, I feared you'd never ask."

While getting up, Benjamiah whispered to Elizabella: "I don't know what else we can do except be curious. Ask as many questions of the dead as you can think of."

So Benjamiah danced with Jem, swirling about the ballroom as the music played. Meanwhile, Elizabella was chatting with a short dead man at another table, pointed out to her by Benjamiah. Jem was surprisingly forgiving of Benjamiah's pitiful dancing, even smiling at him once or twice. It was on their second dance that Benjamiah noticed something rather disturbing.

His hand, perched on Jem's waist, looked bony—as though his skin had grown thinner or his bones more protuberant. Benjamiah gasped, yanking his hand away and comparing it with the other. There was no question his left hand was becoming skeletal.

"What's happening?" he yelled.

"Oh, you can spare just a little life," said Jem. "You have so much of it!"

Benjamiah's head spun. Dancing with the dead was

more awful than he'd imagined. Jem had absorbed some of his life, it seemed. Now he looked closer, her blue eye shined brighter and her smile flashed livelier.

"Don't be afraid, young man," she said, pulling him back to dance. "Tonight is the Grand Masquerade! The Ghoul Ball! It's only for tonight—tomorrow you'll be right as rain!"

Benjamiah danced with Jem, and then danced with Pollus the Eager, then with Osme 'Undred. Elizabella, too, was being twirled and pulled about the ballroom, dancing with the long-deceased while doing her very best to be as curious as possible. Benjamiah's hand was entirely skeletal now, as was much of his wrist. Surprising himself, he was no longer afraid—the Masquerade was wild, spectacular fun. Whenever he and Elizabella caught each other's eye, they grinned like toddlers in a toyshop.

After much dancing had been done, a breathless Benjamiah and Elizabella regrouped on the edge of the ballroom. The orchestra continued through a medley of beautiful numbers, fast and slow.

"Anything?" asked Benjamiah.

Elizabella shook her head, pink in the cheeks. She couldn't see that her own arm had become skeletal, and Benjamiah saw no reason to tell her. Elizabella had plied her many dance partners with every question she could think to ask, just as Benjamiah had, with no breakthrough.

Then Benjamiah saw the Count of Hollyrock. He was performing an autopsy on a canapé at a table in the corner, looking thoroughly miserable. He had a large rusty beard, thick hair, and a hooked nose—at least, the half of his face that lived.

"I wonder . . . ," said Benjamiah.

When Elizabella asked him what he wondered, Benjamiah ignored her and together they approached the Count.

"May we sit?"

The bearlike man looked up, bleary-eyed. On a napkin in his lap were the ruins of a coco tartlet.

"Why?" asked the Count, with a sigh.

Benjamiah and Elizabella sat. "I heard about your son," said Benjamiah.

Fright flashed across the large man's face. Then the Count stiffened haughtily, fastening his lips together.

"Filip," he said. "A good boy."

"Tell me about him," said Benjamiah.

The request provoked mistrust. The Count said, "Why?"

"I'm curious."

The Count of Hollyrock studied Benjamiah for trickery, apparently found none, and commenced chewing an already well-chewed fingernail.

"A good boy," he said again gruffly, staring into his

lap. "What can I say? Quick-witted. Devious but in the best sort of way. A son any father would be proud of. One time..."

And Benjamiah and Elizabella listened—prodding where necessary—as the Count regaled them with stories of Filip, who had lived while the Count and Countess had died. As the Count talked, he loosened up, smiling wistfully, even erupting into syrupy belly laughter at times. Throughout it all, the Count circled—without actually mentioning her—the Countess with whom he no longer spoke.

When the Count lapsed into silence, Benjamiah mouthed to Elizabella that she should ask him to dance. When she looked confused, he leaned over and whispered in her ear.

"Keep him talking about Filip. Don't mention the Countess. Let him find his own way there."

In much better spirits than when they'd approached, the Count gladly accepted Elizabella's offer to dance. Benjamiah then went looking for the Countess.

He found her on one of the balconies overlooking the ballroom. She was rosy-cheeked and had more gladness in her eyes than her husband, tapping her fingers and swaying gently from side to side as she watched the blur of waltzing below.

"May I sit?" said Benjamiah.

The Countess proved trickier to draw into talking about Filip; though cheerier, she had a talent for wriggling away from the topic no matter what Benjamiah tried. Finally, though, he made a breakthrough. The Countess began revealing her own memories of the beloved son she'd lost. Like the Count, she couldn't bring herself to acknowledge her spouse's presence in those happy times—though he saw it in her eyes.

"Would you like to dance?" asked Benjamiah.

After a pause came a smile. The Countess said, "Why not?"

Benjamiah had put all his hopes into this. If, as he suspected, Jem *did* know about the witchstone, then maybe she'd given them a clue. That clue being, Benjamiah hoped, the story of the heartbroken Count and Countess of Hollyrock. Through asking questions and showing curiosity, could he bring the couple back together? What if he was wrong? The sky was darkening above, the Masquerade reaching a crescendo. There wasn't much time left. This had to work, or Benjamiah might never wrest the witchstone from his face. And what would that mean for Manfred, the Minotaur, Bo . . . ? There was so much at stake.

Back on the dance floor, Benjamiah waltzed with the Countess. Whenever possible, he kept her talking about Filip, trying not to worry about the deadness that continued to creep up his arm, now reaching his shoulder:

Jem had said it was only for tonight. They chatted as they wove circles about the ballroom, bringing Filip back to life.

The time came for Benjamiah to put his plan into action. It took a while to spot Elizabella and the Count amid the twirling masses. When he did, he steered the Countess toward them. Elizabella caught his eye and instinctively understood. The children maneuvered their partners through the chaos until—in the center of the ballroom, beneath the ghostly glow of the fading Midsommer sun—they crashed into each other.

Benjamiah and the Countess fell. Standing above them were Elizabella and the Count. The Count and Countess locked eyes, their gazes traveling back through time—seeing again, suddenly, through the heavy fog of grief, the person they once loved.

The Count held out a hand. The Countess took it. The Count trembled, biting his lip. He went to release the Countess's hand, but she wouldn't let him.

"Do you mind?" the Countess said to Benjamiah.

Doing his very best not to smile, Benjamiah shook his head. The Countess patted him on the head, smiled sweetly, and set off with the Count—a slow, close rumba three hundred years in the making.

"I would have thought of that if you hadn't," said Elizabella. "In fact, I already had."

"Sure," said Benjamiah. "Shall we?"

He held up his arms—an invitation to dance. Elizabella wiped the stroppy look from her face and accepted. Smiling, laughing, Benjamiah and Elizabella danced and danced among the living and the dead.

Finally, when Benjamiah's legs and lungs could take it no more, they flopped into chairs at the edge of the ballroom.

"What if you were wrong?" said Elizabella.

She—like Benjamiah—was watching the Count and Countess, who were still dancing together, staring a thousand miles into each other's eyes.

Before Benjamiah could answer, Jem materialized above them.

"Being dead is less interesting than being alive, it's true," she said, "but that isn't to say it's entirely *uninteresting*."

And she snapped open a handheld mirror, reached inside, and offered Benjamiah the witchstone fragment.

"Good work," she said before stalking off.

Benjamiah smiled. Elizabella slumped back and gave a noisy, relieved sigh. Then, one final time before the night was done, they joined the dance floor and waltzed together.

FOURTEEN
WITH THE MIDSOMMER GIFTS

Gifts are given on High Dusk, to show somebody you care about them, love them, and know them—or, in the case of Betty Pennythistle, to deliver a curse that turned her enemies into piglets.

—*The Book of Barely Believable Stories*,
Mildred Fogge

THERE WAS MORE relief to come. They escaped the Resplenda without incident and discovered that the way they'd entered—Agatha's eerie slash in the stone—was still there. Benjamiah and Elizabella clambered through and found Mea and Silas unharmed and delighted to see them back safely.

Leaving the abandoned dress shop, Benjamiah and Elizabella described everything that had happened—only omitting Manfred's request that they give up Mea, fearing it would do more harm than good. The story of the Masquerade and the dancing dead made Mea groan with envy at having missed it all; Silas, meanwhile, was rueful.

"The Mapmakers should have been there," he said indignantly. "We are one of the oldest and noblest Companies of Wreathenwold! Couldn't you have given the Viper a good hard kick on the dance floor?"

Benjamiah laughed. Elizabella was aghast that she hadn't thought of it herself.

There was, however, something to darken the mood. Manfred Tarr was behind Bo's campaign to kidnap children. But to what end? And what had he promised Bo in return?

"It must have something to do with the Widow," said Benjamiah. "It's the only thing that matters to him."

Elizabella nodded gravely. Manfred Tarr would stop at nothing to restore his beloved Osmeralda.

"Edwid's secret revealed where she is," said Benjamiah. "Manfred knows, so why hasn't he freed her?"

"There must be something else he needs," said Elizabella. "Something to do with the snatched children. If he has dark magic in mind, Midsommer would be the time for it." She paused. *"Magic forged at Midsommer is the strongest and truest of all magic—both fair and foul."*

While waiting, Silas and Mea had taken a walk outside. A woman selling treacle opples (Mea had eaten three) told them of a splendid hotel on the next street over, so the children walked through the late Midsommer night in search of it. More modest masquerades were taking place on the Wreathenwold streets, but Benjamiah could think of nothing worse than another party.

The hotel they'd been recommended didn't disappoint. It was an old-fashioned steam train, every carriage repurposed as a luxury bedroom. It spanned a track from one end of the street to the other, overlooking a silky stream and a range of bonewood trees. Its chimneys loosed soft smoke, the carriage windows lit warmly from within. Written on the silvery locomotive were the words: *The Dream Express*.

"I didn't know Wreathenwold had trains," said Benjamiah.

If there was one thing Benjamiah loved, it was a good feat of engineering. He'd enjoy nothing more than poking round the steam engine, but it was clear the Dream Express had not traveled for an age.

"Hansel said there used to be trains," said Elizabella. "Before Wreathenwold was a labyrinth. This must be over a thousand years old!"

It certainly looked that way, more a series of snug steel cottages than something that had ever moved. Weeds gripped its wheels and the doors were decorated with knockers, room numbers, and Midsommer wreaths—circular braids of ne'er-do-wells and will-o'-wisps and a few sprigs of barbed wyrm plant.

With their room booked and paid for, the owner, Ms. Frogly, showed them to their carriage. It was wonderful—rendered in mottled bonewood, a squashy bed in each corner and seats surrounding a crackling log fire. Nuisance the capuchin squealed her approval.

When Ms. Frogly had left, the children settled in. Elizabella yawned—Benjamiah knew how she felt. But it wasn't time for bed just yet.

"There's one more thing before High Dusk is over," said Benjamiah. "It's time for gifts."

A nervous thrill traveled through the children. One by one, Benjamiah collected the presents in a pillowcase—without peeking—then returned to the bed. The foursome sat in a circle. Benjamiah emptied the pillowcase between them, revealing four gifts wrapped with varying degrees of competence. Each of them located theirs.

With an ungrateful lurch in his stomach, Benjamiah found his was the smallest and lightest—in fact, it felt like a twist of wrapping paper with nothing inside.

"Who's first?" said Elizabella.

Mea looked like it was the most fun she'd ever had. Silas was trying not to smile, turning over a weighty and clumsily wrapped present in his hands.

"Mea first," said Benjamiah.

Nobody argued. Mea shivered with excitement, pulling gently at the string holding the present together before—unable to contain herself—proceeding to rip the paper into confetti like a frenzied magpie in search of food.

It was a large, beautiful book. Benjamiah recognized it immediately—it was the illustrated edition of *The Book of Barely Believable Stories*, except it was brand-new. The colors were wonderfully bright, making it considerably more expensive than Elizabella's edition.

"It's . . . It's . . . ," breathed Mea, tracing the lettering on the front cover.

Then she burst into tears, crying into her hands. Benjamiah and Elizabella shared a smile while Silas shifted uncomfortably.

"Don't you like it?" said the Mapmaker, his voice tiny.

"I love it," said Mea. "Who bought this for me? It's . . . It's the best thing I've ever seen! I don't even have a single thing, and now I have *this* . . . The best thing ever . . . I don't deserve it."

"Of course you do," said Elizabella gently. "It's the very least you deserve. It's against the rules to ask who bought it, though."

Not that it was much of a mystery to Benjamiah. Silas looked about as buoyant as a blimp beside Mea.

"You choose who's next, Mea," said Benjamiah.

So entranced was Mea with the book that it took her a beat to hear him.

"Elizabella," she said meekly.

Elizabella flashed a crooked smile and deftly untied the ribbon around her gift. The paper fell away to reveal a small box. Elizabella's lips fastened together and her eyes narrowed as she flipped it open.

Though Benjamiah couldn't see the contents, he saw the effect it had on Elizabella. After a gasp, her mouth grew slanted and her eyes gaped, shock splashed upon her face.

"Let's see it," said Benjamiah.

Gently, Elizabella lifted the gift. It was a silver bracelet. Hanging from it were two pendants, each the shape of a poppet. One was clearly Emba, dark blue with tiny marbled eyes and three white strings depicting hair. The other was the opposite—snowy white with a tuft of dark blue hair. This was Cinda, Edwid's poppet.

"Who did this?" said Elizabella, her voice faraway.

Not for the first time, Benjamiah wondered how Elizabella could sound cross about something that moved her so deeply. Nobody spoke up. Mea looked frightened and Benjamiah knew why—she'd asked him three days ago if he knew what Edwid's poppet had looked like, after all.

"Do you like it?" said Benjamiah.

"Yes," said Elizabella. "It's absolutely precious."

Mea beamed. Benjamiah shot her a look and she

quickly tried to look nonchalant. Elizabella saw nothing, the bracelet consuming her attention.

"Help me put it on," she said to Mea.

It was a perfect fit. The two poppet pendants jostled on her wrist, drawn together no matter how she moved her arm. Elizabella sniffed and pretended there was something in her eye.

"I'm never taking it off," she said. "Right, Silas next."

The Mapmaker did all he could to look dignified and grown up as he wrestled with the brown paper and the many lassos of string holding it together. Finally, the gift was revealed.

It was a brand-new spyglass, one which Benjamiah had bought for a small fortune from a CuriOddities shop the previous morning. Mea clapped her hands. Silas smiled from one end of Wreathenwold to the other, lifting the spyglass to his eye and turning it over as though it were pure gold.

"That's very good of you," said Silas. "Whoever it was. My last one was damaged when we were being cleared out by the Hanged Men. Who knows? Maybe it will come in useful one day if the Mapmakers are ever revived."

"The Mapmakers haven't gone anywhere," said Elizabella. "Who could ever stop you lot, honestly?"

Silas nodded grandly at that, his chest puffing out.

"Your turn," he said to Benjamiah.

A simple process of deduction meant Benjamiah's gift had to be from Elizabella, not that her expression revealed a thing. Making a mental note to never play poker with her, Benjamiah tore into the featherlight twist of paper in search of his gift. For a moment, he wondered if Elizabella was playing a trick on him and the wrapping was empty, before something fell into Benjamiah's lap.

It was a noose for his poppet. From above, Nuisance the nightjar squalled—whether delighted or mortified, Benjamiah couldn't tell. It didn't matter to Benjamiah. He thought it was absolutely perfect. It was a silken, silvery weave ending in a neat loop. Sewn in with artful precision was his name: *Benjamiah Creek.*

"The perfect gift for all our sakes," said Elizabella, throwing a look of mock annoyance toward Nuisance.

Nuisance chittered in offense. Benjamiah saw how Elizabella fidgeted, her expression stiff and pained: she was waiting for him to say he liked it.

But he didn't like it. He *loved* it. Now he felt like a real dollcaster. He told the others—but Elizabella really—that it was the best possible gift.

A bright smile flashed briefly across Elizabella's face.

With the gift-giving over, the children ate sweets (Mea ate the most) and played chess (Elizabella won the most) long into the night, the log fire roaring. Laughter filled the train carriage for hours, as warm and magical as the

Midsommer sun. It was getting light by the time they fell asleep, Benjamiah's last thought being that he couldn't remember ever having more fun.

Before leaving the next day, Elizabella had Benjamiah practicing dollcasting.

"No point looking the part if you can't play it," she declared, gesturing to Nuisance—now dangling obediently from Benjamiah's new noose, attached to his belt.

The sky was a hazy pink above the Dream Express as Elizabella led a grumpy and bleary-eyed Benjamiah to the edge of the stream. Morning birds sang their strange songs and the grass sparkled with dew.

"Right, this test is going to be a *little* trickier," said Elizabella, perching on a rock by the stream. She held the spellbooks Benjamiah had been studying in recent days: *Cellar Spider*, *Dormouse*, and *Sparrow*. "The questions will jump around between the three. Remember, it's okay if you get stuck. Needing help isn't a weakness, you know."

Benjamiah, who could smell Ms. Frogly's delicious treacle tea drifting down from the breakfast carriage, said, "Same to you. Let's get on with it."

With a wry smile, Elizabella got on with it, but her joy was short-lived. No matter what she threw at Benjamiah, he was ready. Though he was half asleep and his mouth watered for treacle tea and sweetdough toast, Benjamiah was unflappable and insurmountable. Last night his dancing had been appalling; this was a different kind of dance of which Benjamiah knew every step, in which the music of knowledge flowed through his bones as though he were born with it.

An irritated Elizabella decided to make it more difficult. She demanded he juggle pebbles while answering questions as quickly as possible.

"These things need to be second nature," she said.

So Benjamiah juggled—just about—while discoursing on how cellar spiders wove their webs, and how much a typical dormouse weighed, and out of what a sparrow fashioned its nest. It *was* second nature to him. An exasperated Elizabella finally huffed and gave up.

"Fine," she said. "Well done. We'll practice the spells as we travel."

"Tea and toast first," said Benjamiah.

True to her word, Elizabella worked Benjamiah all day. Thanks to successfully casting an earthworm, Benjamiah was now familiar with the required mental process. Performing magic meant channeling all that knowledge into something whole and harmonious. It was a kind of alchemy, transmuting the components into an elegant construct—it was the point where notes became music, where words became poetry.

Despite a few miscasts, Benjamiah always found a way. Before the day was done, he'd cast a cellar spider, a dormouse, and a sparrow. Seeing Nuisance take each form brought fresh, incomparable delight to Benjamiah. Elizabella was nonplussed.

"What's wrong?" he said.

"I've never seen anybody learn this fast!" she said despairingly. "This isn't right!"

Benjamiah couldn't help but beam. Finally, something he was good at that was absolutely, undeniably cool.

"What's next?" he asked.

Elizabella set him a new, trickier set of spells: *Boa Constrictor*, *Common Octopus*, and *Fruit Bat*. Benjamiah was also made to practice his transitions between the spells, which were not yet smooth. Elizabella would call out the names of spells he'd learned with a snap of her fingers and Benjamiah was expected to transform Nuisance from one to another. It meant slipping his mind in an instant between the mental maps he had of each animal. Sometimes he fell short, resulting in a miscast—where Nuisance would again squeal in anguish.

"Work to do," said Elizabella after the latest miscast.

That was no problem for Benjamiah. He enjoyed homework in his own world—often wishing the teachers would give him more—so this felt like the best possible kind of studying. Nuisance seemed to be enjoying her new forms, too. From the roof of a hansom, Nuisance the cellar spider dangled happily from a thread in front of his face.

"You're a strange one," said Benjamiah.

And it was true. For all the time Benjamiah had spent in Wreathenwold, he still hadn't encountered another poppet like Nuisance—one who could behave so independently, and change form at will. Benjamiah felt that Nuisance was his, but also that there was more to her beyond even her life with Mum.

This inevitably drew Benjamiah's thoughts back to his mum. He missed her so much and wished she were here with him. It would have meant the world to her.

"I wonder what she wanted from Agatha," mused Benjamiah.

"Agatha will tell us," said Elizabella. "And you can tell your mum when you get home."

Home. Where everything had felt so bland and alien, where things in their own way had felt more unsafe than Wreathenwold and Agatha's perilous game. Home had been ripped in two, the halves thrown to the wind. Benjamiah missed Mum, Dad, Grandma, and Once Upon A Time with all his heart, just as he'd missed Wreathenwold, Hansel, and Elizabella with every fiber of his being when stuck in Wyvern-on-the-Water. What did it mean? Where was he supposed to be? The fear that he might not belong anywhere—that he would never feel *right*—spread coldly throughout him.

He looked at Elizabella, lost in her own thoughts. Her situation wasn't so different. Follynook had been taken from her and her father. What did the future hold for the Cottons?

And what was Manfred up to with the stolen children? What fate awaited the Minotaur, apparently dying at the Shrouded Palace? They'd left Ogbo's Rest to play a dangerous game, only to find the stakes were greater than they ever could have imagined.

As always, Elizabella seemed to sense the turmoil behind Benjamiah's eyes without him having to say it.

"One problem at a time," she said. "Agatha first."

Benjamiah nodded. The hansom clattered and rocked onward, piercing the rainy night, as the violet moths dazzled and fluttered outside the window.

Their last stop that day was a street in which the residents had built a giant Midsommer bonfire. Suspended above it, built from wood and rags, was a huge effigy of Agatha Drake. The children watched as the bonfire was lit and the effigy ignited, cheered by the onlookers. After booking two rooms at a quite shabby and inexpensive inn, the children bought cups of treacle tea and sat on the grass, gazing into the pyre as it crackled and spurted embers into the black air.

"Some marshfruits for you?"

A boy had approached carrying a tray of paper bags. Inside were what looked very much like marshmallows. The children bought a bag each, stabbed their first marshfruit with the nearest twig, and toasted them on the edge of the bonfire. Ribbons of sweet-smelling smoke rose from Benjamiah's marshfruit as its shell crackled and its insides melted. Like most things in Wreathenwold, it tasted wonderful—sweet, warm, and gooey.

Full and sleepy, they chatted lazily about things that were neither dangerous nor frightening. They did not speak of Agatha Drake or the Viper or children being stolen, instead talking about food and books and school. At times, Benjamiah tried to explain things from his own world that bewildered the others and often had them laughing at their absurdity.

"So you put plates in a big white box," said Mea, deeply confused by the sorcery of a dishwasher, "that washes them for you, even though you have two perfectly good hands to do it yourselves?"

Silas and Elizabella were rolling around with laughter.

"Well, it means you can go and do something else while it's washing," said Benjamiah, feeling oddly defensive.

"Like watch moving pictures on the big black box?"

Elizabella laughed, still baffled by the idea of a television.

Benjamiah joined in at that point. Maybe his world really did make less sense than theirs.

When conversation tailed off, Mea left to find the boy selling marshfruits. While she was gone, Silas kept glancing around nervously in search of her.

"She'll be back soon enough," said Elizabella, noticing.

"Who?" said Silas defensively.

Elizabella shrugged extravagantly. Benjamiah smiled.

"That horrible snatchling boy is still out there somewhere," said Silas defensively. "We need to be careful."

"Is that the only reason?" asked Elizabella.

"What do you mean?" said Silas warily.

"That you keep looking around for her? Not just tonight. All the time."

"I . . . ," blustered Silas. "I don't know what you mean!"

"It's okay," said Elizabella teasingly.

"What's okay?"

"That you like her."

"We all like her!" Silas half shouted.

"Some more than others," said Elizabella, with another infuriating shrug.

"What does that mean?" croaked a wide-eyed Silas.

"That you *like like* her," said Elizabella.

Benjamiah felt bad for Silas. Elizabella had quite the talent for provoking people. This last comment had left the

Mapmaker melting with embarrassment, spluttering indignantly and incoherently before growing angry.

"Of course I don't *like* her," blustered Silas. "Look at her!"

Silas knew immediately he'd gone too far; Elizabella looked suddenly regretful. But Benjamiah had eyes for neither of them. He'd heard the soft approaching footsteps while the others had tussled. He knew what he'd see when he turned round.

Mea was frozen, staring at Silas. A new paper bag of marshfruits in her trembling hands. Eyes big and full of firelight and a kind of shocked pain that hurt Benjamiah at his core. She stared at Silas and Silas stared back, looking as sorry as anybody ever could. He opened his mouth, but only a croak escaped. Before anybody could say a word, Mea turned and hurried away.

FIFTEEN
WITH THE CROWN OF BONES

The true wonder of life is precisely because of its briefness; to be a momentary spark in an otherwise eternal oblivion, a spark that dances, laughs, loves in defiance of that endless gloom. To live forever is not to live at all.
—*The Book of Barely Believable Stories*,
Mildred Fogge

"You should apologize," said Benjamiah to Silas.

Silas was devastated. The look he threw Elizabella—as he scrambled up—was one of withering fury.

"I'm sorry," she mumbled. "I didn't mean for that to happen. I was just . . ."

Before she could finish, Silas stalked off in search of Mea. Elizabella drew her knees into her chest and let her head fall, a picture of profound regret.

"You didn't mean it," said Benjamiah. "And neither did Silas. Mea will understand."

Elizabella said nothing. Others who'd been sitting round the bonfire had trailed merrily off home. The fire had descended into a pit of white logs and smoking ash. Now the air bit colder and the quiet assumed a new menace.

A few minutes passed before Silas returned. Finally, Elizabella moved, looking up at the Mapmaker with hope in her eyes.

"I said I was sorry," said Silas. "She didn't say much. Just told me it was fine. That I was *right*. I . . . I . . ."

He buried his face in his hands, breathed hoarsely through his fingers, then let his shoulders slump.

"I'm going to bed," he said.

Benjamiah and Elizabella both rose. Elizabella said, "I'll find Mea and explain."

Now it was her turn to walk off into the darkness. Benjamiah and Silas didn't speak as they found the inn, went upstairs, and climbed into bed. A while later, they heard Elizabella and Mea arrive in the next room— Elizabella talking in low tones and Mea apparently silent. Benjamiah chased sleep for what felt like hours, worry gnawing in the pit of his stomach. It had been enormously difficult to persuade Mea that she was one of them, that she was welcome and wanted and liked. Had that all been irreversibly undone now?

From Silas's bed, Benjamiah didn't hear a snore all night.

The children left in the early hours the following day. Trekking through the pale morning, the great beast of Wreathenwold lifting itself drowsily from slumber, the atmosphere was fragile. Silas's eyes were puffy from not sleeping. Elizabella did her best to pretend nothing had happened, that all was business as usual, but it fell flat. Nobody believed that. Nor could anybody find the words to say or the right way to say them.

Following the moths, they crept round Mea as though the slightest movement might knock her over and break her into pieces. She kept her eyes down and trailed at the back, wrapped in a silence so deep that Benjamiah worried how they'd ever pull her out. Every step of the way, Benjamiah, Elizabella, and Silas glanced toward Mea, wondering how to make it better.

They saw a woman selling treacle opples, but Mea wasn't hungry. They passed a street performance of "The Two-Headed Magpie" from *The Book of Barely Believable Stories*, but Mea wasn't interested. At lunch, they tried gently to draw her into conversation, but she neither ate nor spoke, instead giving a brittle smile when she had to and humming a strange, somber tune to herself otherwise.

That afternoon, Benjamiah was left alone with Mea while Elizabella and Silas went for milk punch. They sat on a flight of weathered stone steps joining one street to another. Nuisance was a sparrow, singing from a tree branch above. Mea hummed, a melody that now carried an eerie foreboding.

"Are you okay?" he asked.

Mea made a "mhm" noise.

"He didn't mean it," said Benjamiah. "We were teasing him and he was embarrassed. You know what Silas is like."

"I don't," she said.

There was no quivering or impending sob in her voice. It was flat and toneless.

"You do," said Benjamiah. "You know all of us."

Another "mhm."

"He's really sorry," said Benjamiah. "He didn't sleep all night."

"Really? I slept well."

It unsettled Benjamiah. This Mea was so removed from the one he'd grown to know and love. It showed how much last night had hurt her, just as she'd begun to feel comfortable.

"It was just a stupid mistake," said Benjamiah.

"A mistake that I heard it for once, you mean?"

Benjamiah was shocked, needing a moment to catch her meaning.

"You think Silas says mean things about you all the time?"

"Not just Silas. All of you. Just like Bo said."

Benjamiah shook his head furiously, frustration welling up inside him.

"You're completely wrong, Mea."

"That's me," she said tonelessly. Then, with a smile that had no humor nor any of the true Mea in it, she added: "I'm *wrong*."

Benjamiah saw then that it was not sadness that gripped Mea. She was angry, humiliated even, as though they'd been fooling her all along. How Benjamiah wished she would rage at them instead—release all the fury so they could deal with it together and move on. Instead, with Benjamiah at a loss, Mea went on humming her haunting melody. Even Nuisance grew solemn, abandoning her joyful tune.

Elizabella and Silas returned and they drank their milk punch in awkward silence. Then Benjamiah got them moving again. There was nothing they could do right now except give Mea time and prove that they were friends. Chasing down Agatha's next trial would give them all something else on which to focus and perhaps remind Mea of what she wanted most of all—for the witchstone mask to fall from her face and her memories to return.

So they traveled. That day became the next day. Sun became rain, mist became snow, thunderstorms became fog. Streets became woods and woods became streets. Color-poachers harassed them on a street of shabby taverns, only giving up when a pair of Hanged Men chased them away.

Plumpkin lanterns glowed from bonewood branches. The masked masses of Wreathenwold spoke of the continued Midsommer festivities, but—for Benjamiah at least—it had all begun to feel vaguely chilling.

Children were still disappearing, almost certainly taken by Bo on Manfred's orders. Mildred Fogge said Midsommer was the most magical time of year, so before the month was out Manfred's purpose would surely become clear. What it meant for the stolen children, the Minotaur, and Wreathenwold itself was yet to be seen.

"So many . . . ," said Elizabella.

The four of them stood before yet another town-square bulletin board. Pinned all over it were sketches of missing children, some offering rewards and some not, all with names attached. Penni Lugrose, nine years old. Ten-year-old Errol Culker. Valentina Hartsome, who had left behind the stuffed teddy she took wherever she went.

Elizabella and Benjamiah exchanged a grave look. They knew who was behind it, but who would believe them? Wreathenwold seemed to adore Manfred. Who would stop Manfred and Bo if not them? But they had no time. The witchstone over Benjamiah's eye was a constant reminder of that. The clock was ticking. If he didn't win Agatha's game by Midsommer's end, he'd be a snatchling himself.

With all that to worry about, Benjamiah kept working on his dollcasting while they traveled, studying the *Boa*

Constrictor, *Common Octopus*, and *Fruit Bat* spellbooks whenever Elizabella was there, and studying in secret the *Gray Wolf* spellbook when she wasn't.

"You won't be much good at defending me when things get really dangerous," said Benjamiah to Nuisance, who was then a fruit bat hanging upside down from his hand.

Nuisance, cloaked in her own wings, squeaked in agreement.

The *Gray Wolf* spell was undoubtedly more complicated, but Benjamiah—for perhaps the first time in his life—believed in himself.

Later that day, everything changed.

It was evening and the four children emerged on a drizzly street of thin, crooked buildings. There were no Midsommer festivities here and very few signs of life. Everything was drab, dripping from the incessant rain, most of the buildings derelict. An old bearded man slept in a doorway. A clockwork dog barked somewhere, wolfish and ominous.

Unnerved, Benjamiah wanted to leave as quickly as possible. But Mea stopped as they passed a particular building—the husk of a long-abandoned orphanage called Aeva's Home for Lost Children.

"I remember this place," she said suddenly.

Such was Benjamiah's shock that for a moment he thought he'd misheard—firstly because Mea hadn't spoken all day and secondly because it was an astonishing revelation.

"You *remember* it?" he blurted out.

Elizabella and Silas were likewise stunned. All eyes were on Mea, whose hands shook and who seemed to be grappling with something immense and frightening. Benjamiah looked back at the orphanage: a spindly, slanted building, every window broken and its roof pockmarked with crumbled tiles.

"Aeva's Home for Lost Children . . . ," said Mea, as though it had taken a huge amount of courage to say the name aloud.

The way she'd half shouted it struck Benjamiah as very peculiar. Afterward, she wore a look of great fear and agitation.

"Aeva was one of the last magi," said Elizabella. "One of the less cruel ones, I think. What do you remember about this place, Mea?"

Mea looked spooked and uncertain, looking around one way and another before drifting toward the orphanage. While she climbed the steps, apparently entranced, Benjamiah swapped a look with Silas and Elizabella. Was Mea remembering something about her life before becoming a snatchling? They joined her as she rested a shaking hand on the orphanage door.

Mea said nothing, every breath a great shuddering thing like shutters rattling in a fierce wind. She pushed open the door and walked inside. The others followed.

They found the home for lost children long forsaken, gripped in dust and cobwebs. Everything was damp and rain leaked through in steady trails. In front of them was a staircase. To the left was a large playroom where they found an ancient rocking horse and a doll's house inhabited by mice. On the walls were empty picture frames and a looking glass that had lost its shine. There were chalky scrawls on the walls where children had drawn pictures or written their names.

"Have you been here before?" said Silas, a croak in his voice.

Benjamiah tensed. It was the first time Silas had spoken directly to Mea since the night before last. Mea flinched upon hearing his voice, didn't look at him, and instead made for the staircase. It was as though she were sleepwalking.

She led them, slow and agitated, round the house. She muttered to herself, and the others didn't disturb her. She drifted into various rooms, up another staircase, back down again. Her eyes were glassy and faraway and she trembled like a dying leaf on an autumn branch. They found no life in the orphanage, only shabby mementoes of what it once was: a music book, a pair of boys' boots, a porcelain doll.

"Wait here," said Mea abruptly.

They were on the second-floor landing. Benjamiah, Elizabella, and Silas did as they were told, anxious not to rush her. While they stood bunched together, Mea disappeared round the corner. Benjamiah looked at Elizabella and Silas, finding the same anxious hope in their eyes.

The longer Mea was gone, though, the more Benjamiah began to worry. When a minute or two passed without her return, he felt a troubled squirm in his stomach. Though he couldn't put his finger on it, something felt wrong. Not only had Mea not come back, but they couldn't hear a sound—save the trickle of leaking rain—from anywhere in the house.

"What's going on?" he whispered.

Silas was biting his nails. Elizabella's face was twisted up with troubled thinking.

"Let's find her," she said.

"She asked us to wait," hissed Silas.

"Something isn't right," said Benjamiah.

Though Silas was reluctant, they went together in search of Mea. They found her sitting by the window in a long room of rusted metal bedframes, whimpering to herself and staring out of the window.

"Mea?" said Benjamiah. "Are you okay?"

She flinched and whirled round, her eyes ballooning. She stood up. Then her breathing raced and shallowed as she worked herself into a wild passion before bursting into furious tears. Her hands clamped over the eye sockets of her witchstone mask.

"We have to go!" she suddenly screamed.

And she bolted the length of the room, snatching at the others like a wild animal as tears streamed down her mask. Over and over, she screamed the same thing—that they had to go.

"Mea, stop!" shouted Elizabella, gripping a flailing Mea by the shoulders. "Stop! Calm down. Breathe. Tell us what's going on."

"Please, please . . . ," she whimpered. "We have to go, we have to go. . . ."

"Not until you tell us what's going on," demanded Elizabella.

Mea sucked in a series of quick, greedy breaths, regaining an element of calm.

"I'm so sorry," she said, sobbing.

Benjamiah's stomach turned. "Sorry about what?" he said quietly.

"I've made a horrible mistake!" she wailed.

Elizabella pulled her hands away from Mea and studied her carefully.

"You don't remember this place, do you?" said Benjamiah.

Agonizingly slowly, Mea shook her head.

"Then why did you say you did?" asked a baffled Silas.

Elizabella's eyes had narrowed, her mouth a tense, flat line.

"To trick us," she said.

Like Benjamiah, she'd caught on. Suddenly she was danger and fury incarnate.

"No, not to trick us," said Benjamiah. "To *trap* us."

Mea cried, sniffing thickly through a blocked nose, big watery eyes traveling manically between Elizabella, Benjamiah, and Silas.

"*That's* why you said the name of this place aloud," said Benjamiah. "So Bo would know where we are!"

"What do you mean!" shouted Silas.

"She wants us all caught," said Elizabella, dangerously quiet. "To punish us for what happened."

Mea howled. "I was just so upset!" she cried. "He's always in my head, always saying horrible things. That he was right all along, that you all think I'm a joke, laughing about me when I'm not there. I'm sorry—I'm so sorry. As soon as I did it, I regretted it. Please, you have to run! I'll delay Bo and the others. It's me he wants! *Please!*"

"How could you do this?" said Benjamiah.

The betrayal had hollowed him out, leaving only a cold vacuum at his center.

"I'm so sorry," Mea whimpered. "Please, run! *They're coming.*"

Elizabella gripped Emba, seething. Silas's expression was

all shadow and loss. He took a few steps back from Mea as though she were something particularly unpleasant.

"We thought you were one of us," said Silas, icy cold. "But you were always one of *them*."

It left Mea dazed and heartbroken, paralyzed on the spot. Benjamiah felt the anger too. But all that was swept from his mind in an instant.

They heard footsteps downstairs and the four of them froze. Benjamiah's heart swelled, thudding violently in his ears. Another footstep. Then a different sound, as though something were scrabbling on the wall outside. Before they could investigate, they heard a noise from above—somebody was in the house.

Then they heard Bo.

"Come out, come out, wherever you are!" he crooned through the hollow orphanage.

Elizabella released Emba, who fell cartwheeling before springing into the form of a bluish bear. Silas likewise cast Griffyn as a lion. Nuisance was already a capuchin. Mea reached for Hope.

Mea cried silently to herself, head drooping and shoulders rocking. Hope still dangled at her hip. Benjamiah wanted to reach out and tell her it was okay, that they'd fix it. But Bo interrupted.

"Here for you," he taunted. "Here for *all* of you. We'll be one big, happy family. From this day until the end of time."

It was impossible to tell where Bo was. There were more sounds from below, above and from the walls outside. Footsteps, scrabbling, creaking. Benjamiah knew what it meant—a plague of snatchlings upon the house, and nowhere to run.

"We escaped them once before," whispered Elizabella. "We can do it again."

Benjamiah swayed, completely unconvinced. Silas stared at Mea, his eyes empty sockets. Mea wiped fresh tears away, took a deep breath, and resolved herself.

"I'm really sorry," she said. "It was a terrible mistake. Thank you for . . . everything. It's been the best time of my life."

Before Benjamiah could stop her, Mea stormed out of the room.

"I'm here!" she screamed. "Come and get me!"

She went charging through the house, stomping up the stairs to the attic. Instantly, the snatchlings swarmed. It sounded more like the scuttling and baying of wild animals. They came smashing through the walls and roof of the orphanage like cannonballs, howling. The flapping and scampering and roaring of poppets accompanied the plague's descent.

Every terrifying sound was gravitating toward Mea at the top of the house.

"We can't leave her behind," said Benjamiah.

Elizabella and Silas hadn't moved and he had no patience for it.

"We *can't*!" he yelled.

Benjamiah and Nuisance darted out of the room toward the staircase snaking upward. Already there came the din of violent fighting—crashing, barking, howling. What chance did poor Mea stand? Behind him, he felt the presence of Elizabella and Silas, who had come with him, after all.

Suddenly Emba snarled and Benjamiah whirled. Rushing toward them were two snatchlings, their witchstone masks gleaming and their toothy mouths drawn in leers, eyes yellowed and watery and bloodshot. Each aimed a crossbow. Racing along the corridor were their poppets—hounds with naked skulls for heads, barking and slobbering and violent.

Emba and Griffyn charged. The poppets clashed. A crossbow bolt fizzed through the air and bit into the doorframe beside Benjamiah's head, spitting splinters. While the poppets struggled, Elizabella dashed forward. Benjamiah never saw the drowsipowder vial. One moment the snatchlings were aiming their crossbows at Elizabella, the next they were sinking to the floor, a splash of yellow dust upon their masks.

From above came an almighty thud before quiet fell.

"We've got her!" a happy, ashy voice called. "We've got her!"

Benjamiah's stomach fell. Mea had been overwhelmed. "We have to try," he moaned.

But Elizabella and Silas didn't move. Their eyes were a tangle of emotions—fear, hopelessness and anger. They hesitated too long.

"New friends," came a voice.

Turning, Benjamiah finally laid eyes on Bo Greaves, the fabled and nightmarish child from "The Witchstone Tree."

He was tall and rangy, wearing a tunic cut off at the shoulders to reveal long pale arms wired with purplish veins. A witchstone mask that tapered to a pointy chin was fixed to his face, eyes of seaweed green—rheumy and bloodshot and ancient—staring out of the sockets. On his head was a crown. It took Benjamiah a moment to realize it was made of bones, a ghastly bonfire of yellowish shards. In his hand, he wielded the great sword of bone. Strolling beside him was an enormous wolf, its head a furless skull. Two devastatingly sharp tusks curved upward from the poppet's jaws.

"I'm so happy to finally meet you," said Bo. His voice was dust and dread. "To welcome you to my family."

He walked slowly along the corridor, boots creaking. More snatchlings joined him. They approached from the stairs above, too, fresh from subduing Mea. Benjamiah, Elizabella, and Silas were surrounded by the dead eyes and cranked crossbows of Bo's horde.

"Let us go!" shouted Elizabella.

Bo only smiled, his poppet growling, the tip of his sword scraping ominously closer.

"Come quietly," he said, "and I will only hurt her a little. Make this difficult and you will all suffer much more. I offer you friendship and family. I offer you forever. Don't be afraid. It is death that should frighten you. Only I can take that fear away."

"You'll never take us," said Elizabella. "We'd rather die."

Benjamiah's knees felt weak as the snatchlings closed in, crossbow bolts ready to fly, poppets ready to spring. Emba and Griffyn snarled, but they were outnumbered and outflanked. The witchstone upon Benjamiah's face had never clung so tightly. Was this his final moment as Benjamiah Creek? All of him would be erased, swept away like ash in the wind.

Then he had an idea. Quick as a flash, he slotted into Nuisance, transformed her into a sparrow, and plucked the drowsipowder from Elizabella's hand. Benjamiah saw through her eyes as she wheeled between the snatchlings, splattering the yellow dust over them. It didn't knock many of them out, but it created enough chaos—as Bo let out an animalistic scream—for the three of them to run.

They could go neither up nor down, so they darted back into the bedroom. They had no choice but to go out of the window. They clambered through as the snatchlings screamed and chased and grabbed. The frame still bore a few teeth of glass that cut their hands and legs as they slid across it.

This time they were too high to jump. So they scurried upward, scrabbling on to the half-crumbled roof, bloodied and shaking. Snatchlings followed. They scampered up the building like eerie, howling spiders, their witchstone masks moonlike and terrible in the rainy darkness. Their poppets whirled and chased.

Emba, Griffyn, and Nuisance fought them off as the children ran, striking a course across the greasy roof. They navigated holes and thrumming crossbow bolts and skull-headed beasts of all kinds, racing from one roof to the next, fleeing for their lives. The snatchlings hunted them. Benjamiah had never known such fear.

But they did escape. Only Mea was left behind.

SIXTEEN
WITH THE BEAST OF FARTHING TOWN

> Old Tum would outdo himself, then. He would fashion a beast so astonishing, so terrifying and breath-taking that all of Wreathenwold would be powerless to ignore his brilliance. It was this ambition that sealed his doom.
> —*The Book of Barely Believable Stories,*
> Mildred Fogge

IN A PEACEFUL STRETCH of woods puddled with early-morning sunlight, the children recuperated. For a long time, nobody spoke. They sat together but not close. Everything felt wrecked, shattered, overturned. They were three, but Benjamiah felt a fourth among them—a living, breathing absence.

"We have to save her," he said eventually.

They'd spent the entire night on the move, so ferociously had the snatchlings pursued them. Long after there had been neither sight nor sound of the murderous children, they'd kept going. To Benjamiah, it was all a nightmarish blur. The trembling had not yet passed.

"We don't know where they've taken her," said Elizabella.

She sat on a stump with her back to Benjamiah. Silas was balled up at the foot of a tree, Ariadne playing round his fingers. It struck Benjamiah that she was offering comfort, but it wasn't working: Silas looked a phantom of his former self, hollow-eyed and less substantial, as though a strong wind might suddenly scatter him.

"The Witch Wood," said Benjamiah.

Nobody responded. Birds twittered. Nuisance was a dormouse, curled up in the breast pocket of Benjamiah's grubby, torn waistcoat.

"She sold us out," said Silas, his voice pale and empty.

"She made a mistake," replied Benjamiah. "Everybody makes mistakes. Think about what she's been through. How Bo has made her feel."

Benjamiah knew all too well what it was like to feel alone, an outsider, to not really believe anybody could actually want to be his friend. A little gingerly, Elizabella pulled herself up. Emba was cast as a fox, her fur bluish and her bushy tail white.

"We don't have time, Benjamiah," she said. "If we don't reach Agatha before Midsommer is over, you'll be one of them too. The best we can do for Mea is win Agatha's game and ask her to end the curse. That's how we save her."

"If she's still alive by then," said Benjamiah.

Elizabella said nothing, staring off into the distance. Silas brooded. They were hurt and afraid and Benjamiah shared those feelings. But surely they had to help Mea?

"We have to go on," said Elizabella. "It's our only choice."

Benjamiah felt his confidence drain. It didn't *feel* like the only choice. Though he, too, was angry, leaving Mea with Bo and the snatchlings struck him as an exceptionally cruel punishment.

"She's our friend," he said.

Silas stood, brushing dirt and mulch from his clothes. The stare he leveled at Benjamiah was dark and cold.

"Friends don't do that to each other," he said.

Elizabella fidgeted. Benjamiah knew then that she wasn't going to back him up. Maybe Benjamiah was in the wrong, after all.

"We find Agatha," said Elizabella, "and ask her to end the curse. Then Mea is free."

"And we never have to see her again," croaked Silas bitterly.

Benjamiah swallowed awkwardly. Outnumbered by the others, he gave a weak nod. It changed nothing for him, though, as the three of them set off again. Despite everything, continuing without Mea felt wrong, right down to his bones.

Two days of somber traveling, during which Benjamiah, Elizabella, and Silas hardly talked, ended at a secret door.

The moths flurried excitedly round a thicket of creeping vines laced over a stretch of stone wall at the end of an alleyway. Nearby were empty barrels, an old spinning wheel, and a stack of sodden timber pallets. When the moths settled on the vines, flexing their wings, Benjamiah looked to the others for help.

Together they struggled with the braids of parched vines, leaves rustling and stems snapping. They found only stone beneath. While Elizabella huffed impatiently, Benjamiah ran his hands carefully across the wall until he felt something press into the palm of his hand.

"Here," he said.

It was a tiny metal point, needlelike, buried in the stone. It ended in a rusty loop of iron.

"I think it's a key."

So minute was the key that Benjamiah struggled for purchase. Finally, he clasped it between finger and thumb and turned it counterclockwise, feeling it struggle through the rust. The soft trill of something being wound up emanated from within the stone. When the pressure brought the contraption to a stop, Benjamiah took a deep breath and let go.

Dust flurried and a melodious ticking rang out. A seam split the stone with a puff of stale air, a column of rotating cogwheels stretching up high, each turning the next. Benjamiah realized the gears formed the hinge of a door, which now yawned open out of the blank stone. When it was ajar, the cogwheels stopped and silence fell.

"Clockwork," breathed Elizabella, examining the gears. "What does it mean?"

Something stirred from the murky depths of Benjamiah's mind. Sliding his knapsack from his shoulder, he withdrew his battered copy of *The Book of Barely Believable Stories*. A pang traveled through him at the sight of it, reminded painfully of Mea. He leafed through until he found a story he'd read a few days ago. He showed Elizabella and Silas the title: "The Clockworker of Farthing Town." Elizabella's mouth formed an O.

"The Clockworker of Farthing Town" was the story of Old Tum, a bumbling old man who made for a poor clockworker. Though he worked hard, he lacked the skill, patience, and dexterity needed to master the craft.

Mildred Fogge wrote:

> Old Tum fell onto a stool in his workshop and wept.

"What I would give to be the finest clockworker in Wreathenwold!" he said in despair.

Just then, the shop bell pealed. In stepped a magus, tall and shimmering and unearthly.

"Do you mean it?" she asked.

"Of course," said Old Tum once he'd recovered from the shock. "What clockworker would not wish for such a thing. Can you make it so?"

"I can," said the magus, "but there is a price. I will make you the master of this art, but you will be alone. People will cease to see you, or hear your voice when you speak. Your neighbors will leave, compelled by some unseen force to get away. Is this a price you are willing to pay?"

Old Tum, so tantalized by the gift on offer, scarcely heard this dire warning. With a wave of her cane, the tricksy magus transformed Old Tum's life. From that moment onward, he was a master of clockwork, a maestro of cogwheels and springs and sprockets. The magus's sorcery enhanced the inherent magic of clockwork to an extent that Old Tum could fashion anything to which his mind turned, from sublime little clockwork bugs to ingenious devices that would baffle and bewilder the finest of minds.

But, as the magus had promised, despite Old Tum's fantastical creations, nobody marveled. On the street, he was ignored when he called out greetings, buffeted by the people of Farthing Town as though he weren't there at all. Old Tum became an apparition, out of sync with the world, unreal.

Gradually, everybody deserted Farthing Town. Old Tum was left entirely alone amid the network of little lanes, bereft and miserable, with nothing but his clockwork wonders for company. Refusing to accept this, he set about conjuring yet wilder and more dangerous contraptions, aiming to create something so magnificent it would be impossible to ignore.

It was this pursuit, wrote Mildred Fogge, that proved Old Tum's undoing. The clockworker was killed by a monstrous machine of his own making. So dangerous was the beast that Farthing Town was sealed off from the rest of Wreathenwold.

"Well, it can't be worse than Crokerley," said Elizabella.

Benjamiah put the book back in his knapsack.

"I'm doing this one alone," he said.

"Oh, for goodness' sake—"

"No," said Benjamiah firmly. "I mean it this time."

Elizabella's eyes went small and dangerous and her hands landed on her hips.

"What are you talking about?" she demanded.

Benjamiah unhitched Nuisance and dropped her. He transformed her into a sparrow. She fluttered up to his shoulder and twittered encouragingly.

Thinking of Mea, and how the others had decided against going to save her, Benjamiah said: "Turns out we're all on our own, anyway."

Elizabella's cheeks flashed with color. Silas's expression slackened into a waxwork face of wordless despair.

"Have it your way," said Elizabella, stung.

This wasn't the way he wanted it, Benjamiah thought to himself. But the anger he felt at Mea had been dwarfed by the anger he felt at the others. Not saving her from Bo was utterly wrong. He knew it, and he felt sure they knew it too.

Elizabella turned her back to Benjamiah. Silas only stared vacantly.

"Come on, Nuisance," said Benjamiah.

To the melody of the sparrow's fortifying chirrups, he passed through the stone door and entered Farthing Town.

A bright sun sprawled above a very narrow, very charming lane. At first, it seemed a picture-perfect scene: rows of quaint cottages with thatched roofs, slender shops with colorful awnings, bonewoods, and streetlamps. There was a bakery and a small pond and a bookshop. A weathered sign read FARTHING TOWN. A stiff breeze trailed through the overgrown flower beds, and fallen leaves rattled and wind chimes sang.

Closer examination revealed the dilapidation. Windows were broken. Thatch was torn away or fallen through. One building around the corner was rubble. An oily smell pervaded everything, and strewn across the cobbles were shards of metal, tiny cogwheels, rusted springs. A faint cacophony of ticking carried on the air too—a sound that reminded Benjamiah horribly of the snatchlings.

A web had been built on a sprawling, unkempt rosebush. A fat pinkish spider sat in the middle. Leaning in, Benjamiah realized—with a happy, bewildered jolt—that it was clockwork. In other circumstances, it would have been an utter delight to investigate how clockworking, this synthesis of horology and magic, actually worked. A clockwork butterfly fluttered by, ticking. Walking on, a clockwork mouse peered out at him from the frame of a broken window, then dashed out of sight.

It was then that Benjamiah began to notice, with a rush of powerful, confused emotion, the whisperwicks. Here and there—hanging from the bough of a tree, or from the rafters of a half-demolished house, or from the roof of a well—were lanterns inside which flickered small flames. Whisperwicks held words, memories or secrets spoken long ago. With a key, they could be opened and those words heard—but only once. Afterward, the candle would go out forever. Benjamiah spotted lanterns of all different forms: one like a tiger's head, another like a heart, one in the shape of a galloping horse.

Seeing the whisperwicks brought back, raw and sharply, the memories of Benjamiah's last adventure with Elizabella. They'd followed a trail of whisperwicks left behind by her brother, Edwid, who had hidden in them a terrible secret from Manfred Tarr.

What did these whisperwicks mean? Why were they here? Benjamiah didn't have to wait long for an answer. He came to a shop called Old Tum's Clockwork Wonders. Depicted beneath the name was a round, genial face with a large gray beard, surrounded by a ring of cogwheels. The shop was a high, narrow building, the windows shadowy with grime.

Extending from the wall was a witchstone branch. Hanging from it, alongside the usual wooden sign, was a simple copper whisperwick. A candle flickered inside. Approaching it, Benjamiah heard again on the wind the faint, creepy chanting of children: *Agatha Drake, Agatha Drake, beneath the witchstone tree . . .*

The rhyme read:

PURSUING BRILLIANCE NEVER EARNED,

THE CLOCKWORKER WAS LOST,

> DESTROYED BY THAT WHICH HE DESIGNED,
> TOO SLOW TO RUE THE COST.
>
> SO CLASP THE WITCHSTONE LIMB AND PICK
> THE LOCKS THAT LIGHT THE WAY.
> BEWARE THE FOOLISHNESS OF YOUTH
> AND THE BEAST NO ONE CAN SLAY.

Instantly, the witchstone upon Benjamiah's eye squirmed, softening and wriggling along his cheek, then down his neck in a way that made him claw at it in panic. Down his arm it snaked, coiling round his index finger. There it stopped, encasing it and ending in a fine point like a knitting needle—chalky white, wrapped in violet threads.

Benjamiah knew it to be a key for whisperwicks. Edwid had left one behind very much like it.

"I suppose this is the cleverness trial, then," he whispered, casting nervously around for signs of monstrous beasts.

Nuisance twittered. The town ticked. The whisperwick on the branch creaked in the breeze. Unsteadily, Benjamiah raised the witchstone key on his finger and slid it into the lock. It clicked, one of the violet threads traveling inside, filling the lock with a flash of bright purple light. Then Benjamiah opened the lantern. A woman's husky voice flowed out, one he recalled with a shiver:

*A face without eyes, hands without fingers,
Sometimes hurries, sometimes lingers.*

Then quiet fell, save the town's symphony of ticking and the chattering of wind chimes.

"Agatha Drake," he said.

Nuisance chirped in agreement. Benjamiah committed the words to memory. For a moment, everything was a blur, his mind slipping and sliding around the looming threat of Old Tum's mysterious monster. Then he settled himself.

"It's a riddle," he said. "And we have to open the *locks that light the way*. So . . ."

He cast around, begrudgingly missing Elizabella and Silas. A clockwork swallow sang. A clockwork beetle climbed a mossy wall toward a whisperwick shaped like a plumpkin.

"The riddle tells us what the next whisperwick is," he said to Nuisance.

But what did it mean? *A face without eyes, hands without fingers* . . . Creeping through the eerie town, Benjamiah racked his brain, peering carefully round every corner and checking over his shoulder whenever something creaked or shivered in the breeze. A mechanical cat chased a rat and he flinched. The tension ratcheted up with every step. He saw whisperwicks resembling many different things, but none that suited the riddle.

"What has a face but not really?" he whispered. "And hands but not real hands? Sometimes fast, sometimes slow..."

They passed a splashing fountain, crossed through the remnants of a derelict home, beneath the branches of a half-fallen bonewood tree. Everywhere little things ticked.

Ticked...

Inspiration flourished like a firework in Benjamiah's mind. "A clock!" he said excitedly.

And too loudly. Somewhere, amid the maze of streets, something stirred. Something, judging by the way the ground itself seemed to quiver, and the hush that fell across Farthing Town, very large. Benjamiah froze, heart hammering. His ears strained, reached. Silence now. But there was no doubting what he'd heard. The beast was here. What a fool he felt, in that moment, for doing this without his friends.

Desperately quiet, Benjamiah crept through the warren of streets, expecting at any moment to be ambushed by Old Tum's murderous creature. Finally, relief washing through him, he spotted what he was looking for: hanging from a streetlamp was a whisperwick shaped like a clock.

Nuisance was a dormouse, poking a quivering nose out of his breast pocket. Benjamiah hurried to the whisperwick and slotted in the key. The thread crawled, purple flashed, and suddenly he was listening to Agatha Drake's next riddle:

I live in the ground and live in the sky,
Undress in the cold, dead when I lie.

A baffled Benjamiah recited the riddle to himself as the whisperwick's flame perished.

"What does *that* mean?" he moaned.

The ground shook. A clutch of clockwork crows erupted from a tree, squawking in fright. Somewhere, something rumbled—like the distant, throaty threat of a thunderstorm gathering on the horizon.

"We need to hurry!"

Benjamiah darted inside an old bookshop, Nuisance quivering in his pocket. The place was full of clockwork spiders and their webs, mildewy books strewn all over the floor. Benjamiah caught his breath, feeling sick. The building shook. The ground shivered. The stormy sound gathered again, then died. Whatever it was, wherever it was, the beast of Farthing Town was stirring.

"What lives in the ground *and* the sky?" he whispered to Nuisance.

The dormouse climbed meekly out of his pocket, jumped, and in midair sprouted feathers and a fanned tail. She landed on the bookshop counter as a nightjar.

"A bird?" he pondered.

He supposed some birds nested on the ground. But what about *undress in the cold*? Uncertain, Benjamiah crept out of the bookshop. Nuisance perched on his shoulder. He thought, and wondered, and worried at the puzzle. But nothing came. Farthing Town shivered in the wind, ticking gently. When the ground shook again, Benjamiah's fear won out and he started to run, looking for bird-shaped whisperwicks.

He found one dangling from the wing of a grotesque. The lantern was shaped like a puffin. Plagued by doubt, Benjamiah reached up, slotted in the key, and opened the little door.

An ear-splitting, gut-wrenching scream spilled out of the whisperwick. It was an abominable, deafening caterwaul that pierced the town, the flame straining angrily on its wick as Agatha's treacherous wail rang out. Benjamiah slammed the lantern door shut, but the scream didn't end, continuing for what seemed like an age.

When it finally stopped, Benjamiah's ears rang. His heart thundered. Then he heard it—and felt it. The dreadful march of the beast. Walking and then running. The world rocked. Shards of glass tumbled from broken windows. A weathervane fell from a cottage roof. Benjamiah was stuck in place, feeling blood drain from his muscles, eyes drawn to the end of the lane.

It appeared then, blotting out the low sun. Silhouetted there, for a moment Benjamiah could make no sense of the monster—he saw only a looming, terrible blackness.

Then it dropped back onto all fours, with a crash that Benjamiah felt in his very soul, and he understood what he was seeing. It was a polar bear, of such monstrous dimensions that Benjamiah's mind could barely process it. When it stood on its hind legs, it towered over the buildings; on all fours, padding toward him, it could scarcely channel its bulk through the width of the street. As it came, Benjamiah perceived dimly the *clunk* of its clockwork heart—like the thick, slow metronome of a clock tower.

It roared and Benjamiah melted. It came like an earthquake. From somewhere, he found the strength to run. The bear's roar deafened him. Benjamiah hurtled into a building as the bear charged. He ran right through the house and out the back, the bear smashing the structure to ribbons behind him.

Benjamiah pelted, weaving through buildings and along lanes, until the bear lost sight of him. He scrambled behind the trunk of a bonewood tree. His legs shook and his breath raced. Behind him, he heard the bear, prowling now. Every fall of a paw sent tremors through the ground.

Benjamiah dared a peek. The bear's size defied all sense. Its fur was unerringly lifelike, shivering in the breeze, slightly yellowed. Everything about it looked real, save for the enormous eyes socketed above its snout: like all clockwork contraptions, the eyes, no matter the artistry of the creator, failed to capture the magic of real ones. Benjamiah also noticed an unfinished gap along its left flank through which he could spy a medley of cogwheels and chains. Presumably, the bear had killed Old Tum before he'd finished.

Nuisance nuzzled Benjamiah's ear. Benjamiah let his head rock back against the bonewood, gathering his breath. He'd never been so grateful for a tree.

A tree...

"A tree!" he hissed.

A tree's roots lived in the ground, but the canopy lived in the sky. It undressed in the cold when losing its leaves over winter. And it was dead when it lay on the ground. He felt a fool for not thinking of this earlier.

When the bear had lumbered away, Benjamiah steeled himself. He *had* to do this. So much would be lost if he failed. Himself, his friends, perhaps all of Wreathenwold. He lifted himself onto unsteady legs, heart rampaging, then went looking for a whisperwick shaped like a tree.

He found it on the second floor of a half-fallen cottage, sitting on the fireplace. Benjamiah slotted in the key, tensing in horror at the thought of another scream bursting out of the lantern. Tentatively, he opened it:

> *I chatter and jump, and gallop and thump,*
> *And break in silence, with no sign of violence.*

As quickly as the candle died, Benjamiah had the answer. He'd already seen this whisperwick, in fact. He actually smiled.

It was a heart.

He turned to tell Nuisance the good news, but stopped dead.

The window was filled with a monstrous false eye, as big and terrible as a wrecking ball. Benjamiah teetered. Nuisance squawked. Then the bear roared, spouting hot, oily air into the room. The monster cranked back a paw and, before Benjamiah could so much as move, cleaved it through the house.

Everything was chaos. Pain, spinning, falling. The house was ripped in two and Benjamiah fell with it, dragged in an undertow of bricks and beams and sprawling dust. He fell, with a crunch, into a tangle of ruins. Somewhere Nuisance crooned mournfully, but Benjamiah had lost his bearings. Something had struck his head and his sight flickered in and out. Wooziness reigned, which felt almost blissful—until another bloodcurdling roar hauled him back from the brink.

Benjamiah scrabbled through the wreckage, every part of him throbbing. Dust stung his eyes and his head rocked. His hands waded through splintery wood and sharp stone. He crawled through the mess, into the bright sunlight, and turned.

Above him, a tower of fur and fury, was the monster. It dropped from its hind legs with a crash and advanced upon Benjamiah. He wriggled backward, but it was hopeless. The monster's head was above him, jaws parting: he saw rows of horrible teeth, and a synthetic tongue flapping wetly, and—down the throat—a network of gears and chains. Its breath poured out, petrolic and greasy.

Before it could bite down, the beast was distracted.

Another bear threw itself between Benjamiah and the monster, this one with bluish fur and marbles for eyes. Emba. The monster paused only momentarily before widening its jaws again and lowering them to snap up Elizabella's poppet. The difference in size between the two bears was not unlike that between a human and a mouse. Emba gave her fiercest roar, but it was lost amid the clockwork monster's rumbling. Before the bear could attack, Emba transformed into an eagle.

It flew up and raked its talons at the monster's eyes, but the effect was minimal. Griffyn came, then, as a barn owl. The birds scratched and pecked at the bear, but it proved no more than a minor annoyance, as it roared and reared, swiping its paws.

"Benjamiah, come on . . ."

It was Elizabella, hooking her hands under his arms. Silas joined her, dragging Benjamiah out of the rubble. A dazed, half-concussed Benjamiah found little substance in his legs, wobbling into the grip of his friends. Relief that they'd come had him on the verge of tears.

But the monstrous bear wasn't done. It came for the three of them, brushing aside the powerless poppets. Silas whimpered. It swiped a paw and the children scattered, caught up in a tsunami of rubble and ruin. Benjamiah fell, and Elizabella was thrown.

Hopping over a lump of stone came Nuisance, a capuchin now. Benjamiah met her button eyes, all the breath squeezed from his body. Then Benjamiah also saw, amid the wreckage, a fire poker.

Instinct took over. Benjamiah slipped into Nuisance's mind and she was off, grabbing the poker. Benjamiah had two minds now, two pairs of eyes. Through his own, he saw the bear smash and claw at his friends, where a single blow would wipe them from existence. Through Nuisance's, he saw the world rushing by as the monkey scampered, and leaped, and finally landed on the bear's leg. She ran up its side, fire poker in hand, and slipped through the hole in its flank.

He heard the droning machinery through Nuisance's ears. Inside the bear was the most fabulous complexity of cogwheels and steel ribbons and springs. And, at its very center, a great silvery orb of gears and sprockets, from which came the enormous ticking sound. The great bear was moments from clamping Silas in its jaws when

Nuisance struck, jamming the fire poker between the gears of its heart.

A screeching sound followed, before every mechanism within the bear ground to a halt. Chains burst and cogs bit suddenly into nothingness. Nuisance fled as the bear shut down, staggered, and finally fell—crashing into Old Tum's shop and ripping most of the building down in the process. It was over.

Benjamiah groaned, throbbing all over. He rolled gingerly onto his side. Nuisance jumped on him and ran her little paws all over his body, apparently checking for injuries. Then she hugged his face. Having lifted the monkey away, Benjamiah saw Elizabella and Silas standing over him—scratched and dusty, disheveled, wide-eyed, and breathless. They helped him up.

"Thank you," he mumbled.

"You'd have done the same for us," said Elizabella.

"I'm so happy you never do what you're told," said Benjamiah to her.

She flashed a crooked smile.

They found the heart-shaped whisperwick together. Benjamiah unlocked and opened it. This time no words flowed out. Instead, the candle flickered and transformed into something solid. Falling from the wick was the witchstone fragment, which Benjamiah promptly gathered up and fitted to the mask once it had returned to his eye.

Then, though bruised and shaken, he turned defiantly to the others.

"I don't care what either of you say," said Benjamiah, "I'm—"

"We know," said Elizabella.

Silas, kicking a dead leaf around with the tip of his boot, said, "I was a cad. I should have listened to you."

"We *both* should have," said Elizabella.

Benjamiah looked from one to the other, feeling relief blossom. Before he could stop himself, he'd laced his arms round their necks and pincered them in a delighted group hug. They both laughed, squirming—embarrassed—from his grip.

"We should never have left Mea behind," said Elizabella, finally extricating herself and straightening her hat.

"And we should have gone back for her," said Silas.

"There's nothing we can do about it," said Benjamiah. "We can only do something now."

"There's just one thing," said Elizabella, gesturing to the witchstone upon Benjamiah's face. "You have to reach the last trial, or you'll be lost. What if there's not enough time?"

"I don't care," he said. "Agatha's last trial is about loyalty. Saving Mea isn't the one she wants us to face, but it's the only one that matters. If we don't save her, I'd rather forget everything, anyway. Ariadne?"

At last, it was Ariadne's moment and the thread rose theatrically and wonderfully to the occasion, uncoiling grandly from Elizabella's straw hat as though she'd been waiting an eternity to be called upon. Elizabella smiled and Silas looked fiercely proud and quite emotional.

"Take us to the Witch Wood," said Benjamiah.

Ariadne gave a regal bow, swung to the stone wall of the clockwork shop, and led the way.

SEVENTEEN
WITH THE WITCH WOOD

> Should the child fail, they will join the wicked Bo as another lost child of Midsommer—as another snatchling of Agatha Drake, memoryless and undying, condemned to the most bleak and unhappy eternity.
> —*The Book of Barely Believable Stories*, Mildred Fogge

FOR THE FIRST TIME, it was Silas pushing the pace—with Ariadne, the navigator, perched on his shoulder. The Mapmaker was like a smoldering coal, lit from within by the need to save Mea. Even when they rested, Silas fidgeted and tutted. Benjamiah knew how he felt. Nothing would be right unless they pried Mea from Bo's clutches. The distance to the Witch Wood was a mystery and an agony; the only recourse was to push on tirelessly.

Along the way, Elizabella tested Benjamiah's dollcasting.

Any playfulness was gone from the sessions. The situation was grave now and Benjamiah needed to be prepared.

"Quicker, quicker!" she snapped when Benjamiah hesitated between transformations.

He tried again.

"A miscast at the wrong time could mean death," she said as Benjamiah fumbled the *Common Octopus* spell and set Nuisance squealing in pain.

Benjamiah focused, but Elizabella groaned.

"No, you're doing it *wrong*," she said after she'd demanded Benjamiah rotate in clockwise circles while making Nuisance the capuchin rotate counterclockwise.

Despite a throbbing pain in the center of his forehead, Benjamiah tried again. And secretly, during those rare moments when Elizabella was not working him furiously, he practiced another spell.

Three days passed with no sign of the Witch Wood, then four. Midsommer was running away from them, which meant time was running out for Benjamiah. Above him, the moths and their trails of shimmering violet looped, trying to draw him toward Agatha's final trial—and his only chance of salvation. The witchstone gripped fast to his eye, but it meant nothing to him now. Mea was all that mattered.

"There's only a couple of days of Midsommer left," said Elizabella.

She watched Benjamiah, her expression a pattern of stress. But Benjamiah was resolute. Agatha could wait. He would sacrifice himself if need be, no matter how terrifying the prospect.

As if that weren't enough to worry about, they found at every turn more news of missing children. Posters and flyers, anguished guardians and siblings shouting and searching the streets, a mustached man preaching from an upturned crate that the Minotaur himself was eating the children of Wreathenwold.

"What does Manfred want with them?" said Benjamiah, seething.

Elizabella shook her head, only reciting once again, *"Magic forged at Midsommer is the strongest and truest of all magic—both fair and foul."*

It never failed to make Benjamiah shudder. Manfred's designs would be foul indeed, rooted in his obsession for the Widow's revival and the inevitable terror and devastation that promised. Benjamiah thought of the Minotaur often. Was he still alive? What did Manfred need from him?

The next morning, an idea struck Benjamiah about how they might fight the snatchlings. Elizabella rolled her eyes and said they didn't need a *plan*—instead, she was going to brazenly storm the Witch Wood and dispatch anybody in the way, Bo included.

"Why are you so determined to get us all killed?" said Silas moodily when Elizabella was finished. "I'd like to hear from Benjamiah."

Benjamiah told them. Elizabella sniffed dismissively, though the fact she didn't immediately tear his idea to pieces suggested she begrudgingly respected it. Silas nodded his approval.

With little time to waste, they were at the mercy of the labyrinth's many coils to find what they needed. On a snowy street, they came across a toyshop. There they found slingshots—Benjamiah grabbed four, then handed over a three of diamonds and a five of clubs to the surly teenager minding the shop.

Next, on an industrial street that smelled of soot and smokeberry jam from a looming condiment factory, they found a color-broker's. The proprietor was an oily man with quick fingers and quicker eyes, the latter leaping between every dot of color upon the children as they stood at his counter: Benjamiah's eyes (he had lost his despectacles when fleeing the snatchlings that night at the inn), Elizabella's poppet bracelet, even the bronze of Silas's spyglass.

"We're not here to sell," snapped Elizabella when the color-broker once again made an offer for Benjamiah's eye colors. "We're here to *buy*."

Even after they'd told the man what they wanted, he continued trying for their eyes.

"Save your cards, little ones," he rasped, fingers rattling on the old bonewood counter. "Give up those pretty eyes instead. Even just the one . . ."

Elizabella telling him they'd take their business elsewhere did the trick. Silas paid the man and the children hurried out, inspecting their wares on the smoggy street outside.

They'd bought boxes of hollow glass marbles, used for holding pure color when being transported or sold. Benjamiah recalled mountains of them in the Viper's home. To prove his plan would work, he grabbed one and threw it hard against a wall. It smashed.

"See," he said.

Elizabella shrugged, still unwilling to admit Benjamiah's idea had been a good one.

Silas nodded gravely and said, "We're wasting time."

Ariadne led them to a small rock bridge cresting a stream, along a woodland path growing ever more shadowy and wild, then yet deeper into the forest where no birds sang and the trees crowded them, the bracken barbed and the ground slippery with moss. Toadstools with bright spots grew in clumps, sweating and pungent.

Ahead, the ground ran out. The forest floor fell over the edge of a cliff. A quivering Ariadne spidered between bramble and branches and stems before dangling over the precipice. From there, she jabbed her tail downward. The children battled through the undergrowth and peered down.

The cliff overlooked a swamp, the water pockmarked with purplish algae. Trees climbed from its depths and in those trees a town had been fashioned, a treehouse city rendered from ancient bonewood and suspended above the depths. Connecting the treehouses were rope bridges and ladders. Flaming torches burned in the gloom. At the heart of the city was a bonewood tower, spearing into the murky air like a crooked skeletal finger.

Snatchlings crawled everywhere. On the bridges, in treehouses, keeping watch from crow's nests above like those of a pirate ship. They were armed with the signature crossbows, though Benjamiah couldn't help wondering why they felt the need to defend the Witch Wood so heavily. Nobody in their right mind would come here.

"Look," said Elizabella. "The water."

For a moment, Benjamiah was confused. Then he saw a shadow stir in the swamp, the arc of something blackish and slippery breaking the surface.

Silas groaned. *"River wolves."*

"Great," said Benjamiah. "Snatchlings above the water

and wolves in it. Even Agatha Drake wouldn't be this cruel."

"Look for Mea," said Elizabella.

They did so, straining through the gathering darkness. The air was heavy with the smell of algae and brackish water. Benjamiah heard the clicking of strange insects and the splashing of river wolves. Sometimes snatchlings shouted and occasionally laughed, high-pitched and eerie.

"I think *there*," said Silas, peering through his spyglass.

At the base of the tower was a set of bonewood steps leading toward a series of small structures. Two armed snatchlings patrolled.

"We can work out a route from up here."

Elizabella talked the boys through the plan, beginning with crossing the main bridge from the cliff, then following a series of ladders and bridges to reach what they very much hoped was indeed Mea's prison.

"Stay together," said Elizabella. "Follow my lead. Be *quiet*. We'll be absolutely fine."

After this, she was up and off. Benjamiah would have preferred a little more strategizing, but knew it was hopeless with Elizabella. She was already creeping through the undergrowth, skirting the edge of the cliff toward the main bridge. The closer they drew, the heavier Benjamiah's heart throbbed. It was full dark now and the Witch Wood—with its bonewood treehouses and witchstone masks—hovered like a wraith world in the darkness.

There were no snatchlings on the main bridge, but two in crow's nests above it. Crouched behind a tree, Elizabella unhitched Emba and threw her into the air. She flapped off into the darkness, a vampire bat. Benjamiah released Nuisance, casting her as a fruit bat. Griffyn likewise took off into the blackness as an owl.

Using their poppets to distract the watching snatchlings, the children broke cover and bolted across the bridge, really a long, dipping streak of bonewood slats suspended over the wolf-infested swamp. Now they were on a bonewood walkway, with smaller bridges spearing off in different directions. Above them came a series of creaks as a snatchling strolled a higher scaffold.

Elizabella beckoned them on. They snuck, and crept, and hid. Benjamiah very much hoped Elizabella recalled the route, as fear had tangled up his own mind. Everywhere snatchlings moved, creaking and muttering and laughing.

They had edged round a treehouse, a fire pit crackling within, when Elizabella froze. Peering over her shoulder, Benjamiah saw why. Barring their way was a pair of snatchlings, leaning over the rope bridge and talking in ashy, gravelly voices—that these children sounded hundreds of years old still disturbed Benjamiah.

Elizabella gestured for Silas and Benjamiah to wait. Then she drew her slingshot from her belt and counted silently down from three. Benjamiah gulped as she reached "one."

They whirled round the corner, slingshots aimed. Loaded in them were the color-spheres they'd bought earlier, filled with drowsipowder. By the time the snatchlings had raised their heads, three pellets were pinging through the air. Silas missed but Elizabella struck one mask and Benjamiah the other, the balls smashing in a flurry of yellowish dust.

One snatchling groaned and the other half shouted something incomprehensible. Before either could string a sentence together, they staggered. By this point, Benjamiah, Elizabella, and Silas had darted forward and taken hold of the drowsy snatchlings, ensuring they didn't fall with a crash or career over the edge into the wolfish waters below. Both were snoring by the time they were set softly onto the platform.

"We need to hide them!" hissed Benjamiah.

"Where?" said Elizabella with a shrug.

"Somebody's coming," whispered Silas.

They had no choice but to scamper away. As soon as the sleeping snatchlings were discovered, an alarm would surely sound. How would they ever escape?

Onward was their only option. Between using their poppets as distractions and well-aimed drowsipowder, they made progress, reaching the base of the bonewood tower.

"That must be where Bo lives," whispered Benjamiah, peering up and shivering.

"Look!" said Elizabella, her gaze trained in the opposite direction.

A walkway threaded downward, bordered on either side by rows of boxy structures with barred windows. Patrolling here were the two snatchling guards they'd seen from the cliff. The girl was fiddling with her crossbow and the boy was whistling, his poppet cast as a skull-headed jaguar. Benjamiah struggled to swallow as Elizabella dragged them into hiding, mouthed more silent instructions, then gave the signal.

Benjamiah staggered out and pinged a drowsipowder pellet. It missed the girl's mask by a foot and a half and smashed on a bonewood post. Benjamiah's stomach sank. But, when the girl went to inspect it, Silas struck her with his own missile. Elizabella had already downed the boy with another plum strike in the mask's slitted nostril.

"Who's there?" said a small voice.

It was not the dusty croak of a snatchling. It had come from one of the cells. Benjamiah rushed over and peered through the bars. Inside was a small boy, eight or nine years old, thin and ragged, his eyes big. Every cell held children, some shared by two or three.

"The children they've been taking . . . ," said Elizabella, wide-eyed.

An excited, urgent chorus traveled through the prisoners, hissing to be let out, begging for freedom. Benjamiah shushed them. Time was running out and there was no sign of Mea.

Silas frisked the fallen snatchlings and came up with what must have been a key, though to Benjamiah it resembled a tiny steel mace. The Mapmaker tried it in the lock of the nearest cell. With a *thunk*, the lock submitted and the door swung open. A girl with light brown skin and her hair in a headscarf stumbled out, shivering from the cold.

"Let the others out," said Elizabella. "We'll find Mea."

Silas continued releasing prisoners while Benjamiah and Elizabella followed the walkway, surrounded on either side by desperate children. From somewhere above, they heard a snatchling call angrily across the Witch Wood.

Benjamiah moaned. "They know something's up!"

"Then we should hurry."

The walkway ended with another cell, another door with a barred window. All the darkness and terror of recent days swelled in Benjamiah, gathering into a frenzied crescendo as he neared the cell, the ugly and suffocating fear that they were too late to save Mea—that all was already lost.

Through the bars, Benjamiah saw her, crouched in the corner. Mea's cell was particularly cruel—most of the floor had rotted away, leaving her crammed onto a single bonewood plank at the edge, overhanging the wolf-infested swamp below.

Mea looked up and the relief was dizzying.

"B-Benjamiah . . . ," she whimpered. Then, when Elizabella joined him, she added, "You . . . You . . . You came for me?"

"Of course we did," said Benjamiah, hands gripped on the bars. "We're so sorry, Mea. Sorry we didn't come sooner. Can you forgive us?"

Mea's amber eyes stretched and wobbled. Behind him, Benjamiah could hear the murmuring and moving of children, the increasingly loud and angry howls of snatchlings. The opportunity to escape undetected had careered hopelessly out of reach.

With a groan of pain, Mea lifted herself and edged toward them.

"I'm so sorry for what I did . . . ," she cried, fingers reaching through the bars.

"It's forgotten," said Elizabella.

Then Silas came running. Upon seeing Mea's witchstone mask, he nearly toppled over with relief. With trembling hands, he used the macelike key to open her cell. Behind Silas was a gaggle of freed children, thin and cold and terrified, some as young as five or six.

Before Silas could say a word, the sound of an eerie horn lanced the Witch Wood, rousing the snatchlings into a formidable and sinister passion.

"Time to go," said Elizabella.

"All the children are still here," said Benjamiah, looking

at the dozens gathered behind them. "We have to get them to safety before Manfred uses them for whatever he has planned."

The Witch Wood was now an almighty din of horns and howls. Benjamiah, Elizabella, Silas, and Mea readied their poppets.

"We're getting out of here," said Elizabella to the crowd of children. "All of us. Stick together. Older children, look after the little ones. We'll lead the way."

With that, she strutted to the head of the column. Benjamiah, Mea, and Silas joined her. The other children unhitched their poppets and cast spells: tigers, bears, wolves, a stag. Griffyn was a lion, Emba a bear. Hope became an eagle. For now, Benjamiah kept Nuisance in doll form, gripped in his trembling hand.

They ran. The snatchlings came, crossbows in hand, poppets cast. At the front, Elizabella, Silas, and Benjamiah downed two of them with drowsipowder pellets. After that, it was chaos. Snatchlings came screaming and howling from every direction, crossbow bolts singing murderously from all sides, poppets crashing into one another, teeth and claws, screams and roars and snarls.

There was great variety to the ways in which Benjamiah nearly died: a crossbow bolt whipping past his eye; a snatchling's poppet hound launching itself at him with its jaws gaping; grappling with a gangly snatchling, which left

him crashing toward the edge of a rope bridge and nearly plummeting to the wolves below.

Benjamiah and Nuisance fought on together. His poppet was a capuchin and Benjamiah used her to wrestle crossbows from snatchlings above, prying them loose and throwing them into the swamp. When Benjamiah could get his bearings, he used the slingshot to drive snatchlings from their path. The snatchlings kept coming, pouring upon them from every direction, climbing from below and leaping from above. The liberated children fought valiantly and with a ferocity that only comes when battling for freedom.

The turning point came when Mea, perhaps the clumsiest girl in the world, tripped over her own poppet and crashed into a snatchling girl. The snatchling stumbled, falling over the edge.

Benjamiah lurched forward and grabbed her, and, with Mea, hauled the snatchling to safety. A pigtailed girl, one of the freed prisoners, looked furious.

"What are you doing?" she demanded.

The snatchling panted, old eyes narrowed.

"They're *us*," said Benjamiah. "They're just lost. They don't deserve that."

Other snatchlings had seen Benjamiah save the girl. A moment of hesitation and unease carried through their ranks. Though the battle raged on in places, some snatchlings—including the one Benjamiah had saved—seemed to have woken from a deep and ancient stupor, unwilling to fight on, in some cases fleeing. Some now actively helped the children escape.

Bloodied and bruised, Benjamiah, Elizabella, Silas, Mea, and the dozens of freed children reached the bridge leading away from the Witch Wood.

Standing on it was Bo, flanked by a few other loyal lieutenants. Their crossbows were cranked and steady, poppets cast as skull-headed predators. Bo had his great curved sword drawn, his own poppet a monstrous tusked wolf. A lull fell as the children bunched at the bridge, all eyes on Bo. Flaming torches set his eerie witchstone mask to gleaming in the darkness.

He lifted his sword and pointed it at the crowd. Directly at Mea, who was quickly shielded by Elizabella, Benjamiah, and Silas—the latter having drawn his cutlass, though Benjamiah saw how it shook in his hand.

"You," called Bo.

"If you want her, you'll have to go through us!" shouted Elizabella.

Bo kept his sword pointed at Mea, ignoring Elizabella. His poppet howled and the river wolves joined in.

"I will kill you for what you've done to my family, girl," said Bo to Mea.

Mea shoved the others out of the way and stood alone.

"Come and get me, then!" she screamed.

Bo and his lieutenants came. Meanwhile, the last vestiges of loyal snatchlings attacked from all sides. The battle resumed. Benjamiah took out one with a drowsi-powder sphere. Mea, Elizabella, and Silas closed in upon Bo and his monstrous poppet. Emba, Griffyn, and Hope sized it up, while Bo bolted in a bloodthirsty blur—sword raised—toward Mea.

Silas intervened with his cutlass, but Bo was far stronger and utterly savage. His sword fell like a hammer upon Silas's parries; he staggered backward. Elizabella and Mea tried to bring Bo down with their slingshots, but he was too quick and too determined to kill them all. Meanwhile, his poppet, jaws snapping and tusks thrusting, was making short work of their poppets.

Silas tripped, cutlass clattering. Bo's poppet scraped Emba's side with its tusks, swiped Hope the eagle down from the air, clamped its jaws round Griffyn, and threw the lion across the bridge. Bo gave a furious shriek, raised his blade, and charged at Mea.

Benjamiah crashed into him, wrestling him sideways. Bo was far bigger and stronger, but Benjamiah held on, arms wrapped round Bo's midriff, breathing in the rancid smell of dust and bone as Bo screamed and tried to free himself. Benjamiah fell. Bo raised his sword, meaning to plunge it through Benjamiah.

Then Nuisance came. Except Nuisance was cast as a spell nobody but Benjamiah had seen. Nuisance was a wolf and she was magnificent: black fur, tinged with red around the throat and the paws, white buttons for eyes. Benjamiah had practiced this spell in secret, knowing Elizabella would disapprove. And he'd mastered it.

Nuisance pounced upon Bo, sending his sword cartwheeling through the air. While Bo struggled with the wolf, a winded Benjamiah pushed the great bone sword over the edge of the bridge and into the depths below.

With a guttural howl, Bo's poppet attacked. Nuisance backed away, dodging its tusks. The wolves circled one another, while a crazed Bo dragged himself up, upper arm bloodied where Nuisance's jaws had fallen. Emba the bear, Griffyn the lion, and Hope the eagle joined Nuisance, eyeing up Bo's wolf.

"I'll kill every one of you!" screamed Bo, spittle flying from his witchstone mask.

His rheumy, seaweed eyes were poisoned with total, annihilating hatred.

"No, you won't," came a voice.

It was a snatchling who'd said it. The only snatchlings still standing had ceased fighting the children and now watched Bo and his poppet, all alone upon the bridge. Some even had their crossbows trained on the king of the Witch Wood. Bo's hold over them had been broken.

"Kill them!" he shrieked. "Shoot them! I want their heads. Kill them all!"

But nobody followed Bo's orders. The snatchlings and the freed children all stared, watching as Bo spun frantically, spitting and cursing, casting in every direction for allies. He found none. Though his poppet howled and snarled, Nuisance, Emba, Griffyn, and Hope presented a formidable front. Bo had lost.

"It's over, Bo," said Benjamiah. "Give up. We won't hurt you. We're going to end all of this and free the snatchlings, including you. You don't have to be this anymore."

Bo backed off, gibbering and snorting with incomprehensible fury, before bursting into hysterical, ashy laughter. He laughed and laughed, edging unsteadily backward along the bridge. Elizabella made a move to chase him, but Mea stopped her.

"No," she said. "Let him go. He'll kill or be killed. It's over now."

With Bo gone, silence fell, broken only by the disappointed whining of the unfed river wolves. Then, quite spontaneously, a jubilant roar rose from the crowd of victorious children, engulfing the Witch Wood.

EIGHTEEN
WITH THE TOWER ON THE HILL

> It is said that the great witchstone bird took Agatha far across Wreathenwold where she found a lonely tower upon a snowy hill. Here she lived a simple, solitary life—with the witchstone tree standing tall and beautiful in her courtyard.
> —*The Book of Barely Believable Stories*,
> Mildred Fogge

IN A LONG, LIMPING LINE, the children snaked through the dark wilderness in search of civilization. Poppets were ignited to chase back the shadows. Those who were injured—those with broken bones, crossbow wounds or bites and scratches—were helped by others. At the head of the column was Benjamiah Creek, Elizabella beside him. Silas and Mea were a few steps behind, silent but inseparable.

"Nice wolf," mused Elizabella.

Benjamiah grinned, but felt his ears prickle with heat. It wasn't impossible that Elizabella was about to tell him off.

"Would you care to explain yourself?" she said teasingly.

"Just some extracurricular studying," replied Benjamiah, a picture of innocence.

Elizabella gave a "hmph" but nothing more. Both of them held their flaming poppets, the world around them a tangle of brambles and wheeling shadow.

"Well, I've learned my lesson," said Elizabella.

"What do you mean?"

"*Never* underestimate Benjamiah Creek," she said. "It's incredible you can do that already. A *wolf*..."

Now Benjamiah was hit by a full blush, grateful the darkness hid it. Joy swarmed in his chest and manifested itself in a huge smile—one that made his jaw ache, where he'd taken more than one blow during the fighting.

The wilderness began to recede. They climbed a slope, then crossed a rock bridge, then up a rise of mossy steps and through an archway. Benjamiah led the procession of children and snatchlings to a cobbled town square, the same one Benjamiah, Elizabella, and Silas had passed through the previous morning.

Sunrise was on the way, amber gathering at the tops of houses. A scruffy boy in a flat cap, extinguishing the square's gas lamps, spotted the rabble of children. Soon residents flooded out to investigate the bedraggled mass. A pair of middle-aged women—Benjamiah learned later they were bakers—took charge of the situation.

Benjamiah explained that these were the lost children of Wreathenwold, though he left out most of the details—neglecting to get into the Witch Wood, and the snatchlings, and Manfred Tarr. The bakers, Miss Puff and Miss Lattice, were skeptical, but roused the little community into action. Soon blankets were being wrapped round shoulders, and treacle tea and opple pastries distributed. The local physician tended to injured children while the resident apothecary dispensed balms and remedies.

The snatchlings hung back, unsure of their place. Though the residents eyed them warily and whispered about their frightening appearance, Mea ensured they were given everything they needed.

"We're going to be set free," she said to them.

"How?" croaked one, a tiny skeletal boy dressed in a shredded tunic and breeches.

Mea looked to Benjamiah, who lingered nearby.

"We're going to find Agatha Drake," said Benjamiah. "We'll do everything we can to end this."

Nearby, Elizabella crouched with her mouth in a tight line, helping bandage a small girl's hand. When she was finished, she approached Benjamiah.

"We need to go now if we have any chance," she whispered. "Midsommer is almost over. And who knows how far we have to travel?"

"Are you going to leave us?" said a voice.

Benjamiah turned. It was the pigtailed girl from the battle. Though her eyes were thinned angrily, her voice betrayed fear.

"What's your name?" said Benjamiah.

"Claris," she said. "Claris Songwood."

"Where do you live?"

Claris described her street: windy and dry, pleasant and ordinary, a street that could be a thousand different streets in Wreathenwold.

"Is there anything distinctive about it?" asked Benjamiah.

Claris thought for a moment, then said, "The Forty-Third House of the Hanged Men is on the corner. Does that help?"

Benjamiah and Elizabella traded a smile. *That* Ariadne could find.

"We'll be able to get you home," said Benjamiah. "I promise. It might take a bit of time, but it can be done."

"And we'll do it."

It was Silas, Mea at his side.

"It sounds like the work of a Mapmaker to me," added Silas importantly, puffing out his chest.

Mea covered her mouth to suppress a giggle.

"*True* work," said Silas. Then, looking at Ariadne, coiled sleepily on Benjamiah's flat cap, he said, "If you'll help us, that is."

Ariadne must have nodded, for Silas gave a relieved smile.

"First, though," said Mea, "we have to finish Agatha's trials."

Benjamiah watched the purple moths circling frantically above. Did they have time? More children stared at him, wide-eyed and hungry for answers. Many of them were swaddled in blankets, bandaged and stitched, in some cases propped on crude crutches.

"We'll get you all home," announced Benjamiah. "For now, we need you to wait here. The residents have said they'll put you up and keep you safe. Is that okay?"

A frightened murmur traveled through the crowd.

Before Benjamiah could say another word, the magical moths suddenly frenzied. They speared across the square and into an alleyway between Puff & Lattice Bakery and a lopsided cobbler's. Benjamiah gestured surreptitiously to the others and they extricated themselves from the clustered children, racing after him.

The alleyway smelled of churned butter, warm sweet-dough, and treated leather. The moths dazzled and swirled round a stone wall at the end. When Benjamiah drew closer, he understood why.

There was a slash in the stone, much like the one that had transported them to the Grand Masquerade, large enough for the children to climb through. Within was only an empty blackness, a cuttingly cold wind blowing out.

"Agatha's helping us," said Benjamiah.

Elizabella let out a grateful sigh. Benjamiah turned to Mea and Silas.

"You two should wait with the others," he said. "You've been through so much because of me already. And if we all . . . If none of us make it back, they'll never get home."

"We're all making it back," said Mea. "I'm coming."

"Me too," said Silas.

There was no use arguing. Elizabella gave Benjamiah a tight nod. Still, it felt too reckless when all the children they'd rescued needed help getting home. Benjamiah turned to Ariadne, now wide awake on Silas's shoulder.

"Ariadne? If we don't make it, we need you to come back here and get every child home. Can you do that?"

Solemnly, the thread nodded.

Benjamiah took a deep breath, readied himself, then led the way—climbing into the black slash toward more certain danger.

As before, it was a tight passageway of brutish rock, desperately dark. The wind blowing from ahead was Arctic cold, lancing through Benjamiah and plunging straight to his bones. Only the ragged breathing of his friends kept

Benjamiah's courage up. Finally, after another twist, an exit filled with whitish light appeared.

Scrabbling out, they found themselves on a steep hill, a freezing, smoky wind blowing from above. Snow covered everything, the sky a maelstrom of falling flakes and curdled cloud. A forest of naked bonewoods grew crookedly upon the slope, spreading far into a swirling tundra. At the top of the hill, no more than a silhouette amid the blizzard, was a small, circular tower.

"Benjamiah, do you see that . . . ?" said a shivering Elizabella, pointing through the snowstorm.

His attention had been absorbed by the tower, but now he spotted something vast and incredible dwarfing it. Surpassing the tower, branches splayed high across the sky, was the grandest and most majestic tree Benjamiah had ever seen. It could only be the witchstone tree. Even from a distance, he could make out the chalky-white branches and the strands of fluorescent violet.

"This must mean . . . ," he said, before trailing off.

Everybody understood. This had to be Agatha Drake's tower. Was this the setting of Benjamiah's final trial?

The cold bit. The snow whipped. Benjamiah wrapped his arms across his torso, the snow stacked higher than his ankles. Already his hair was slicked to his forehead.

"Let's go," said Elizabella.

They waded through the snow, battling up the hill

toward the tower and the magnificent, looming tree. They passed a small, hardy orchard of smokeberry trees, and a covered well. There was a log shed, an axe wedged in a stump.

When they reached the foot of the tower—sopping wet—the wooden door creaked open.

Silhouetted in the doorway was a woman of quite incredible height, even in spite of the way she hunched over a cane. Benjamiah froze, the others bumping into him. Nobody dared move.

"Come inside, Benjamiah Creek," she called through the snow. "You have traveled all this way."

Nerves squirmed in the pit of Benjamiah's stomach. The woman's voice was from another time: something in the accent and the stresses, the weathered and husky tones. He remembered it, as he remembered the silhouette. She'd appeared in the mirror of Mum's flat. Her voice had flowed from the whisperwicks in Farthing Town. Nudged by Elizabella, Benjamiah found himself moving again, finally close enough to look upon the face of Agatha Drake.

She had a long face and faded red hair that fell to her waist. Most striking was her right eye, which was entirely clockwork—built into the socket was a network of tiny cogs surrounding a false eye of electric blue. Her other eye was likewise blue but real, blanched and watery. She looked old by Benjamiah's standards, but not the many hundreds of years she should have showed. Her skin was deathly white, her veins an unearthly purple. There was something quite mesmerizing and disorienting about her; the air around her seemed to flicker and coil.

She wore a thick fur coat and large lumberjack boots. A poppet hung at her hip, a shabby doll of pale purple with black stones for eyes.

"Come in," she said, turning away. "Before you all freeze to death."

With the help of her cane, she limped inside. The children followed. They crossed Agatha's threshold, stepping mercifully out of the snow. The room was wide and circular, lit by a fire in an enormous hearth and a few weak oil lamps.

"Close the door behind you, young lady," Agatha said to Mea.

Mea did as she was told. Agatha limped her way to a larder. Benjamiah appraised the rest of the room. There was a stove, a small dining table with one chair, entire bookshelves crammed with leathery volumes. Surrounding a basin were myriad jars of herbs, seeds, and leaves. There was also a carpentry bench piled with tools and smothered in sawdust.

"Sit by the fire," she said in her raspy voice. "You'll catch a chill."

The four of them did as they were told, feeling particularly small beside the mighty hearth. They perched on stools, leaving the vast armchair for Agatha. Out of the window Benjamiah could see the tip of a witchstone branch, its violet seams especially vibrant amid the murky snowstorm.

"Here," said Agatha, making Benjamiah jump.

It was a pitcher and some tumblers. Benjamiah sniffed it—smokeberry juice.

"Drink up," she said. "Freshly made this morning."

Was it a test? Elizabella didn't think so, shrugging and pouring everybody a drink. After one sip, Benjamiah couldn't resist more—it was sweet and ripe.

Agatha lowered herself into the armchair with a grunt. She wheezed. Her clockwork eye ticked, though it was a higher pitched and less threatening sound than the thick, clunking tick of her snatchlings.

"Is this the final trial?" said Benjamiah.

Agatha's gaze had been buried in the fire. It took her a moment to look at Benjamiah.

"No, Benjamiah," she said. "It isn't."

"But we only did four," said Elizabella.

"You did five," said Agatha. "When you went to save your friend. Not the fifth trial that was meant for you, but the one that was right—and one far more difficult than I would have devised."

Her eyes were on Mea—one ancient and rheumy, the

other electric and unblinking. Mea fidgeted nervously. Benjamiah's hand drifted absently to the witchstone ringed round his eye. Was it really over? Would it really be coming off?

"So it's all true?" asked Mea meekly. "The story Mildred Fogge wrote, I mean. . . ."

Agatha smiled. "It had been through some changes by the time Mildred wrote it," she replied. "People telling it in taverns and around hearths. Traveling bards. People writing down their own versions, carrying it through time. What really happened was messy, while Mildred's version is neat and tidy. What happened had no real point, but Mildred gave it one, I suppose. In spirit, though, the story is not false.

"I wanted a simple life, my little house in the woods, with the witchstone tree—my family has protected people from it for thousands of years. It has always been a terribly dangerous thing. And it has always wanted to grow. I was weak, wanting to help the children. Every time they failed me, the witchstone grasped me a little tighter. It took hold of me, and eventually, after Bo, I was lost. That set in motion the trials. The witchstone used me. Every Midsommer, I would come to a few of the children who chanted in the mirror. They would play the game. Some succeeded, but most did not. As you know, young lady."

This was said to Mea whose eyes were big and fearful.

"Though you don't remember it," said Agatha, "we have met before. You called upon me. I came. You failed and the witchstone never left your face."

"S-so you know . . . you know who I am?" stammered Mea.

"I do," said Agatha, her voice low and husky. "I will not tell you, though. That's not my place. You will know for yourself."

"What do you mean?" said Elizabella.

"This is the night I die."

The children stared gravely, unsure what to say. The fire in the great hearth crackled and spouted embers.

"We must burn the witchstone tree," said Agatha Drake.

Benjamiah was stunned. Seeing the majestic tree outside, it felt like an act of enormous gravity and almost sacrilege.

"That will free the snatchlings?" he asked.

Agatha nodded. "All the witchstone will die with the tree. I shall die with it. I know what I did to you, young lady. You and all the children. To Bo, too. Though the tree remains coiled round my soul, it cannot stop me. Our time is up—mine and the tree's."

Anxiety flared painfully in Benjamiah's stomach as he next spoke.

"My mum called upon you," he said.

Agatha nodded again. "I remember her clearly. You look like her. That's why the witchstone fits so well upon your eye. She was an orphan, lost in the labyrinth. At Midsommer, she called upon me, told me what she wanted. I reached out of the mirror and gave her the witchstone you wear now. But she never wore it."

Benjamiah felt suddenly light-headed and dizzy.

"What did she want?" he finally managed to ask.

Agatha took an age to answer, her clockwork eye ticking and unblinking. Benjamiah's heart was a hound in pursuit of a hare.

"She wanted to know where she belonged," replied Agatha at last. "A request, I think, you might have made yourself had it been you calling upon me now."

Unexpectedly, Benjamiah felt tears prickle in the corner of his eyes. Elizabella's hand slipped into his. Somehow she always knew.

"And what would you have shown her?"

"Nothing," said Agatha. "I would only have told her what I would tell you now. That belonging is not a question of place. Belonging is comfort. Belonging is freedom. Belonging is not about one house or another, or being with one person or another, or even one world or another. It is the safety to be yourself—to safely need and be needed. Eyla Creek found her answer without me, in another world entirely. She found you. And you have had it all along, young man, in this world and the last. You have it with your friends here. You have it with your family. Treasure it—it is a most blessed thing."

Benjamiah sniffed, sweeping a tear from his cheek. Elizabella squeezed his hand tighter and Silas patted him on the back.

"I will tell you one more thing, Benjamiah Creek," said Agatha. "A terrible darkness lies ahead for Wreathenwold. There is a reason this world will not let you and your doll go. Your part will be a crucial one in the struggle to come."

Benjamiah's heart gathered pace. She could only mean Manfred and the Widow. Nuisance squeaked encouragement from his breast pocket. Deep down, he supposed he already knew he had a bigger part to play in the coming battle. Before he could respond, Agatha levered forward, reached out, and touched the witchstone looping his eye. Benjamiah felt his skin prickle, heard the air sing, before the witchstone slipped from his eye socket and fell into his lap. Relief flooded him. The skin felt strangely soft, as though a plaster cast had been cut away.

"I have something for you, too, Elizabella Cotton," said Agatha. "On the mantelpiece there."

With a crooked smile, Elizabella hopped up and brought down a square, dusty box.

"What is it?" she said, eyes narrowed.

"Look inside."

It snapped open, coughing up a puff of dust. Elizabella's eyes ballooned and she gasped. "Is this *real*?"

Agatha nodded, smiling. Benjamiah, Silas, and Mea stood and peered inside. Sitting on a tiny little cushion was a brooch, the stone comprised of the most astonishing red, blue, and yellow strands.

"They called them kaleidostones in my day," said Agatha. "They are rather rare and worth a small fortune. Enough, I would think, to buy back a bookshop."

Elizabella's eyes glistened as she lifted the brooch, her hand trembling.

"Thank you," was all she could manage.

"And finally our Mapmaker," said Agatha, "whose mission is the gravest and most vital of all. Wreathenwold will never be free until it is mapped. You know this, don't you, Silas Weaver?"

Silas nodded, swallowing awkwardly.

"There is a quill on my workbench," said Agatha. "Bring it here."

Silas shuffled off and returned, quill in hand. Its tip was dry and pointed, the feather large and silkily silver.

"This is a griffin feather," said Agatha. "The griffins are all gone now, but in ancient times its feathers were used as a remedy for blindness. A map drawn with this quill will not change. But it is only a quill, young man. It cannot protect the Mapmakers against everything else that will seek to stop you. However, it is a start. Use it to revive the spirit of your disbanded company. The Mapmakers need neither premises nor permission to succeed. And you *must* succeed, young man."

Silas was transfixed by the quill, stroking the feather with a shaking finger.

"We will not fail, Ms. Drake," he said formally.

Agatha mustered one final, tired smile.

"I won't ask for forgiveness," she said, climbing out of her chair with a chorus of groans and creaks. "I am beyond it. I ask only one more thing of you all. For too long, I have been a servant of that wicked tree, my soul snared among its roots. But that must end and there is only one way out—a path I have been too cowardly to walk until now. Until I watched the four of you fighting for goodness, for true things. You have given me the courage I have lacked for hundreds of years. Will you help me burn the tree?"

This was to be Mea's gift. She looked so afraid, so close to freedom that she dared not hope. Elizabella squeezed her arm and Benjamiah nodded at Agatha.

Agatha led the way through the snow, carving a trench toward the witchstone tree with her huge boots. Above them, the vast, thrusting branches of the tree were spread. Benjamiah knew a lot about trees and this was taller than anything back home, including the coastal redwoods of California. Its trunk was monolithic, wider than a house.

Suddenly the idea of seeing it aflame filled Benjamiah with dread—to torch something so mighty felt frightening and sinful.

Then Benjamiah saw Mea, being held by Elizabella as they walked. Mea and all the snatchlings deserved freedom—to know who they were.

Agatha reached the tree. The children gave her a moment alone, in which she laid her hands upon the trunk and whispered words they never heard. There was a haunting and sorrowful finality to it, the way her fingers found comfort in the wood, the way her posture seemed to slacken further when it was over.

"Would one of you bring some wood from the shed?"

Inside a hollow at the heart of the trunk, a pyre was built—shielded from the snow and wind. Then Agatha ignited her poppet, reached inside, and lit the stack of wood in the belly of the tree.

It took time for the fire to grow. For a while, it looked rather like a furnace built into the trunk, smoke pouring out. Then the flames began to take hold of the witchstone tree itself, spreading irreversibly upward through its heart. Before long, most of the tree was ablaze above them, a terrifying colossus of flame and smoke amid the snow.

Agatha, who never took her eyes from the burning tree, moved them all to a safer spot. Mea stood alone, rubbing her temples. Benjamiah couldn't possibly imagine what she was going through. In a matter of moments, the witch-stone would fall from her face and she'd be reunited with all the memories it had stolen from her. She was about to meet herself for the first time in an age.

Benjamiah was still watching Mea when Bo came storming out of the blizzard.

With the sickening, delirious slowness of a nightmare, Benjamiah saw Bo's poppet—cast as the tusked wolf—ambush Mea. Her bewildered scream made the others look too. But it was too late. The wolf had Mea pinned to the ground and Bo, staggering through the snow, had snatched up Mea's poppet from her hip. The doll was scrunched in his glove.

Benjamiah, Elizabella, and Silas lurched forward. Bo howled, laughed, and showed them something in his other hand. It was a tiny spike of bone. He brought it toward the breast of Mea's poppet and held it there. A threat to make them all stop—if he plunged it through the doll's heart, Mea would die.

"No!" screamed Elizabella.

Above them, the inferno took hold. Branches bent and fell with violent cracks. The heat was searing, the snow awash with fiery light. Bo's mask and his crown of bones glowed, flame-colored, as did his frenzied eyes.

Agatha came limping.

"Bo!" she shouted. "Please! It's over now. It's all over. I

am so sorry for everything. I did this to you. Please, let her go. Let her be free. And yourself!"

"Free?" screamed Bo. "I don't want to be *free*. I had a family and it's gone. I had *power* and it's gone. I had everything and it's gone! All because of *this traitor*!"

Drool sprayed from his mouth as he finished. Mea was whimpering, Bo's wolf snarling to keep her pinned. Benjamiah was dazed, suffocated, and paralyzed. Unable to move, unable to do a thing.

"I said I would kill her and I will!" howled Bo.

He plunged the bone spike through the heart of Mea's doll. Benjamiah thought he might have seen Mea flop lifelessly beneath Bo's poppet, but he couldn't be sure; as in the depths of a nightmare, everything swam in a flood of darkness and disembodying horror and screams, as fire burned, as snow fell, as the entire world was cut loose from the bonds that held it together and fell terribly apart.

NINETEEN
WITH THE KEY TO THE DOOR

Ciaen the Lesser's ugly pursuit of power proved to be his unraveling, for though the glorious souls of children might briefly be turned to witchcraft, there can be no lasting mastery over them. They are much too pure and colorful to be truly contained.

—*The Book of Barely Believable Stories*,
Mildred Fogge

THE SCREAMS WENT ON. Benjamiah never heard them end. His ears were filled with an endless, devastating ringing as he slumped into the snow. He felt ripped in half. The fire had now burned through the very core of the witchstone tree and it had begun to crumble, folding downward into ruin.

Now Bo was screaming. He'd dropped Mea's poppet and clamped his hands over his witchstone mask. It had started to disintegrate. Fissures had struck across it. Though Bo tried to hold it in place, it was over. The curse had ended and Bo's mask fell piece by piece as the snatchling king howled. Benjamiah glimpsed the face beneath it: long and pointed and slanted, the bloodshot, seaweed-colored eyes.

Elizabella went for Bo—bolted toward him with, Benjamiah knew, murder on her mind. Agatha stopped her, her willowy arms snaring, with some difficulty, the screaming and spitting Elizabella. While they struggled, Bo ran, hands still running despairingly all over his naked face. He disappeared beyond the throw of the firelight, into the snowy forest.

Accordingly, Agatha herself was left to absorb Elizabella's mindless fury. Elizabella grabbed fistfuls of her coat and hammered her hands against Agatha's midriff, screaming names, and at one time, before Agatha finally stilled her, trying to bite the woman.

"You did this! You did this!" she shrieked over and over, before dissolving into hysterical sobs.

Silas was crouched over Mea. Benjamiah cried and cried, staggering toward them. This was a nightmare from which he couldn't wake. Grief had ripped a hole in his center and he'd never be whole again.

Mea was perfectly still in the snow, her head propped on Silas's thigh. Her witchstone mask had also cracked and fallen away. For the first time, in the most unimaginably cruel of scenarios, Benjamiah looked upon Mea's real face. She was olive-skinned, with a wide mouth and a button nose and sharp cheekbones. Her eyes were closed.

Elizabella had torn herself from Agatha, dropping to her knees beside Mea. Benjamiah turned to the Witch of Midsommer.

"You have to save her," he begged.

Agatha tried to steady herself on her cane, failed, and rocked backward onto the snowy slope. Tears curled from her living eye.

"It is beyond my power," she said, her voice tiny.

"You have to," said Benjamiah. "You have to, you have to, you have to!"

Agatha only shook her head. "If anybody has the power, it's you," she said.

Benjamiah wondered if he'd misheard. Eyes clotted with tears, he stared desperately at Agatha.

"All of you," she said huskily. "I . . . I don't know, but maybe."

"What do you mean?" demanded a frenzied Elizabella.

Agatha looked at Benjamiah and in that moment something in the chaos of his mind was brought into relief. Something surely hopeless and meaningless and yet which Benjamiah threw his arms round like careering driftwood in a furious river.

"*Magic forged at Midsommer is the strongest and truest*

of all magic—both fair and foul," Benjamiah heard himself saying.

Elizabella was moon-eyed, absolutely lost. Still Silas had not moved. Benjamiah wondered if he ever would.

"But . . . but . . . ," stammered Benjamiah, grasping for how it might help. "It's . . . How do we . . ."

"Magic comes in many forms," said Agatha, staring at Mea. "You forged something this Midsommer, the four of you. Something formidable. Something for the ages. Call upon it now. Call upon Midsommer."

Elizabella stared, baffled, her eyes rimmed with red. Finally, Silas looked up and Benjamiah felt his heart break all over again: there was nothing left of him.

"We forged something this Midsommer," said Benjamiah to the others. "We became friends. You remember Mea's favorite story? 'Bolly Pondwater'? How all the good memories saved her? Maybe that . . . Think about the happy memories now."

Saying it aloud felt absurd, a symptom of the singular foolishness that comes with refusing to accept the inevitability of death. But Elizabella and Silas did as they were told, closing their teary eyes and clasping Mea's hands. Benjamiah grasped Mea's shoulder, shut his own eyes, and begged silently for Midsommer to hear them.

Pictures clamored, each rising with a stab of pain. Mea saving them when the snatchlings had them cornered in the woods, dashing drowsipowder upon their abductors' faces. The way Mea giggled so wildly and joyfully when she first tried a wyrm's egg. Her uncontrolled excitement as she recited the Pyrate Queene story before the first trial, the way she devoured treacle opples as though her life depended on them.

"Please . . . ," said Benjamiah, tears creeping down his cheeks.

Mea being given a name by Elizabella as though it were a tremendous gift. Mea, so broken by Bo, wondering if the others were really her friends. The thoughtfulness of the Midsommer gift she bought Elizabella and how it brought her such pleasure to see Elizabella's joy. Her telling them that this Midsommer had been the best time of her life before she drew the snatchlings away so they could escape.

"Please . . . ," croaked Silas.

"Please," echoed Benjamiah.

Mea: determined and resilient and brave, funny and clumsy, kindhearted and true, and deserving of everything good and more. Mea, their friend. Benjamiah felt the pain of it in his throat, in the center of his chest, an ugly and noisy grief plaguing his body.

Please, begged Benjamiah. *Please.*

A shiver ran down his neck. The hairs on his arms stood up. He pictured Mea gazing at the copy of Mildred Fogge's book that Silas had gifted her, the way she adored it so fully and purely, the way those stories were her window of light in a landscape of gloom. The way their magic formed a trail of hope for her, however unlikely, toward escaping Bo's clutches and setting herself free.

"*Please,*" whispered Elizabella.

Again something shivered the length of Benjamiah's body. The air whispered about him, though whether a trick of the wind and snow he had no way of knowing. Opening his eyes, he saw the others gripping Mea's hands so tightly, tears tumbling, heads bowed in silent prayer. About them all, the air had turned to shivering and curling, an almost imperceptible trembling of the atmosphere itself.

Then, through the sky that was all murk and snow, light bloomed. Though the clouds did not part, it was as though the Midsommer sun beyond them had flared magnificently, dyeing the sky a luminescent silver, pouring a smoky and dazzling brightness over the clustered children. The air around Mea churned and twisted, the light warm upon them all, Elizabella and Silas crying and whispering for Midsommer to please hear them.

And it did.

Mea gasped.

Benjamiah had never experienced a moment like it. A wondrous joy went through him like an explosion as Mea's eyes flew open and she sucked in air. Silas cried out and Elizabella fell back and Benjamiah fell forward onto Mea, sobbing into her shoulder as she breathed in and out, in and out—baffled and soaked but *alive*.

"What happened?" she said.

None of them could speak. They piled upon Mea, crying now with a relief that was dazed and euphoric.

"Would somebody tell me what's going on?" said Mea, her voice muffled by Elizabella's midriff.

Benjamiah, Elizabella, and Silas drew back. Every eye was red and swollen. Benjamiah's throat ached with the force of crying. Mea's hair was soaked by the snow, her eyes flicking between them all as though they were mad. She eased herself into a sitting position. It was then that her hand rose trembling to her face and she realized the mask was gone.

Her eyes bubbled with shock, her fingers testing the nose and cheeks and mouth that had been imprisoned for so long.

"Is it . . . Is it . . . ," she babbled.

"It's over," said Benjamiah thickly, gesturing to the smoking remains of the witchstone tree. "You're free."

Mea breathed sharp and wild, still feeling her face. Her mouth parted and her eyes swam with tears.

"Mea?" said Elizabella gently. "Do you remember who you are now?"

Benjamiah's chest tightened. Everything was quiet, save the sighing wind. Mea cried out abruptly and buried her face in her hands. Benjamiah's heart sank, but then Mea nodded, face still clasped in her hands. She sniffed through her fingers.

Before another question could be asked, she clambered gingerly to her feet and found the bag she'd dropped when Bo's wolf pounced on her. Did she remember any of that, Benjamiah wondered? Did she have any notion of what had just happened?

Rifling through her bag, Mea withdrew her copy of *The Book of Barely Believable Stories*. Sniffing back more tears, she opened it to Mildred's dedication at the front:

> *To my beautiful daughter, Rosa,*
> *claimed by the cruel coils of this labyrinth.*
> *These stories are yours; I pray they reach you.*

Benjamiah gaped, openmouthed. The pieces fitted together then, the reason Mildred Fogge's stories meant so much to Mea, though Mea herself hadn't even known why. It explained why they kept Mea sane and young and hopeful, when all the other snatchlings were so lost. Because they'd been written by her mother.

"My name is Rosa Fogge," she said, clutching the book to her chest. "Mum used to tell me these stories before bed. I think . . . I think that's why she wrote them, after I was lost. As a way to still reach me, wherever I was in the labyrinth."

Something shifted behind Benjamiah. He'd almost forgotten Agatha was still there. Looking up, Benjamiah was shocked. She had aged a hundred years in a few minutes, her skin wrinkled and her real eye blotted with white, her arms thinner and her cheekbones sharper and her hair gray.

"I am so sorry, my girl," she croaked. "So sorry."

Mea—or Rosa—seemed not to hear her. She cradled the book and stared down into the snow. What must it have felt like for her, Benjamiah wondered, to reconcile so suddenly with all her memories, her life, her name?

Elizabella hugged her. Silas hovered nearby, his eyes a bloodshot mess, apparently unwilling to stray more than three feet from her side.

"Benjamiah?" croaked Agatha. "I wonder if you'd be kind enough to help me back inside?"

She was growing more frail by the minute. Benjamiah and Elizabella helped her hobble up through the snow, into the tower, and back in her armchair. Silas and Mea trailed behind, speaking in whispers—Silas seemed to be comforting her.

From her armchair, Agatha let her head fall back with an anguished sigh. She seemed half-blind now, a tremor taken root in her hand.

"Can we do anything?" said Benjamiah.

"You have done everything," she wheezed. "You have

ended all the horror I could not end alone. My time is up. The way you came here remains open."

Though Agatha had indeed caused so much untold misery, Benjamiah couldn't help feeling sadness as he watched her career toward death. He glanced at Elizabella, then over to Silas and Mea.

"Could you open another path for me?" asked Benjamiah.

Agatha tried to lift her head but couldn't, tried to smile but failed.

"To where?" she said.

"The Shrouded Palace," said Benjamiah.

The room was stunned—all except Agatha, who perhaps was not capable of it. Elizabella studied Benjamiah with narrowed eyes.

"Why?" said Agatha.

"It's not over yet," he said. "There's somebody else who needs saving."

"What do you mean?" asked Silas.

"The Minotaur," said Benjamiah. "He's still alive. And Manfred is *keeping him alive*. We overheard that at the Masquerade, didn't we? Manfred is giving the Minotaur an elixir. Why would he do that? It can only mean he needs something from him. And I think I know what it is."

"What?" asked Elizabella.

"Remember what we learned from Edwid's whisperwicks? We—and Manfred—discovered *where* the Widow is. I bet Manfred knows the exact place. But Hansel said that the Widow must be sealed inside it and Manfred can't get to her. Something from the Masquerade also stuck in my mind. Manfred has Grygor from the Company of What Cannot Be Explained scouring the Company archives. It's been nagging me where else I heard about that Company, but now I remember. It was a story from Mildred Fogge—the first one I read—'The Soul Snatcher.' Long ago, a magus stole the souls of children, imprisoned them in his cane, and then used it for dark magic. To bind other people to his will—*or compel them to speak the truth*."

All eyes were on Benjamiah, some narrowed and some wide, some skeptical and some believing.

"Manfred needs a way *in* to wherever the Widow is," he continued. "He needs to break the seal. The Minotaur must know how to do it—he put her in there—but won't tell. Manfred doesn't know how to imprison the souls in his cane, so he has Grygor searching for it. Then he'd have used them to force the Minotaur to tell him. But now we've freed all the children, who knows what Manfred will do next? I have to save the Minotaur."

From the armchair, Agatha watched Benjamiah closely—her clockwork eye looked increasingly large in her sunken skull, whirring bright and eerie.

"I can open a path for you," she said. "If you're sure."

Benjamiah nodded, his stomach knotted. "I am."

"Let's go," said Elizabella.

"I'm going alone," said Benjamiah.

"Then, Benjamiah Creek, you had better kill me dead right now. Because there is nothing else you can do or say that will stop me coming, do you understand that? So what will it be?"

He could hardly remember seeing Elizabella so furious and dangerous—and it was her standard mode for the most part. Despite himself, Benjamiah smiled.

To Silas and Mea, he said, "Not you two, though. Please. Go back to the children. Take Ariadne. We'll come back if we can, but if not then you leave without us. Somebody has to get them home. It's all been for nothing if they remain lost in a strange part of Wreathenwold."

As anticipated, Mea and Silas were outraged, telling him they were coming and there was nothing he could do to stop them. Unlike with Elizabella, however, Benjamiah didn't cave.

"Please?" he said. "It's not that I wouldn't rather you came with me. But we can't leave all those kids stuck there. *Please?*"

When Elizabella nodded solemnly at Mea, it was settled. Benjamiah and Elizabella would go one way, Silas and Mea another. Benjamiah couldn't bring himself to make a moment out of it—to say goodbye with any kind of strength of feeling. Never seeing either of them again was too sad a prospect. The others followed suit, keeping it together, acting as though it were a given they'd shortly be reunited.

Agatha Drake, without even the strength to stand, laced her bony fingers round her poppet. Across the room, Benjamiah saw the aether of the stone wall come to life, shivering and shifting the way he had thought only a magus could achieve. There was a crack, a spatter of stone, a louder smash. A tear zigzagged down the stone wall, a slash of blackness large enough for a child.

Benjamiah swallowed, his throat still sore from crying. He took one final look at Agatha, nodded at Mea and Silas, and set off. Elizabella was right behind him, as she always was.

"Good luck," said Silas.

"Please come back!" called Mea.

Benjamiah and Elizabella climbed through.

Another burrow of sharp stone walls, a coiling blackness that went one way then another, ending in a jagged exit filled with grayish light. Benjamiah climbed out, then helped Elizabella through.

They emerged somewhere Benjamiah both recognized and did not. It was the Minotaur's grand library within the

Shrouded Palace, a great birdcage of a room rising high to a point in the rafters. But all had changed. On their last visit, the library had been opulent and glorious, books curving up to the ceiling, everything gleaming and gilded and palatial.

Now it was a ruin. The books were gone, only a few stray pages and torn leather bindings remaining. All color had leached away; now the bones of the library were black or gray, the air dark and damp, the ground a snarl of wrecked furniture: shafts of timber, the carcass of a fallen chandelier, broken glass and shredded paper. Benjamiah's heart sank to see the beautiful library so destroyed.

There was only a single source of light. Beyond the smashed hulk of a huge bonewood desk, a fire crackled in a makeshift steel pit. Hunched over it was the Minotaur.

He made for a sight no less sorry than the library. He was birdlike-thin, wrapped in a ratty blanket that surely offered no real defense against the punishing cold. Indeed, Benjamiah saw how the old man trembled, craning as close as possible to the dancing flames. When Benjamiah had last met him, the Minotaur had worn a mask. Now that was gone and Benjamiah, by the soft glow of the flames, saw a square head, the skin milky white, split with wrinkles and a tuft of thin gray hair on the crown.

"Hello," said Benjamiah.

The Minotaur turned slowly as though dragged from a

reverie. In a frail voice, peering into the shadows, he said, "Who's there?"

Benjamiah stepped forward, Elizabella at his side. The Minotaur's eyes, filled with firelight, widened and he gasped. "Can that be Benjamiah Creek?"

Benjamiah nodded. The Minotaur sat, stunned, shivering. A smile lifted the corners of his mouth, though even that seemed a struggle.

"Goodness," he said, "however do you manage it? Come closer, my friend. My eyes are not what they used to be. And who might this be with you?"

Elizabella introduced herself with a kind smile. They shook hands—the Minotaur's was all pointy knuckles and liver spots.

"I am glad to see you again," he said. "I rather enjoyed our last conversation. I'm only sorry my situation has somewhat diminished, otherwise I'd fetch you something to drink."

"Manfred," said Benjamiah.

The Minotaur's eyes flashed with fear before he nodded grimly.

"He calls it love," said the Minotaur, "but it is a most abhorrent madness that compels him. He'd have you believe he and Osmeralda are great lovers for the ages. But my mother never loved a thing. Only ruin. In the name of a love that does not exist, he has condemned me here."

"That's why we came," said Elizabella. "We want to help."

"We worked it out," added Benjamiah. "Most of it. He doesn't know how to free her. He planned to use the souls of stolen children to force you to tell him. Don't worry, we found them."

The Minotaur croaked with joy, then regarded Benjamiah as though he were a living miracle.

"You *found* them? And they are well?"

Benjamiah nodded. The Minotaur croaked again, wiping a tear from his eye.

Elizabella said, "We'll get them all home safely. Promise."

"I don't doubt it," said the Minotaur. "What could stand in the way of the two of you? Neither labyrinths nor magi, it would seem."

"We heard he's giving you an elixir to keep you alive," said Benjamiah.

"It's more a poison," said the Minotaur, his voice feathery. "I will live until I divulge the information he wants, which is the location of the key. He will grow more manic, more cruel in his methods. I . . . You know, I'm rather unsure what to do."

The Minotaur tried to laugh, but it was the quiet hysteria of despair. Benjamiah traded a glance with Elizabella. She nodded.

"Tell us where the key is," said Benjamiah. "Then you'll be free. Able to . . ."

A great sadness blew through Benjamiah then, like a sudden stormy wind, preventing him from finishing the sentence. He didn't want the Minotaur to die.

"Out of the question," said the Minotaur, shaking his head as furiously as his frail neck would allow. "He would only turn his attentions to you."

"He'll never know we were here," said Benjamiah. "Can you think of another way to end this? He'll come up with another plan, or otherwise you'll live forever like this. . . ."

"You would really do this for me?" said the Minotaur.

Benjamiah and Elizabella nodded.

"I . . . ," said the Minotaur, before pausing to brush away another tear. "I do not deserve you, Benjamiah and Elizabella."

He took a long look around, taking in the dusty wreckage of his grand library, eyes afire.

"I have lived a long time, you know," he said. "Longer than anybody has a right to live. And yet I am afraid of . . . of what comes next. Will it be dark, do you think?"

Benjamiah felt his eyes heat up with tears yet again. Rather than say a word, he stepped forward and hugged the Minotaur. It caught the old man off-guard, until he finally laced his feeble arms round Benjamiah in return. Benjamiah could hear the Minotaur's heart whispering beneath his ribs.

"I don't know what's next," said Benjamiah. "But if there's a good place to go, you'll be going there. I promise."

To underline the point, Benjamiah took out his fifty-pence piece—the same one he'd brought with him on his last adventure in Wreathenwold—and placed it in the Minotaur's hand. A coin was a promise in Wreathenwold. The Minotaur gripped it, hand shaking.

Behind Benjamiah, he felt a tug and heard a rustle. Elizabella withdrew a book from Benjamiah's bag: *The Book of Barely Believable Stories*. She gave it to the Minotaur.

"For you to read," she said. "You know, afterward. All your books are gone."

"This is my very favorite book!" exclaimed the Minotaur, grasping it tightly. "That's very kind of you. The books were the first thing he took from me. Is there a more hopeless world than one without stories? If so, I am glad I do not have the imagination for it."

When that was done, Benjamiah and Elizabella stood side by side. Benjamiah's eyes and throat were clotted with a grief all too familiar that night. The Minotaur leafed slowly through the book, mumbling happily and nostalgically. Then finally he found the courage to look up.

"You are sure?" he said softly.

The children nodded.

"The Widow is sealed away," said the Minotaur. "A

magical seal requires a magical key. And a keeper of the key. It is this name that Manfred Tarr seeks."

Benjamiah swallowed nervously, finding Elizabella's hand. Their fingers locked.

"Tell us," he said.

After a deep, rattling breath, the Minotaur did so.

"The key-keeper is Bird Song of the Root Folk," he said. "She can be found in the very depths of the Weird Wood."

Silence followed. Then the Minotaur let out a long, relieved sigh, as though poison were draining from his veins.

"It is over, then," he said.

His hands shook, gripping the book in his lap. Benjamiah thought about hugging him again but was frozen in place by a sound from up high.

All three heads swiveled upward, peering through the shadows. Something had moved on the balcony above, Benjamiah felt sure. Just when he had begun to calm down, something—*somebody*—dashed across it. They only heard a nasty giggle, only saw a flash of pink gown and ginger ringlets, but it was enough to send Benjamiah's mind into meltdown.

"Oh no . . . ," groaned the Minotaur. "It's that rotten girl! She's been listening. You have to stop her. You have to . . ."

But he was too feeble to lift himself. Even his voice had little substance. Benjamiah found Elizabella's eyes, saw in them the same cold horror spanning his own chest.

"Gertrid!" she seethed.

"Have to . . . stop her . . . ," breathed the Minotaur. "Forget about me! You *must* stop her, or all of Wreathenwold is in danger. . . ."

Elizabella and Benjamiah ran. Gertrid must have been instructed to spy on the Minotaur. It meant that somewhere on the balcony was a way out. Benjamiah and Elizabella blundered through the wreckage, raced up to the balcony, and found Gertrid's secret opening: a blackened panel that slid in and out of place. Benjamiah's mind was a whirlpool, his ears filled with its rushing.

They raced on. Benjamiah could scarcely believe their surroundings. On their last visit to the Shrouded Palace, all was a ruin save the Minotaur's library; now it was reversed, the rest of the palace restored. The corridors were threads of gleaming black stone, carpets and tapestries of blood-clot purple, opulent chandeliers. There were paintings of glorious color, and fires lit in brackets, and stone sculptures of fabulous hues.

Up ahead, they saw Gertrid—giggling, ringlets bouncing, her violently pink dress flapping as she hared onward. Their pursuit was in vain. They came to a wide flight of marble stairs and Gertrid disappeared up them.

When a breathless Benjamiah and Elizabella followed her, they found themselves in the throne room.

Like the rest of the palace, it was rejuvenated. The walls and dais were rendered in gleaming blackish glass, the domed ceiling inlaid with writhing stone sculptures, a mass of limbs, and howling mouths. Huge stained-glass windows streaked the length of the walls. Tapestries tumbled down the vast height, luxurious purple fabric depicting coils of green vipers.

Up ahead on the dais were the twelve thrones of the last magi set at different heights. Where before they had been half crumbled, now they were rebuilt. Sitting on ten of them were huge figures of black stone, some hooded and some crowned, armed with swords or axes fashioned from shimmering black metal.

In one of the lower thrones sat the relatively smaller figure of Manfred Tarr. A breathless, jubilant Gertrid was panting beside him, her eyes on Benjamiah and Elizabella.

"How wonderfully helpful the two of you continue to be," drawled Manfred.

It echoed through the throne room. Emba snarled. Benjamiah had his hand on Nuisance, hanging from her noose.

"Bird Song of the Weird Wood," said Manfred, rising. "I'd never have thought the old fool would trust Root Folk with something so important. That, I suppose, rather proves him wiser than he looks."

Tall, straight-backed, waxy-skinned. His cane clacked as he strolled down the dais and Gertrid fizzed with excitement. She plonked herself in the throne Manfred had vacated and licked her lips.

"Now I'll get my eye colors," she said, giggling and swinging her legs.

"A deserved prize, my cherub," said Manfred, not taking his eyes from Benjamiah and Elizabella. "You have done well."

"Where's the Viper?" asked Elizabella.

"My wife-to-be has important city business to which she must attend," said Manfred. "You have, I think, just secured her ascension."

"Do you even know what you've done?" Benjamiah shouted to Gertrid. "He wants to bring the Widow back. What do you think that means for you and your mother?"

Gertrid giggled again, still swinging her legs. Manfred smiled as he drew closer, cane clacking. A black flower sat in the crook of his collar. His eyes were inkwells.

"Do not think them so oblivious," said Manfred. "The Murdstones are quite aware of my ambitions. Ours is an arrangement of convenience."

"That's stupid," said Elizabella. "The Widow won't share power."

"What would you know of my darling Osmeralda, Miss Cotton?"

Manfred waved his cane. Behind them, the vast bone-wood doors slammed shut. The boom bored through Benjamiah's midriff. They were trapped.

"You knew too much already," said Manfred, fiddling with the flower at his throat, "but now you *certainly* cannot be allowed to leave. I thank you, not for the first time."

"She never even loved you!" shouted Benjamiah, hating himself the moment he said it.

For the first time, Manfred Tarr was wrong-footed. Something rippled across his face, a twist of the mouth and a flash of the eyes, the rest of him completely still.

"The Minotaur told us," continued Benjamiah. "You love her, but she feels nothing for you. For anybody."

Manfred's colorless lips fixed into a grim smile. He raised his cane and pointed it.

"Your deaths will be lonely and miserable," he said, cold and quiet. "Only your eye colors will survive, for which I believe Miss Murdstone has plans."

"A new dress!" squealed Gertrid, clapping her hands.

Benjamiah and Elizabella moved closer together. There was nowhere to run. Manfred drew closer, looming, his eyes the blackest of depths.

"I did advise you to make our previous meeting the last," he said. "It seems you cannot help yourselves. Now you will pay the ultimate price."

He waved his cane, swinging it round and round as

his eyes swam like droplets of dark blood in water.

Then Benjamiah heard a thunderous splitting sound. Another followed, and another, until the throne room was filled with a cacophony. Then his eyes found the source, though his mind struggled to accept it. The magi statues, ten of them, had risen from their thrones. Gertrid whooped and cheered. Aether shivered and curled round them, their movements oddly liquid despite the black stone. The entire palace seemed to shake. Each of them was ten feet tall, their eyes craters, and armed with mighty weapons.

They came slowly, the ground shuddering. Manfred smiled as his soldiers marched. Benjamiah held Nuisance, but fighting would be a hopeless endeavor. Emba the bear was no more than a speck in comparison, though she roared regardless. Manfred and Gertrid laughed.

Benjamiah and Elizabella backed away, whirling around fruitlessly. There was nowhere to go. The magi came, hooded and crowned and soulless, dragging their glassy, deadly blades.

A splitting sound came from behind Benjamiah, but he dared not turn. Manfred's monsters loomed over them. The nearest, dragging a great axe, cranked it backward. But then they stopped. Beyond the statues, Benjamiah spied Manfred. The magus was perplexed, staring at something behind them.

Benjamiah turned.

Staggering out of a split in the wall, barely able to walk, came Agatha Drake. Her entire weight was folded upon the crook of her cane, which looked on the brink of buckling. Benjamiah had never seen anybody so old. Her face was a collapse of wrinkles, her good eye and mouth almost entirely lost. Only her clockwork eye seemed alive. Otherwise, she was all bones and a fur coat and lumberjack boots.

"Behind me, children," she croaked.

Stunned, Benjamiah had to be dragged by Elizabella. They positioned themselves behind Agatha Drake as she hobbled forth toward the looming magi statues.

"Back, you devils!" she tried to shout.

But there was nothing left of her, neither voice nor body. How she could even move was a wonder to Benjamiah. Behind the statues, Manfred had tucked his cane beneath his arm and clapped his hands together.

"A marvel," he said, smiling. "It will be my honor to kill you, too, Witch of Midsommer."

With a wave of his cane, the statues marched again. Benjamiah watched with horror as they lurched forward to destroy Agatha Drake where she stood.

A feat in itself, Agatha plucked her purple poppet from her hip and dropped it.

What followed, even for Wreathenwold, defied explanation for Benjamiah. The tiny doll exploded outward into a shape so large and so strange that Benjamiah felt he could no longer trust his eyes. The transformation went on and on, the body and neck extending outward endlessly in a flowing river of lilac flesh, assuming a shape so massive that suddenly Manfred's statues were dwarfed.

Agatha had cast a wyrm, a long, wingless dragon with four legs like a giant lizard, a tail that speared into a barbed wrecking ball and a mane around her throat. From where he stood, Benjamiah could feel a devastating heat emanating from her center, a hotness that filled his nostrils and throat. Her movements made everything—Benjamiah included—tremble. Even Manfred looked bewildered. The wyrm formed a barrier between Agatha and the statues, her body armored and snakelike, a snout and rows of teeth like a crocodile's beneath stony eyes.

The wyrm roared. Manfred flinched. The heat was unbearable, as was the way the sheer magnitude of magic seemed to shred the air to ribbons. Gertrid hid behind one of the thrones.

"Run, children," Agatha said over her shoulder.

The statues lurched forward. The wyrm unleashed a torrent of fire so hot and bright Benjamiah was forced to jam his eyes closed. Elizabella was dragging him backward. The throne room was volcanic, the air rippling, smoke flooding. Manfred's statues drove at the wyrm. It smashed one with its tail, closed its jaws round another. But there were too many. One drove its gleaming sword into the wyrm's scaled flank and it reared up with a terrible scream.

Agatha fell to her knees.

"Benjamiah, come *on*!" pleaded Elizabella in his ear.

The wyrm did all it could to slow the march of Manfred's statues as Benjamiah and Elizabella ran toward the slash through which Agatha had arrived. Behind them was fire and stone and death. Manfred howled furiously. The floor beneath Benjamiah's feet ripped upward and became long arms of stone, snatching, smoking with aether. Manfred did not intend to let them leave.

They scrabbled through the swirling debris. Elizabella dived into the slash first, pulling Benjamiah on. The last thing he saw before following was the wyrm die, Agatha Drake falling to the ground beside it. Then they surged through the blackness, away from Manfred's raging, blood-curdling screams.

TWENTY
WITH FOLLYNOOK

To reward the Hero, the Magi Queen said she would grant him a single wish.

"I wish for a bookshop," said the Hero, "in which every book is the story of another bookshop, filled with thousands more stories to be read."

The Queen reproached him. "But you will not live long enough to read them all," she said.

"It is enough that they are there," said the Hero.

—*The Book of Barely Believable Stories*,
Mildred Fogge

THE AUCTIONEER WAS a stiff, nervous type, a freckled young man in a bland, ill-fitting suit and a bow tie that a parent had surely tied for him. He stood awkwardly at his makeshift podium, for a moment unable to quiet the crowd. They were arranged in rows of wooden seats, with more onlookers gathered behind—some perhaps considering a bid, others merely curious.

It was the Hanged Man beside the auctioneer who finally hushed the crowd.

"Enough," he said—not loud, but clear and effective.

Quiet fell.

"Well then—lovely," gibbered the auctioneer, fiddling with his bow tie and dabbing sweat from his forehead with a lace handkerchief. "Here we are, then. Thank you for . . . I mean, thank you to those who have . . . Well, shall we get on with it?"

Perhaps it was his first day. Certainly, his sweaty and fidgety demeanor was already proving irksome to the crowd.

"Well, this is it, as you all know," said the auctioneer, gesturing behind him.

It was Follynook, a tall, narrow bookshop, a face of pale stone and a hat of grayish slate and a beard of black vines. The auction was being held in the bookshop's courtyard, beneath the branches of a crooked bonewood tree. A few plumpkin-shaped paper lanterns still hung from its boughs, rocking in the swift breeze. Above the tree, the sun peered through strips of cloud.

A great chain was lashed across Follynook's front door. A sign declared it had been repossessed by the city. For weeks, potential buyers had eyed the rather idiosyncratic bookshop, appraising it inside and out. Some turned their noses up at its shabbiness; others were rather charmed by it.

Then there were those neighbors loyal to the former inhabitants, who shamed anybody thinking of purchasing and renounced the entire process as a sham.

Still, the auction could not be stopped.

The auctioneer began the bidding at fifty thousand bits. A woman with a nose sharp and hooked enough to gouge out eyes flashed up a spidery hand.

"The bid is fifty thousand bits, do we have fifty-five?"

A round man in a pinstriped suit bid fifty-five thousand. Others joined in as the price soared: a young couple, each with a baby in a sling; a farmer-type man who had brought an actual pitchfork to the auction and smelled powerfully of mudnips; a woman with dark-lidded eyes and tattoos of spiders swarming up her arms. Soon the price was at eighty thousand bits, then eighty-five thousand. The young couple were the first to drop out, then the spider-armed woman. The others seemed intent on winning.

Then a new bidder joined. From the back, a woman with light brown skin, one eye hazel and the other gray, her hair long and dark, raised a hand. Inspector Halfpenny wore her dark blue Inspector's tunic, complete with a navy derby hat and a new clasp holding her black cape in place— the silver head of a viper, fangs bared.

"A new bidder!" called the flustered auctioneer, who seemed rather bereft that the process was not yet over. "The bid is ninety thousand bits. Do we have ninety-five . . . ?"

Up and up the bidding went, passing one hundred thousand bits. It was at this point that Benjamiah began to squirm. Alongside Elizabella and Hansel, he watched the proceedings from a second-floor window across the street. It was the house of an Erbie Rogwash—an old friend of the Cottons whom Hansel had taught to read many years prior.

"Come on," moaned Benjamiah, fingers clawing the windowsill.

Elizabella was perfectly still beside him, her mouth disappeared inward, fraught with worry at the spectacle. They'd sold the kaleidostone for 124,000 bits. Any higher and they were out. Halfpenny was bidding on Hansel's behalf—the Hanged Men overseeing the auction would have surely excluded him. When the farmer bid again, Halfpenny glanced up anxiously toward the window.

"The bid is one hundred and ten thousand. Do we have . . ."

The sharp-nosed woman bid again. Then the round man. Then Halfpenny.

"Do we have one hundred and eighteen thousand? Ah, we do . . ."

The farmer with his pitchfork had bid. The round man spat noisily on the cobbles and waddled off in a huff.

The sharp-nosed woman bid. Then Halfpenny. A quite visceral panic coursed through Benjamiah, twisting like a corkscrew. They were going to lose. . . .

"One hundred and twenty-one thousand is the bid. The bid is . . ."

The woman with the nose kept her hand down, shaking her head ruefully. The farmer wasn't done, though, jabbing his pitchfork upward to signify another bid.

"What does a farmer even want with a bookshop?" hissed Benjamiah.

"It's okay, my boy," said Hansel from behind, dropping a hand on Benjamiah's shoulder. "What will be will be. . . ."

Slowly and horribly, the bids went on. Halfpenny, then the farmer. The jumps between the bids were diminishing, the auctioneer sensing that both final bidders were nearing their maximum. Halfpenny shot another despairing look toward the window as the farmer offered 124,000: all the money they had.

"Going once, going twice . . . ," babbled the auctioneer.

"One hundred and twenty-five!" shouted Halfpenny.

"We don't have that much . . . ," whispered Elizabella in horror.

"The bid is . . . ," continued the auctioneer.

Though he gave the farmer plenty of time, finally the auctioneer declared Halfpenny the winner.

It should have been a celebratory moment, but the atmosphere in the room was tense. The crowd began to disperse as Halfpenny made her way over to the auctioneer. Benjamiah looked up at Hansel, who was pale and exhausted, his hair a mess from having raked his fingers through it incessantly.

"Let's go and see the Inspector," said Hansel.

They'd only just made it back in time.

From the Shrouded Palace, they'd stumbled back across the slope of Agatha's snowy estate, then scrambled through the slash that led to the town square. There they were reunited with Mea and Silas, the rescued children, and the freed snatchlings, whose masks had cracked and fallen and whose memories had flooded back. Every one of them now remembered themself and their former life—though for most their families were long dead.

Once Benjamiah and Elizabella had recovered, a plan was agreed. Ariadne would lead all four of them back to Follynook, before Silas and Mea—and Ariadne with them—would return for the children and get them home one by one. Exactly how long that would take was a complete mystery, but it was work that needed doing and Mea and Silas were ready to do it. Elizabella and Benjamiah would have helped, too, were it not for the business of saving Follynook and, in Benjamiah's case, getting home himself.

The journey back with Mea and Silas was not without its perils. Along the way, the town criers hit the streets of

Wreathenwold, ringing their bells and declaring that the Minotaur had died peacefully in his sleep. Wreathenwold would enter ten days of mourning, after which the Viper would assume rule of Wreathenwold—as ratified by a vote between the Captains of the Honorable Companies, something Benjamiah very much doubted had unfolded fairly.

"Are you okay?" Elizabella had asked Benjamiah when they first heard the news.

Benjamiah nodded, but he wasn't. He carried with him an ache for his lost friend, one he expected would stay with him for some time.

The city changed around them. Respectful black fell like a shawl upon Wreathenwold: black gowns and cravats, black flowers and black ribbons, black flags and wreaths. Not many really mourned the Minotaur in truth; to Wreathenwolders, he would always be a child-eating monster at the center of the maze, the last vestige of an uncivilized age. To Benjamiah's horror, the people seemed to quietly rejoice at the Viper's ascension. That the Minotaur was thought of so poorly, and the Viper so highly, was grossly unfair.

What danger the Viper had posed to Elizabella and Benjamiah had therefore increased significantly. Now she had all the power in the world, and Manfred Tarr very much desired their deaths. The four children traveled cautiously and sensibly back to Follynook, avoiding trouble and attention, filtering away whenever they spotted Hanged Men. They would not be easy for the Viper or Manfred to find. Wreathenwold was still a labyrinth, after all, and Benjamiah had never been more grateful for it.

Before reaching Follynook, they collected Hansel from Ogbo's Rest. They found him outside the manor, smoking his pipe on a tree stump beneath a bonewood tree. Upon seeing them, he squinted and staggered up, seemingly afraid his old eyes were playing tricks. Then he hugged Elizabella, hugged Benjamiah and Silas, and even gave Mea a hug, despite the fact they'd never met.

Benjamiah told Hansel how sorry he was that they'd left again, saying it over and over until Hansel finally quelled him with another hug.

Elizabella showed Hansel the kaleidostone.

"We can get our home back," she said.

Hansel regarded it, the color filling his eyes.

"What a thing . . . ," he said. "But it's hopeless, my dear. The Viper will never let us win. Even if we reclaim Follynook, it isn't safe. She knows where to find you. And, therefore, so does the magus."

Though Benjamiah couldn't fault his logic, Elizabella was steely and unwavering.

"We'll worry about that after," she said. "Follynook is ours. We can't let anybody else have it! I'll do it without you."

That sealed it. Hansel knew better than to doubt his daughter's determination once an idea had taken root, when her eyes flamed and her hands were fastened to her hips. With a defeated yet admiring smile, Hansel nodded.

With that, it was time to say goodbye to Mea and Silas. And, Benjamiah realized with a pang, to Ariadne, too.

Mea engulfed both Benjamiah and Elizabella in a breathless, long-armed clamp, tripping over a rock as she rushed forward. She sobbed into their ears and thanked them for everything intensively and effusively. Teary-eyed, she finally stepped back, somehow stumbling again over the same rock. Though Benjamiah still hadn't quite got used to Mea without the mask, it was a joy to look upon her real face. Mea was still processing everything she'd been through, he knew. She'd likened it to being reunited with a dear friend after decades apart, except the dear friend was herself. For now, she'd chosen to keep the name Mea. Rosa had been her name when she was lost, she said, while Mea had been her name when she was found.

"Well, um, I suppose this is farewell," said Silas stiffly, unsure what to do.

Elizabella smiled and held out her hand and Silas shook it, nodding gravely. Then he and Benjamiah likewise shook hands.

"We'll meet again," said Benjamiah, out of nothing more than sheer hope.

Silas nodded formally, but the same hope was in his eyes—that they would see each other again.

Finally, Benjamiah dipped a finger into the breast pocket of his waistcoat and lifted out Ariadne. She snaked round Benjamiah's finger and met his gaze. Elizabella leaned in close. Nuisance, a nightjar on Benjamiah's shoulder, twittered sadly.

"You have a big job to do now, Ariadne," said Benjamiah. "All those children need to get home, okay?"

Head drooping, Ariadne nodded glumly. Elizabella stroked her neck with a single finger.

"We'll miss you," said Elizabella. "You'll take care of Silas and Mea, won't you?"

Ariadne nodded again. Benjamiah felt a fresh wave of melancholy. Nuisance dropped onto Benjamiah's wrist and embraced Ariadne—as far as a bird and a thread could do so, of course.

"We'll see you again," said Benjamiah. "I know it."

He couldn't know it, of course. As Silas, Mea, and Ariadne departed through the snow, Benjamiah wondered if he'd ever see them again. After all the children were safe, Silas would find Captain Josabella and, alongside Ariadne and his griffin-feather quill, set out to finally map Wreathenwold. Mea was hugely excited to meet Josabella too—as a descendant of Mildred Fogge, she was Mea's family.

When they were gone, and Benjamiah had chased one final tear from the corner of his eye, he looked at Elizabella and Hansel.

"Let's get Follynook back," he said.

They met Halfpenny and the auctioneer inside Follynook. If the auctioneer was surprised by their arrival, Benjamiah never saw it. He had eyes only for the bookshop, which represented so much happiness for him. It was largely undisturbed, though a little messier and dustier: the columns of dark leather-bound books, the rafters festooned with cobwebs, the smell that was at once inky and papery and homely.

Elizabella was mute, thrown off-balance. Benjamiah didn't blame her. He only stood nearby in case she needed him.

"Well, that is . . . all concluded then," gabbled the auctioneer.

He gathered the briefcase that Halfpenny had handed over, the one Hansel had given her earlier, jammed with stacks and stacks of playing cards. Inspector Halfpenny had in her hands a sheaf of parchment. When the auctioneer had hurried away, Halfpenny gave it to Hansel.

"The deed," she said. "It's in my name, as we agreed. But this is your home and always will be. The moment it's safe, we'll transfer it back."

"But your final bid was . . ."

"I brought my own savings along," said the Inspector, "just in case."

"I cannot—" began Hansel.

Halfpenny raised a gloved hand. "There's nothing I'd rather spend it on," she said. "You've lost enough. I'm only glad that Follynook is safe and yours when you're ready to return. For now, though, you and Elizabella will come with me. Unless you're minded to go back to your brother?"

"You know, I'd rather not," said Hansel, with a wink toward Benjamiah. "Just between us, I find him rather odd."

They all laughed, but it was restrained. It was so cruel, Benjamiah thought, that home was no longer safe for Hansel and Elizabella.

"Could we stay?" said Elizabella suddenly. "Just for one night?"

Hansel and Halfpenny exchanged a grave look.

"Yes," said Hansel. "We can and we will. And if the magus should come, he'll have me to deal with."

Though it was a terrifying prospect, Benjamiah couldn't help but beam.

Hansel cooked while Benjamiah and Elizabella tidied the bookshop, Nuisance and Emba hopping and scampering and fluttering about. Dinner was a feast, a tagine of smoking toadstool casserole, crispy phantom leaf drizzled in oil, slices of freshly baked sweetdough, and spicy plumpkin tarts. Hansel and Halfpenny drank poppysyrup while Benjamiah and Elizabella shared a jug of milk punch.

Throughout the meal, they laughed heartily as Benjamiah and Elizabella recounted their journey, the feisty Moggie Blueheart at the bottom of the lake and Mea gorging on treacle opples and Silas trying to charm Ariadne. At other times, the atmosphere turned graver as Elizabella described the Other-Way-Ups and Bo Greaves until finally, as though following the flows and currents of the labyrinth itself, they arrived at the events of the Shrouded Palace: Manfred, Bird Song, the Widow.

By now, Benjamiah had fallen silent, playing with his food, his appetite drained away.

"Are you okay, Benjamiah?" said Hansel gently.

Benjamiah looked up. "Nobody can stop them," he said.

Everybody stared at him. Benjamiah felt his ears burn, but was undeterred.

"Nobody's doing anything," he continued. "Nobody even could. Agatha cast a *dragon* and it barely slowed Manfred down. How can anybody fight him? He'll already be searching for Bird Song. He'll find her and he'll get the key and the Widow will come back. And *nobody's doing anything!*"

The sentence had careered into a high-pitched falsetto, a symptom of profound fright and frustration. For a moment, all was quiet, save Nuisance the sparrow's oblivious chittering from atop the cupboards.

"May I show you something?" said Hansel. "All of you, in fact."

Having set down his napkin, he led them out of the kitchen and into his study—a room Benjamiah had never seen. It was just as messy and buried in books as Benjamiah would have expected. The desk was a cityscape of stacked leather volumes. Propped on one stack was the upturned top hat housing the monkeys-of-the-inkpot. In the center of the desk was a typewriter.

"You might have noticed a couple of these at dear Clover's," said Hansel, patting it. "It looks like a typewriter, but is something different, actually. We call them typeflighters."

Benjamiah wondered if he were being fooled. It looked just like an unloaded typewriter.

"Ah, you are skeptical!" Hansel smiled. "I'd expect nothing less from the brilliant mind of Benjamiah Creek. Allow me to show you. . . ."

Hansel sat. For the first time, Benjamiah noticed a dial above the keys—they displayed a random array of numbers between zero and nine, which, as Hansel demonstrated, could be changed.

"You see here," he said, pointing to a six-digit number in the bottom corner of the typeflighter. "These are the coordinates for *my* typeflighter. With this dial, I can instruct it to send a message to another, no matter how far away. I need only the coordinates. For example..."

He flashed through an address book filled with what seemed to be thousands of names, each with a six-digit number beside it.

"... here are the coordinates for Clover. I shall send him a message. *Dear brother. We would very much love to return to your home and stay there forever. I assume we are welcome? Your brother.*"

Hansel clattered the keys as he typed. Though Benjamiah heard and saw the hammers flash, there was no paper on which the message could be written. Instead, the hammers struck thin air.

A moment passed in which Hansel whistled. Benjamiah and Elizabella swapped a glance—like Benjamiah, she seemed to be wondering if Hansel had lost the plot.

Then, suddenly, a piece of paper rose out of the typeflighter, unfurling from nowhere and imprinted with a message. They all leaned closer and read:

Hansel—I am considering moving.
Will send new address anon. Your brother.

Everybody laughed.

"But what does this have to do with Manfred?" said Benjamiah, wholly unconvinced.

"The Widow's reign was the darkest of times," said Hansel soberly. "But do not think it passed without resistance. Do not think that good people sat idly by while she ruined and murdered and burned our world. It will not be so now, either. It was with typeflighters that resistance was coordinated, that the good soul of Wreathenwold was fortified through the gravest of years. Work has already begun and will continue. Good people are already gathering, ready to fight the darkness again. Words are the best and truest of birds, and already they fly far and wide. I'm a bookseller, after all, and a bookseller has many friends."

To underscore this point, Hansel flicked through his address book again.

"So you're going to fight Manfred Tarr with a typewriter?"

Benjamiah looked skeptical, but Elizabella's face broke into a lopsided smile.

"Oh, Benjamiah, my dear boy," said Hansel, good-humored. "You have never disappointed me before and I ask you not to disappoint me now. Don't tell me that you, Benjamiah Creek, doubt the power of the written word! That you do not harbor in your heart the same reverence for it as I do myself! That you do not see the word for what it is—all the hope and power and light in the world when the darkness gathers! When evil descends, it strikes first and hardest at our words because it fears those more than anything else. Do not break an old man's heart by telling me you feel differently...."

A smile sprawled across Benjamiah's mouth. He didn't feel differently and never would.

Morning meant more goodbyes. Hansel and Elizabella would go with Halfpenny. Outside was a wagon loaded with their possessions, Hansel's poppet cast as a horse to pull it. Benjamiah would go home.

The morning, like every morning on Where We Live (the streets of Wreathenwold had no real names), was sunlit and breezy. It was enough to make Benjamiah forget all the danger of Manfred and the Viper and the specter of the Widow—enough to make him hope, however fragile a hope, that all was not lost.

"I would feel much better to be sure you'd found your way back," said Hansel, spinning his flat cap anxiously.

"Nuisance will show me the way," said Benjamiah, looking up at the nightjar. She was perched on the bonewood tree outside Follynook. "Isn't that right, Nuisance?"

She unleashed a confident squawk and Hansel laughed.

"You and that doll...," he said, shaking his head. "You

are quite the pair. Wreathenwold is a poorer world without you. But so, too, my dear boy, is your own. Last time, I was not so sure, but this time I am: we will see you again, Benjamiah."

Before he could stop himself, Benjamiah had rushed into Hansel and hugged him. Hansel enveloped him softly and warmly, patting him on the back of the head.

"Send my love to your mother, won't you?" he said.

"I will," said Benjamiah.

When they'd separated, Halfpenny hugged him.

"You get home safely, you hear?" she said, keeping a hand resting on his shoulder. "You're a good boy, though trouble does seem to come whenever you're nearby. . . ."

Benjamiah laughed despite the injustice of this.

Then it was time, yet again, to say goodbye to Elizabella.

Her eyes were glassy with restrained tears, her mouth fixed in an uneasy line.

"Make sure you study your books," she said, a tremor in her voice.

Benjamiah's knapsack was swollen with Follynook spellbooks.

"Agatha was right," she said. "You and Nuisance have got a part to play in all this. You have to come back. Do you promise?"

Before she let Benjamiah see her cry, she lurched forward and hugged him. They stayed that way for quite some time and yet it was nowhere near enough for Benjamiah.

"I don't have my coin," he said. "But I promise."

She smiled and he smiled back. They locked hands, squeezed, then let go.

Nuisance fluttered down to Benjamiah's shoulder as he watched them go, surrounding the wagon as they set off down the cobbled lane. Benjamiah grieved as they grew smaller and smaller, Elizabella turning every few seconds to wave. Benjamiah waved back, despite the increasing weakness he felt at the sight of them leaving.

Then he and Nuisance were alone. She nuzzled his ear with her beak and he scratched her feathers.

"Let's go home," he said.

TWENTY-ONE
WITH HOME

> And with her wicked stepfather taken away, Bolly Pondwater returned home to the family castle and lived a long and wonderful life. And, no matter where she traveled, she found other homes—welcomed by friends far and wide across Wreathenwold.
>
> —*The Book of Barely Believable Stories*,
> Mildred Fogge

Nuisance led Benjamiah to a poky Wreathenwold library and a door in its basement. They emerged the same way they'd left, through the impossible door in Smythe's study in the Wyvern-on-the-Water library. The moment they were through and the door closed behind them, Nuisance fell. She was a doll again. The magical nerves in Benjamiah's mind flailed blankly in the void. The pain was considerable.

With the doll stowed in his knapsack, Benjamiah set off. He'd been gone nearly a month and that meant trouble. No doubt another nationwide manhunt was underway. Unable to face it all right now, Benjamiah made a decision: he'd find Mum first.

Avoiding detection would prove challenging, though. The library was busy, a beehive of the elderly and schoolchildren and everything in between, from the librarian stamping books to the boy being tutored at one of the colorful study tables, from a toddler chewing a picture book to an old man reading a newspaper. Benjamiah was still plotting a safe path through when Hassaan, eating a bag of potato chips, clattered right into him.

"Oh, sorry, I . . . ," mumbled Hassaan, before his eyes widened. "Ben? You're *here*? Everybody's been looking for you for, like, ages. . . ."

A realization hit Benjamiah in that moment. He'd pushed Hassaan away because of how much he missed Elizabella. But that was wrong. Having other friends didn't diminish what he had with her. Silas and Mea had proved that. It was time to live in the real world, which didn't mean forgetting Wreathenwold. Like Agatha Drake had said, belonging wasn't about place—it was the safety to be yourself.

"Yeah, I've been . . . ," mumbled Benjamiah, unable to finish. "Listen, do you want to come round for dinner this week? Don't worry if you're busy or whatever, or you don't want to. . . ."

"I'd love to!" blurted Hassaan.

Benjamiah smiled and Hassaan smiled back.

"Cool," said Benjamiah, before telling himself he'd never say the word again. "One more thing, which is going to sound a bit weird. Could you help me get out of here without being spotted?"

Hassaan took to the task without question and with absolute brilliance. He stalked to the middle of the library and, in one of the most ridiculous things Benjamiah had ever seen, faked a very loud, and very dramatic, heart attack.

Benjamiah, laughing, escaped the library and hit the lanes of Wyvern-on-the-Water. Everywhere he looked he saw his face. Guilt coursed through him. Like a fugitive, Benjamiah snuck all the way to the quay and the horseshoe of flats surrounding it. He slipped inside Mum's building, hurried up the stairs, and took out his key.

He let himself in and called out, "Mum?"

She came running with a shocked shriek, stopped to drink him in with her eyes before crushing him in a hug. Then she cupped his face and looked into his eyes.

"Tell me everything," she said.

So they curled up on the sofa while Benjamiah described all that had happened, from the moment he laid the witchstone upon his eye to the moment he said goodbye to

Elizabella and Hansel. This time he left nothing out, not any of the more dangerous parts nor the peril he feared lay ahead for Wreathenwold. His throat hurt by the end.

It was a lot for Mum to absorb. He found her pale, stricken with the same fears he felt himself. She reached down and squeezed his hand.

"You've been incredibly brave," she said. "Incomprehensibly reckless and stupid, but brave nonetheless. Try not to worry too much. Hansel's right—he usually is. There are good people there, far more good than bad."

Benjamiah considered pointing out that it didn't matter when the bad people were Manfred Tarr and the Viper, but left it for the time being. He rested his head on his mum's shoulder; she smelled of such safety and goodness that it was overwhelming.

"I'm sorry," he said.

"Mm?"

"For coming here and taking the witchstone," he said. "That wasn't right."

"It was my fault," she said. "If I'd only explained, none of this would have happened. I was just so frightened that you wouldn't move on from Wreathenwold. I don't want to lose you to another world. But I was wrong, and I'm sorry. I handled it badly."

For a moment, all was still and quiet.

"Mum?"

"Yes, sweetie."

"You do belong now."

Mum reached out and squeezed him closer, kissing the top of his head.

"I know," she said. "And so do you—no matter where, no matter what."

Benjamiah asked one final thing of Mum before she rang the police. Initially, she looked skeptical of his plan, but agreed nonetheless. She made a call, set down her phone, and studied him with thin eyes.

"You sure about this?" she said and Benjamiah nodded.

It only took a few minutes for Dad and Grandma to arrive. Mum opened the door and they stormed inside, falling upon Benjamiah with an intensity that reminded him of the Van Craggs. But their hugs and kisses were the best thing in this world or any other, even when mixed in with a healthy dose of reproach for having disappeared on them again.

Grandma seemed thinner and Dad looked ten years older. He couldn't do this to them ever again. Even though Mum had strongly suspected where Benjamiah had gone, she hadn't told Dad and Grandma. How could she?

But Benjamiah would. Having finally escaped their barrage of affectionate scolding, he made them sit down at Mum's kitchen table. Then he set Nuisance down between them all. Grandma, all cardigans and tortoiseshell glasses, cocked a suspicious eye. Dad frowned through his own spectacles, his widow's peak damp with the sweat of dashing here.

"What's going on, Ben?" he asked.

Benjamiah took a deep breath and told them about Wreathenwold: about this journey and the last, about Nuisance, about the world beyond the impossible doors. It didn't take long for the expressions around the table to change. Grandma looked sympathetic and Dad unbalanced.

"You're tired, love," said Grandma, reaching out a hand.

"He's telling the truth," said Mum, who throughout it all had been leaning against the sideboard, sipping coffee. "I should know. I was born in Wreathenwold."

While Dad and Grandma stared blankly, Mum told her own story. Quiet swelled after she was finished, broken only by a ticking clock and the droning of the dishwasher.

Dad and Grandma swapped a glance. So too did Mum and Benjamiah. He knew then that they didn't believe it. Perhaps they thought they were being tricked, or otherwise that Benjamiah and Mum were suffering some strange folie à deux. Benjamiah didn't blame them. Before Wreathenwold, he would have thought the same—nothing could have persuaded him otherwise.

Then it all changed. Suddenly, right there on the table, Nuisance the doll sprouted back into Nuisance the nightjar.

Dad fell off his chair and Grandma screamed, stumbling backward with a hand on her heart. Nuisance hopped about and squawked. Benjamiah's heart swelled like the most stunning of sunrises. He slotted into Nuisance and transformed her into an octopus, and a spider, and a dormouse.

"You're here," he whispered, holding out a finger.

Nuisance nibbled it affectionately. Mum joined Benjamiah, her eyes big and fogged over. Nuisance had been her doll, so seeing her come back to life must have been wonderful. Nuisance squeaked happily to see Mum, springing up onto her hand. Mum laughed, and stroked and kissed her.

"Hello, you," she whispered, a sob in her throat.

Dad had clambered up from the floor and peered at the dormouse, hair and glasses askew, goggle-eyed and mumbling incomprehensibly.

"That's impossible," he gasped.

"Not impossible," said Benjamiah. "Just magic."

Grandma said, "I think I need a cup of tea."

While Mum put the kettle on, all eyes remained on Nuisance—not least Benjamiah's. His heart was full, all music and color. Having Nuisance for company was the most wonderful and unexpected blessing. Benjamiah knew Wreathenwold wasn't done with him yet, that his most dangerous adventure was still to come—but for now all that would have to wait.

ACKNOWLEDGMENTS

Writing the second book in a series is a very different thing from writing the first—and in many ways more difficult—so I'm doubly grateful to a lot of people for helping me navigate the new challenges I encountered along the way.

Thank you to my agent, Chloe Seager, for your help with everything, your great advice, and your positivity, and for very patiently handling my various anxieties. Huge thanks also to Kelly Chin and the rest of the team at Madeleine Milburn.

This book was made infinitely better by my editor, Carmen McCullough, whose support, enthusiasm, and wise suggestions made all the difference in shaping and improving the story. Thank you also to the many other people at Puffin who have been so supportive, enthusiastic, and generally brilliant—Alice Grigg, Maeve Banham, Susanne Evans, Beth Fennel, Clare Braganza, Aisling O'Toole, Anda Podaru, Stella Dodwell, Ellen Grady, Sophia Pringle, Sarah Doyle, Lottie Halstead, James McParland, Josh Benn, Katy Finch,

Kat Baker, Becki Wells, Rozzie Todd, Toni Budden, Michaela Lock, Minnie Tindall, Memoona Zahid, Sophie Marston, and Amy Wilkerson—and to my copy editor, Jane Tait.

Across the Atlantic, thank you to my editor, Alyza Liu, and the whole team at Simon & Schuster—Justin Chanda, Anne Zafian, Kendra Levin, Lizzy Bromley, Hilary Zarycky, Amanda Brenner, Chava Wolin, Amaris Mang, Tara Shanahan, and Victor Iannone—and similarly to the many other publishers around the world that have so passionately taken The Whisperwicks into so many territories and languages.

Vivienne To's cover and illustrations continue to blow me away: thank you for capturing everything so beautifully and adding so much to the book. Likewise a huge thank-you again to Isobelle Ouzman for the stunning US cover.

Thank you to all my friends and family for supporting and encouraging me, especially my wife, Caroline, and daughter, Violet.

Finally, I want to thank all the booksellers (special mention to Robbie Mann, who I believe was the first-ever reviewer of The Whisperwicks and who has been an incredible supporter ever since), librarians, parents, teachers, and readers who have been so generous in championing The Whisperwicks. It's meant the world to me to have your support, and I am humbled and very grateful.